RAVE REVIEWS FOR *TURTLE BABY*, ABIGAIL PADGETT, AND BO BRADLEY

*

"A series protagonist of note . . . Padgett constructs a complex, multilayered plot with ease, using the conventions of the classic detective novel."
—*San Francisco Sunday Examiner & Chronicle*

*

"Unusual . . . a marvelous feel for character and place. Her people live and breathe, and her evocation of our border and back country is as good as any I've encountered. . . . Gives customers their money's worth."
—*San Diego Union-Tribune*

*

"An unusual and exceptional protagonist. . . . A powerful novel with complex characters, a sophisticated love story, evocative descriptions, and heart-stopping action."
—*Minneapolis Star Tribune*

*

more . . .

Novels By Abigail Padgett

*Child of Silence**
*Strawgirl**
*Turtle Baby**
Moonbird Boy

*Published by
The Mysterious Press

ABIGAIL PADGETT

TURTLE BABY

THE MYSTERIOUS PRESS

Published by Warner Books

A Time Warner Company

Excerpts from the *Popol Vuh*, translated by Dennis Tedlock, copyright © 1985 by Dennis Tedlock, used with permission of the Balkin Agency, Inc.

Turtle glyph from *Maya Hieroglyphic Writing: An Introduction* by J. Eric S. Thompson, copyright © 1960-1971 by University of Oklahoma Press, reprinted by permission of publisher.

MYSTERIOUS PRESS EDITION

Cover design and illustration by Wendell Minor

The Mysterious Press name and logo are registered trademarks of Warner Books, Inc.

 Mysterious Press Books are published by
Warner Books, Inc.
1271 Avenue of the Americas
New York, NY 10020

Visit our web site at
http://pathfinder.com/twep

 A Time Warner Company

Printed in the United States of America

Originally published in hardcover by The Mysterious Press.
First Printed in Paperback: April, 1996
10 9 8 7 6 5 4 3

To Jean

...ted in Paperback April 1996.

Acknowledgments

To Rigoberta Menchu, Maya writer and
Nobel Peace Prize Winner,
for the inspiration of her work.

To Kay Redfield Jamison, Ph.D.,
Johns Hopkins University School of Medicine,
for her work on manic-depressive illness.

To Dennis Tedlock, translator of
The Maya *Popol Vuh*, for bridging two worlds.

To Douglas Dennis, Staff writer, *The Angolite*,
Louisiana State Penitentiary,
for technical advice on Louisiana prisons.

bones, a fear of the loneliness she endured before A.
black eyes told her how empty she was. How needed.
Cline had not known that she was alone, or cared, until
those eyes melted the walls around her and called her back.

Prologue

Daybringer

The darkness behind the hills grew pale and silver, like the hair of an old woman brushed down from the sky. The Milky Way, which the Maya called the *Sac be*, faded and then vanished. Where before there had been that wide, white road above, now there was only a moist gray chill. A transitional queasiness in which night terrors were almost, but not quite, forgotten.

Chac had followed the Milky Way all night, barefoot on the streets of Tijuana. A smooth brown stone, loaf-sized, hung in a sling between her thin shoulder blades from the *mecapal* cutting into her forehead. She could not put the stone down in the dark. That much was clear, a self-imposed rule she could not explain and did not question. The stone with its weight borne in the woven band across her brow kept her rooted in the world with her baby, Acito. This world, now. A place so lonely that at twenty-two she sometimes felt ancient and hollow. Used up. Disconnected from everything except Acito. Just the ghost of a ruined Maya Indian, following a road in the night sky.

But it was all right. The burden of the stone kept her away from the drug, the white powder that was like a warm, blind wind in her veins. She had not used heroin in over two years, but the fear she felt now made a hunger for it shriek in her bones. A fear of the loneliness she endured before Acito's black eyes told her how pretty she was. How needed.

Chac had not known that she was alone, or cared, until those eyes melted the walls around her and called her back.

1

Now there was nothing but fear of losing him. And now, unless she was smarter and more careful than she had ever been in her life, that was going to happen. She was going to lose him.

But the stone kept her feet on the road of rutted dirt and her mouth breathing darkness in and out for Acito, just as her mouth had breathed air for him when he lay curled and squirming in her belly. She wouldn't give up, wouldn't break. Only a few more days and she could escape with her baby. There would be money. Just a few more days.

For now, light had come, and her burden could be put down. She'd made it through another night. On the potholed street a stream of fluid splashed to the ground from between two gnarled feet visible beneath a corrugated tin wall. The city called "Aunt Jane" was waking.

Chac raised the woven strap from her forehead and placed the stone from its fabric sling on the ground near a pile of old tires. She had left hundreds of stones in the streets of Tijuana, each a relic of her survival and a prayer for her baby's future. Each a burden of time carried honorably, as befit a Maya woman.

"My white nun," her father, Tomás, had called her the popular name for the cream-colored orchid that grew in the Petén rain forests of Guatemala. "My little white nun."

And her mother, Joseña, had called her *mi chica linda*, "my pretty girl," so that she would know she was a fine little girl and not just an animal born to slavery in the baking fields of the *fincas*. Her mother, who wore the purple-embroidered white *huipil* of their village near Lake Atitlán, even though she was from Cobán where the traditional loose blouse was made of lace and embroidered in many colors.

"What you are hides in your heart," Joseña Bolon had told her nine-year-old daughter only days before a soldier's bullet tore through Joseña's heart. "The dress you wear is like a mask for your soul. If you wish to keep secret what is inside, cover yourself outside like all others about you and make no noise."

Chac's mother had taught her to speak and read Spanish, and explained the dishonor of a woman who would sell her body to a man. A dishonor to the woman's soul, which was like the surface of water, a bridge between the physical and spiritual worlds.

The rhythm of her long arms swinging at her sides as she strode toward Chris Joe's little room reminded Chac that she was still alive in spite of all that had happened. She had dishonored her soul in ways her mother could not have imagined. She had sold her body to a hundred faceless men who stank and dripped sweat and then were gone. She had sung for them and straddled them, her mind afloat on the sky she'd pumped from a needle into her arm. But not one of them had touched her secret self, hidden inside. No one had touched that self, ever, except Acito, whose eyes were like her father's.

With his eyes Acito had told her she was that white orchid again, the *monja blanca*. She was his mother. Acito had given life to her, as much as she had given life to him. They were bound in that giving, equals even though he was new and helpless, waiting for her to set the terms of his world.

And she would. Soon. There was already money, saved in a San Diego bank under the name Elena Rother. She had chosen the surname in memory of a missionary priest murdered, like her mother, by Guatemalan soldiers. The Maya had sent his body back to Oklahoma for burial, but had cut out his heart, which they loved, to keep near Lake Atitlán forever.

Soon there would be a contract with an American recording company. Enough money to ensure that Acito's belly would never be swollen with starvation or with the million white pinworms Chac had seen kill her little brother on a hot afternoon while their parents worked in the *finca*. They'd buried him in a cardboard box beside one of the fields at night, so the foreman wouldn't know. That night Joseña Bolon had chewed her hands in the dark to muffle her sobbing, and weeded coffee plants the next day as if nothing had happened.

The American record company would give enough money to shelter Acito, keep him clean and safe. The money would send him to school where he would speak English and play games. He would grow in a place with no white worms, where soldiers would not come and blast out the heart of his mother. Only a few more days.

Until then Chac would carry her fear like a stone on her back, and keep her baby hidden where no one would find him. Away from her. Over the border in America where brown-skinned people lived in hidden webs across the two great cities of San Diego and Los Angeles and moved by night, always telling softly where they were, where they would be tomorrow. Chac could find her baby in that web at any time, but most anglos couldn't even see it. Acito was safe there, she was sure.

Chapter One

"Let it be this way; you must go."

　　—Popol Vuh

"How does this look?" Bo Bradley asked from a kneeling position atop her desk in the offices of San Diego County's Child Protective Services. "Can't you just *hear* that sax?"

Bo's officemate and Spanish-speaking child abuse investigator, Estrella Benedict, turned to glance at a five-by-seven enlargement of a black man in suspenders and a dated tie, playing a saxophone. "Who is it this time?" she sighed, conveying an absence of interest that could, Bo thought as she positioned the Xeroxed photo among others pinned to her bulletin board, almost be construed as hostility.

"It's Charlie 'Yardbird' Parker, probably the greatest jazz composer and alto sax improvisationist of all time. Just looking at him makes me long for New Orleans." Bo sat on the edge of her desk and gazed into the yellow-edged acoustical tile of the ceiling. "Steamy nights, jazz riffs drifting from a hundred musty doorways, the scent of bourbon, chicory coffee . . ."

"Bo!" Estrella choked, dabbing her upper lip with a tissue.

". . . mixed with pungent Creole spices and crawdads boiling in brine."

"Please stop talking about *food!*" Estrella had placed both hands over her mouth and looked wildly at Bo through moist, dark eyes. Beneath a dusting of peach-colored blush, her cheeks were suddenly pale.

Alarmed, Bo slid off her desk and crossed the closet-sized room in one large step. "Es, are you sick? You look like you're going to toss your cookies. Here's the wastebasket. I'll

5

go get some wet towels for your head. Don't worry, I'll drive you home and then pick up Henry so he can get your car later. Should I get Madge? Es, what's the matter with you?"

In the three years they'd shared an office, Estrella Benedict exhibited a robust vitality that simply ignored the possibility of ill health. She'd never even had a cold. Bo entertained the possibility that her best friend might be dying. Probably food poisoning, she thought. Or maybe something worse. Some exotic, foreign disease contracted from the migrant-worker population that comprised Estrella's Spanish-speaking caseload. Malaria, maybe. Or leprosy. A weak but encouragingly familiar grin pulled at the white-edged lips.

"Don't overreact, Bo," Estrella warned. "I'm not dying, I just need a Coke or a 7-Up, something carbonated, okay? And it'll help if you stop describing cooked crustaceans."

"I'll get the Coke," Bo agreed, sprinting out the door and through the two-block maze of carpeted ramps leading from the court investigators' hallway, past the adoptions office, the typing pool, record room, and glass-enclosed child abuse hotline control center, to the deserted cafeteria. The soft drink dispenser was, as usual, out of order.

"It's an emergency," she told the humming machine, and folded her left hand deftly through the catch-tray at the bottom, found a rack she hoped held anything but root beer, and bent the sliding aluminum bar just enough to grab a cold can. Sprite. It would do.

Their unit supervisor, Madge Aldenhoven, had commandeered Bo's office chair and did not allow it to swivel in the direction of the door when Bo returned with the purloined soft drink. A new case file lay in the supervisor's lap, obscuring the detail of a stitch-pleated skirt in khaki twill saved from its serviceable look by the addition of a wide red tartan scarf at the waist. With a crisp white blouse and penny loafers, Madge lacked only the pith helmet to complete a Miss Jean Brodie look that Bo found herself envying.

In this lifetime, she mused, there would be no more bright scarves at *her* less-than-lithe waist. Not even with the new medication Dr. Broussard had prescribed for the manic depression. Something called Depakote, which was really something called valproic acid. Fewer side effects than lithium, at least for Bo, but still the weight problem. An annoying reality, but not exactly the end of the world.

"An eight-month-old boy, poisoned," Madge was explaining to Estrella, "probably a household substance. Clear negligence on the part of the baby's caretakers, whose name is Cruz. Natalio and Ynéz. They told the intake worker at St. Mary's that the baby's mother is a singer in Tijuana named Chac, who made arrangements for them to care for Acito, as he's called, about three months ago, but they don't know anything else about her. She visits the baby frequently, was just there this morning, in fact. St. Mary's put a hold on the baby, who fortunately survived, but we need to file a petition right away. There's no telling when the mother will show up again. I'd like you to complete the initial investigation today."

"Sure," Estrella answered. As she reached to take the case file from Madge, Bo noticed a quivering of narrow gold bracelets circling Estrella's wrist. "Uh, excuse me. I'll be right back."

Tossing the manila file folder on her desk, Estrella hurried out, leaving a trail of spicy perfume in the air. In seconds Bo and Madge Aldenhoven heard the click-bang of the loose pneumatic closer on the women's room in the hall.

"Is Estrella sick?" Madge succeeded in making the question sound vaguely ominous.

"Probably gout," Bo answered, jamming her hands into the pockets of long, partridge brown knit culottes that with huarache sandals either created an illusion of slenderness or made her look as if she were standing in a hole. Bo wasn't sure which. "I hear it's going around."

Madge sighed. "I assume that you *are* taking your medication, Bo, and that this puerile attitude so unbecoming in a woman your age is actually you and not the 'disability' you claim to have."

Bo couldn't decide whether to take offense at the "woman your age" part, or the more serious slur on the concept of brain disorders deserving equal footing with, say, congenital hip displacement. Since coming out as one of the fifteen million Americans treated yearly for severe depression or manic-depressive illness, Bo had noticed a new chill cloaking the already strained relationship she endured with her supervisor.

"The pills are in my purse, bottom drawer on the left," Bo intoned. "Since you're so interested, let me explain that this particular medication, actually an acid, seems to complement the inhibitory qualities of another acid, naturally present in the brain, whose name is gamma-aminobutyric—"

"I haven't got time for this, Bo," Aldenhoven snapped, rising from Bo's chair. "Tell Estrella when she returns that I'll need to give her case to someone else immediately if she's not up to it. I want that petition filed today."

"Why? We've got forty-eight hours to do the initial investigation. The baby's safe. What's the rush?"

But Madge Aldenhoven was gone.

Bo stared at a photograph of Georgia O'Keeffe in profile over her desk until Estrella came back, her normal coloring restored.

"Es, you must have the flu or something. I think you should go home. Madge said . . ."

"Bo, I have a beet of news," Estrella began, her accent deepening with nervousness. "I . . . Henry and I . . ." She leaned against the desk and took Bo's hand. "We want you to be a godmother."

"Godmother," Bo repeated blankly. "You go to the bathroom, come back, and tell me you and your husband want me to be a godmother. Rejecting the devil and all his works, that sort of thing?"

"I mean *the* godmother," Estrella tried again, her free hand unconsciously touching the belt of her poppy red shirtwaist.

The subtle gesture was, Bo realized, absolutely poetic.

"Es," she yelped, leaping up to hug her friend, "a baby! When did you find out? God, that's *great*. Henry must be thrilled, he's wanted to be a dad all along. No wonder you're barfing, it's morning. They say that goes away after a while, right?"

Estrella attempted a game smile and then burst into tears.

"Oh, Bo, it's awful. I just feel awful. I've been sick for days and then last night we did the pregnancy test thing and it was positive and Henry's so happy, and my whole family's delirious with joy and I should be, too, but I just want to crawl in bed and never get out, and I don't know if I can keep working and I have these weird dreams. It's awful, and there must be something wrong with me because—"

"Ah," Bo interrupted, leading Estrella to her chair and popping open the Sprite. "This has a familiar ring. Hormonal changes with pregnancy and all that."

Estrella took a sip of the Sprite. "Huh?"

Bo grinned conspiratorially at a picture of Edgar Allan Poe on her bulletin board. "It's not the same, but *we* . . ." She gestured at the collage of photos above her desk. ". . . can relate."

"Bo, I'm not crazy, I'm pregnant," Estrella began and then grimaced at the *faux pas*. "I'm sorry. I didn't mean to say 'crazy.' You know what I mean. Those people you're collecting, they were all . . ."

" 'Crazy,' occasionally," Bo conceded. "Mood-disordered, guests of the best psychiatric hospitals of their times, a few suicides. But my point is, it's a matter of degree. What you're going through is because of a big change in your chemistry. It's affecting your brain, but you'll adjust to it after a month or so. In the meantime, I'm going to help."

Estrella examined a mummified fly in a gauzy web decorating the upper corner of the office window. "There's nothing you can do. I've got myself into this, but . . ." She mashed the heels of her hands against her eyes, smearing mascara into the semblance of a narrow mask. "I mean, I thought I wanted this, but now . . ."

"You look like the Lone Ranger." Bo grinned. "And of course you want this baby. Just try to ignore any negative thoughts until you have a chance to adjust."

"How do I ignore my own thoughts?"

"That's the hard part," Bo agreed. "Poe drank, O'Keeffe painted, Hemingway blew his head off. For you I suggest a day in bed with a stack of magazines. Meet me back here at three-thirty. *I'm* going to do the preliminary investigation on this case for you."

"Since when do you speak Spanish?" Estrella's look gave new depth to the term "skeptical."

"I don't need to, just to get records from St. Mary's, take the required look at the kid, and glance at the house where these people were keeping him. Besides, I can say, *'Dónde está otra cerveza?'* with the best of them. Trust me."

"Where is another beer? Such a useful phrase in child abuse investigations. Bo, it won't work."

Bo grabbed the case file and stuffed it into a briefcase on her desk. "Yes, it will. My cases are caught up, I'll tell Madge I'm going out to check on that new family crisis intervention center that's halfway to Los Angeles, and you'll go home and relax until three-thirty when you can draft the petition from my notes, go over to court and file it, and call it a day."

Estrella actually smiled. "I owe you one, Bo."

"How many times have you and Henry helped *me* over rough times, Es? Ten? Twenty? How about pretty much consistently, all the time, for nearly three years! I know it's not easy being friends with somebody like me. Let me do something for you for once, okay?"

Estrella glanced at the long-dead fly once again. "Just be careful then, Bo. You never know when one of these easy cases is going to get messy. And you don't know anything about dealing with Mexican people. I shouldn't let you do this . . ."

Bo raked her silvering auburn hair with both hands and refastened a cherrywood clip that strained to corral too many curling wisps. "That's just your wacked-out chemistry again. Too much estrogen or something. Go home and research diaper services over a tall glass of lemonade. Lie in the sun, if it ever comes out. Take a nap. I'll see you at three-thirty."

In the parking lot Bo threw her briefcase onto the passenger's side bucket seat of an almost new Pathfinder with four-wheel drive. She'd bought it with the insurance compensation for her BMW wrecked only a month earlier. Haze-filtered sunlight swam on the pinkish beige surface of the vehicle's hood, a color named "champagne pearl" by the manufacturer. Bo polished a smudge of dust from the left side panel with her thumb. Estrella's case was going to be easy. At least something different. An eight-month-old baby who'd gotten into the laundry detergent or something. Hardly a quagmire of murderous intrigue.

Chapter Two
The Little Turtle

Safely belted in the Pathfinder, Bo drove sedately through the chain-link gates of the CPS parking lot. No sense in irritating Madge with a display of boisterous driving.

From the console between the gray leather seats, not one but two gear levers indicated the vehicle's readiness to take Bo anywhere she wanted to go. Off the roads. Into the desert where an ancient silence that either terrified or bored other people invariably flooded her mercurial brain with peace.

She'd go out to the desert soon, she promised herself. She would have gone already, but she'd been driving a cheap rental car until the little vehicle turned up a week ago at a police auction. Dar Reinert, the child abuse detective who'd worked a recent big case with her, had alerted her to its sale. Probably out of macho-cop-guilt, she thought, because he hadn't *really* believed she was in any danger. Hah.

"Only a coupla years old," he told her paternally over the phone. "Been used to transport cargo in from a little airstrip the Tobacco and Firearms guys found out in the desert near Borrego. Wheel rims look like pastry crust, but they're chrome steel so I can hammer 'em out for ya. Want it?"

Bo knew the "cargo" had been drugs, fleeing Mexican gang kingpins, and the occasional corpse, and didn't care. A four-wheel drive would be her passport to earthly nirvana, well worth the small sacrifice in symbolic principle. And the lousy gas mileage would do for penance.

"I want it," she told the detective.

And even though the end of June was too late for anything resembling comfort in the arid wilds surrounding San Diego, she was going to get out there at least once. Just once before

11

the hammering heat of July, August, and September that could mummify an already dehydrated human body in one day.

Bo had seen it. One of her first cases involved a runaway fourteen-year-old girl, already an open file with Child Protective Services. The teenager's active CPS status was the result of her frequent calls to the child abuse hotline claiming that her parents were abusing her by not allowing her to date a twenty-year-old reject from the navy with a history of arrests for kiting checks.

The girl, Stacey, had sneaked away with the young felon, Ron, for a romantic motorcycle trip to the desert. Alone at last, they had explored the joy of sex on a greasy tarp and feasted on four six-packs of Corona and a bag of jalapeño barbecue chips. When Ron, as he explained later, declined Stacey's offer to move in with him the next day, she hopped on his Yamaha Virago 535 and sped away into the desert, furious. He didn't worry too much because he passed out.

When she hadn't returned by the time he woke up the following morning, he assumed she'd ditched the bike somewhere and got a ride back to San Diego. Visions of statutory rape charges precluded his phoning her family to see if she'd made it home after he hitchhiked back. By the time Stacey's frantic parents found him to ask, it was hours too late.

Sheriff's deputies located the body that evening, less than a mile from the fallen four-hundred-pound motorcycle, which had simply been too heavy for the hundred-and-five-pound girl to upright. Coyotes had found the body first. What was left, Bo noted when she accompanied Stacey's father to the morgue for the identification, was a mottled husk that looked like a wizened old woman. She hoped he didn't see the barrel cactus spines imbedded in his daughter's hands from what must have been a last, frenzied attempt to find moisture.

To the Pathfinder's rear door the previous owners had welded a wire frame that held a five-gallon can of water. An unsightly addition that, in light of Stacey's demise, Bo welcomed. Five gallons of water could buy at least two extra days in the summer desert, in an emergency. Plenty of time for somebody to find a stranded camper.

Rounding the corner from Linda Vista Road onto Genesee Avenue, Bo slowed to admire a long vacant lot full of thistles.

Their blue flowers dried on the gray-green stalks every year, retaining a color that reminded Bo of forest ponds on Cape Cod. That same inscrutable amethyst. An artist away from the job that paid her rent, Bo envisioned a painting in which blue thistles covered an entire canvas. Maybe she'd stop on the way back and pick a bouquet for Estrella, to celebrate the forthcoming blessed event. Except the spiky flowers were probably full of ants, or earwigs, or the larvae of centipedes. Maybe she'd just buy a couple of carnations at the florist near the hospital.

By the time she found a parking space in St. Mary's Hospital for Children's inadequate front lot, Bo was entertaining doubts about the new medication Dr. Broussard had said might work better than the lithium. The side effects did seem less noticeable. That sloppy, awkward slowness that seemed to accompany all the medications was a little less annoying. And there was no hand tremor, or not much, anyway. But the singular thoughts characteristic of manic depression were heartily in evidence despite the scrim provided by the little pills. Objects seemed more than usually anxious to reveal covert aspects of themselves. Bo regarded the parking lot's asphalt pavement, thought of dead dinosaurs melting into the primordial crude oil from which asphalt would be made, and sighed.

"I can only imagine," she told an audience of invisible dinosaurs at her feet, "what a life without these endless scenes from PBS specials might be like."

The baby called Acito was, Bo ascertained at the fourth-floor nurses' station, still classified as "guarded" after presumably ingesting a toxic substance that had caused violent diarrhea and vomiting. "Rule out hemolytic anemia," her copy of the medical chart suggested. What it meant was, "*Don't* rule out hemolytic anemia; hemolytic anemia is a possibility here." Bo whistled critically at medical jargon that seemed intent on obfuscation.

"What kind of poison causes hemolytic anemia?" she asked the nurse who'd politely duplicated the chart.

"I don't know." The young woman smiled beneath a haircut

too short and chic to hold a nurse's cap even if she owned one. Bo tried to remember when nurses stopped wearing those starched white relics, and concluded that the actual date was probably a secret. "But sometimes it's a symptom of malaria."

"Malaria? I thought this baby got into some kind of toxic substance."

"It looks that way," the nurse answered, leaning conversationally on the counter. 'We've got whole blood on standby, just in case he needs a transfusion. He came in pretty sick."

Pretty sick. The usual euphemism for "potentially near death." Bo drew a sharp breath and felt a halo of sudden sweat forming at her hairline. The hall with its bright colors, its stuffed animals and Disney pictures, was a facade, a set. Behind it desperate battles were being fought. Nothing new, but the reality seemed oddly shocking.

"Thanks," she told the nurse. "I'll just take a look at the baby and get on out of here."

And straight to a phone where you'll call Dr. Broussard and tell her this medication has about as much clout as a mint patty. You're not scouting for a documentary here, Bradley. Stop seeing dramatic camera angles.

Acito was asleep, the tiny, terra-cotta-colored fingers of his right hand wrapped snugly around the large thumb of a male special-duty attendant Bo knew from an earlier case. The baby's left arm was taped to a white plastic support into which snaked an IV drip.

Bo glanced at the bottle upended from a steel rack at the head of Acito's crib. Pedialyte. Gatorade without the flavoring, meant for dehydrated little people. A quart of the chemically enhanced water sat in Bo's refrigerator at all times. Her old fox terrier, Mildred, was prone to scarfing up rancid delicacies found on the beach, with resultant gastrointestinal chaos. Fortunately, Mildred loved Pedialyte. Among San Diego's fox terriers, she was perhaps the least likely ever to suffer an electrolyte imbalance.

Bo watched air bubbles drifting up the clear IV tube toward the bottle. A fast drip. They were putting a lot of fluid into Acito, to water down a poison. The special-duty attendant,

Rudy Palachek, wore alarmingly deep furrows in a wide, tanned forehead.

"What is it, Rudy?" Bo whispered.

"Kid damn near died," the fifty-year-old ex-Marine growled, "and where's his mother? This little dude needs his mama right now, not a bunch of strangers."

The words carried a judgment that ruffled and snapped like a flag in the wind. Rudy Palachek disapproved of absent mothers.

"I'm just doing the initial investigation for Estrella," Bo said softly. "I don't know anything about the mother except that she's apparently in Tijuana. Is he going to be okay?"

"Looks like it," Palachek breathed as the baby stretched and grimaced in his sleep. "But his gut's gonna feel like he ate barbed wire for a while. If you're going to be here a minute, I'll run to the head."

"Sure," Bo replied, her focus on the baby in the crib. His reddish brown legs were long and still chubby, smooth and unmarked by scars. Above the elasticized waist of a disposable diaper decorated in cows jumping over moons, his round baby stomach rose and fell with each breath. The little brown hand that had held Rudy's thumb now curled against ribs barely visible under healthy, filled-out skin. Gently Bo rolled him to the left, so she could check his back for any evidence of abuse.

People who hit babies, she knew from the experience inherent in her job, often hit them on the back in the deluded belief that blows to kidneys or spine couldn't do any real damage. Acito's back was unmarked, but the movement had disturbed his sleep. Blearily he opened the blackest eyes Bo had ever seen, and blinked with long, feathery lashes.

"I'm sorry," she explained as he struggled to sit up. "I just had to make sure nobody'd hit you. A crummy job, but somebody's got to do it, right?"

The face that looked back was unusual. A rosy brown face faded to rust in sickness, but unmistakably different from the parade of babies Bo saw constantly. Not just different from the black babies and the white babies, but different from the Latino babies, too.

Probably an Indian, Bo thought, from one of the demoralized Mexican tribes routinely seen begging in the streets of Tijuana. A higher forehead, higher cheekbones, glossier raven hair so straight it stood out uniformly from his skull, peaking in a fierce cowlick that made him look like an Indian version of the "Little Rascals" character called Alfalfa.

And his nose. Even though the cartilage was still soft, Bo could see the subtle outline of a bend at the bridge. A Barbra Streisand nose, sort of. Unconsciously Bo began to sing the chorus from "People," and then bit her lip. The ballad ranked high in her personal list of Truly Awful Lyrics. Now it would sing in her head, all day.

In his struggle to sit up, Acito had rolled onto his taped arm and couldn't get enough leverage with his right arm to rise from a kneeling position. His diapered rump wobbled like a balloon with the effort. Sleepy baby mutterings melded into an irritable cry.

"I know, it's the pits," Bo said as she lifted him over the crib's side, careful not to disturb the IV. Against her chest he whined and nuzzled like someone much younger than eight months. Regressing, Bo thought, because he was sick. All kids acted younger when they didn't feel well. Adults, too, for that matter. His right hand clutched at the knit fabric of Bo's blouse, and then at her hair. Somehow it was obvious that this wasn't the fabric, or the hair, that he wanted.

Bo breathed the faintly sweet-and-sour baby smell drifting from the little form in her arms and kissed the top of his head. "I know you want your mom," she said into soft, black hair. "You're scared and sick and nobody else will do. Maybe we'll try to find her, huh?"

An anticipatory shiver of joy seemed to animate Acito's small frame. It occurred to Bo that she had just made a sort of promise to an infant Indian who, if he comprehended words in any language, did not comprehend words in English. A desperately important promise that on some primitive level he appeared to understand. A promise she would have to keep.

When Rudy Palachek returned, Acito was again asleep beneath a spill of Bo's unruly curls, drooling copiously down the front of an ensemble intended to create the illusion of chic.

"Teething." The burly attendant grinned as he took Acito from Bo. "See?" He pointed to two perfect incisors in the center of the baby's otherwise toothless lower gum. "But it's these up here that're hurting." Bo saw the almost transparent white edge of an upper incisor, already through the skin, and another beside it, not quite erupted.

"One more thing for him to deal with." She nodded. "Have you heard any theories about whatever he got into? Clorox, tile cleaner, somebody's stash of tequila?"

"Nothing like that," Palachek answered, tucking a miniature white thermal blanket around Acito's shoulders and settling into a rocker. "Andy told me toxicology can't seem to identify the substance. It's something unusual."

Andy was Dr. Andrew LaMarche, pediatrician and director of the hospital's child abuse program, old Marine Corps buddy to Rudy Palachek, and enigma to Bo. At the sound of Andrew LaMarche's name, her scalp began to feel like a warm hat, unaccountably shrinking. She hoped she could complete this leg of the investigation without running into him.

"Thanks, Rudy," she said, and stashed Acito's file in her briefcase as she left the room.

A cup of coffee would be nice, she decided, for the trip to San Ysidro, San Diego's southernmost community smack on the Mexican border. And the hospital cafeteria provided free coffee for the county's child abuse investigators.

Bo loped into the cafeteria appreciatively and then stopped short halfway to the coffee. To her right a display of small, wholesome salads nestled in a bed of crushed ice beside overlapping watermelon slices under plastic wrap. The watermelon slices were accentuated with artful clusters of parsley. To her left Dr. Andrew LaMarche in dazzling white lab coat and equally white French cuffed dress shirt sat at a table with a woman Bo could only describe as stunning.

"Bo!" he greeted her, standing and holding out his hand as if he expected her to climb over the chrome bar that routed cafeteria patrons past the display of delicacies. "I didn't expect to see you today. Please, won't you join us?"

His companion stood also and brushed nonexistent crumbs from the bodice of a perky little silk dress in an art deco print unwearable by anybody weighing more than a coatrack. Bo fought an awareness of the dark baby-drool smear down the front of her own blouse, now the color of dried mud, and the silvering clumps of red hair pulled loose on one side of her head by Acito's little fingers.

You look like a haystack on feet, Bradley. But don't let it bother you.

"Thank you so much for your time, Dr. LaMarche." The woman smiled, exiting. "I hope to discuss this with you further once our program is established." Her elegant nose crinkled in a disarming mock grimace. "There are bound to be kinks we'll have to iron out."

Kinks? Bo feared that the idiot smile distorting her face might appear frozen. She actually felt its chill until she realized that the heel of her left hand, swung back in surprise at LaMarche's greeting, was a half-inch deep in crushed ice.

"Andy," she sighed, "we've got to stop meeting like this."

Over coffee and a slice of watermelon Bo felt compelled to buy because she'd smashed seeds all over its little plate, she explained her role in Acito's case. Andrew LaMarche nodded approval.

"I'm so pleased for Estrella and Henry," he said quietly. "But I think it might be a good idea for Estrella to let somebody else handle this case after all. It may get complicated."

"Why?" Bo asked. "The baby got into the toilet cleaner, or somebody's marijuana brownies, or swallowed some roach pellets. It happens all the time. What's complicated, besides the fact that the Immigration and Naturalization Service people are going to want to deport him back to Mexico and nobody knows how to find the mother? Es deals with the INS all the time."

"It may be more serious that that." Andrew LaMarche's gray eyes were troubled. "The toxin involved has so far eluded analysis, but it's clearly something unusual. *So* unusual and deadly that I don't think we can write this poisoning off to accident. At least not until we know more."

Bo stared at the man whose surprising proposal of marriage she had rejected only a week ago. He continued to look like an attaché to the court of Victoria and Albert, aloof and foppish as a society mortician. A gold collar pin beneath his handwoven gray linen tie caught the cafeteria's fluorescent light. Bo felt something akin to panic at the thought of his succumbing to stress, sliding into an embarrassing eccentricity. "You can't mean you suspect that somebody tried to *kill* Acito." She frowned. "That's crazy."

"I've been advised not to use that term in casual conversation." He smiled beneath a graying military-style mustache. "Let's just say I recommend caution and an exhaustive investigation. Since there's insufficient evidence as yet for the police to become involved, the task must fall to Child Protective Services. You can see why it may be too much for Estrella at the moment."

Bo thought about the strange baby three floors above, ill and lonely amid alien noise and unfamiliar touch. Why would anybody want to murder a little Indian baby already lost in the shifting cultural landscape created by an international border?

"And by the way," LaMarche interrupted her reverie, "the lady who just left is the administrator for a grant which will fund training for volunteers in our pediatric AIDS unit. Very important work. I was delighted to see that you were a bit jealous."

"I wasn't jealous," Bo replied, snapping the lid on her Styrofoam coffee cup. "Something, but not jealous. I wish you'd stop this game, Andy. We have to work together from time to time."

"It's not a game, Bo. Will you have dinner with me tonight?" He made the request as if it were perfectly ordinary. As if he weren't hell-bent on a quaint courtship that made Bo feel like an antique paper doll, complete with parasol.

"Sorry, it's Thursday," she answered, rising. "My poker night."

In the hospital's parking lot Bo paced thoughtfully beside the Pathfinder, smoking. She'd decided not to smoke inside, at least until the vehicle's newness wore off. She'd keep the little vehicle sparkling, an oasis of tidiness on wheels. It would be a statement. Or something.

From a slowly passing car whose driver obviously coveted her parking space, Bo heard an old Patti Smith song that promised to supplant the first two lines of "People" repeating themselves in her head. Turning on her own radio, she scanned the dial for "Because the Night" and found it, although something was different.

The music was the same, the whiskey-voice similar, but the words were in Spanish. Intrigued, Bo headed away from the hospital and onto I-805 toward the border, listening to a San Diego phenomenon generically called "Mexican radio." The next song was a Roy Orbison hit she'd loved in seventh grade called "Crying." She sang along in English, wondering if the Spanish words were the same, and how they could do that. Don't copyrights extend over national borders? Maybe not.

By the time she reached the last U.S. exit in San Ysidro, an unfamiliar song had begun. A poignant tune accompanied by only a guitar and some sort of flute. The woman singer's voice resonated with controlled power. A trained voice, deliberately speaking of feeling. Bo wished she could understand the words. One, repeated several times, was *corazón*. And at the song's end Bo could have sworn she heard the phrase *mi Acito*.

"Nah," she told the station's announcer, who was booming something involving numbers. "I'm imagining it, or else Acito is just a common endearment, like darling."

That had to be it, she reassured herself as she parked near a nondescript San Ysidro apartment complex where people named Natalio and Inéz Cruz had cared for an eight-month-old baby that was not theirs. A baby who had, accidentally or deliberately, been poisoned.

"Thees ees Rrrrahdio Rrrromántico," the announcer crooned in heavily accented English, "where the secrets of the heart are hidden."

Bo turned off the ignition and clambered to the gritty street. A quarter mile away the sprawl of Tijuana climbed uphill from the valley border, clearly visible. The two cities were, geographically, one. But which held the secret that had thrown an Indian baby up on the shores of high-tech Western medicine, and left him there, alone? Bo sucked air through her teeth and stared at the Mexican city, a jagged web of streets in the distance. The secret lay there, she thought. In Tijuana, where she could legally investigate nothing.

Chapter Three
A Wood Man, a *Duende*

Chac stretched uncomfortably on Chris Joe's aluminum-frame camp cot, and punched at the pillow. It wasn't really a pillow, but a canvas bag full of clothes. An odor of eucalyptus clung to it from the leaves he kept inside so his T-shirts would smell good. Chris Joe acted as though doing things with leaves and herbs were something new. As if the Maya hadn't used medicinal plants since long before the birth of the Christian god.

Chac sighed. She knew she'd been asleep and that it was too soon to wake up, but something was wrong. A ringing in her ears. A clammy fear that made her shiver in the overcast mid-morning light. There had been a dream, but she couldn't remember it. Or else this was the dream.

"Go back to sleep," he said without turning to look at her. "Everything's okay."

For a moment she forced open her eyes and watched him. A strange gringo boy with the long hair of a woman and thin, pale hands that could make a guitar sing like the soul of a sparrow. As she watched, those hands sewed tiny, glittering stars to the sleeves of a white blouse he'd made for her from a bedsheet bleached in the sun. Row after row of silver flashes on sleeves shaped like wings. The light from the open doorway reflected the little specks and made her eyes close again.

The dream was still real.

Her father, Tomás, stood at the edge of a small cornfield in his purple and white striped pants, playing a reed pipe as huge clouds blew close down on the surrounding forest. The little field was her family's *milpa* near Lake Atitlán in Guatemala, and the leaves of corn and squash seemed to whisper.

In the dark wind Chac held Acito up for her father to see. So he would see the peculiar deformity that would show all the Maya how blessed her baby was. How alike with the gods no matter what Chac had done wrong.

And when Tomás saw, a hundred other Indians were there, too, and a sound of her mother's heart in the wind. But there was something else. A *duende*, a dead thing from the cemetery or some other evil spirit, moving through the forest from the north. A noise signaled the *duende*'s presence. It buried her father's music in scratchy shrieks that became an ugly song she couldn't understand, like the noise from the loudspeakers on the evangelical church in Panajachel.

Tomás and the others vanished, fleeing the sound. And Chac realized the heartbeat filling her ears was her own. The *duende* was coming for Acito!

The baby seemed to weigh nothing as she ran, stumbling in squash vines. Some of the vines were snakes, watching her with furious eyes. The eyes froze her legs so she couldn't run, and suddenly Acito wasn't in her arms at all. Nothing was in her arms but her own heart, huge with terror.

A bitter scent that was like wasps came from the evil spirit chasing her, and Chac saw one of its white feet running between the forest shadows. The foot was on backward! The *duende* ran toward her with its terrible, wrong feet and she screamed and screamed as parrots flew up and turned black against the sky.

"Chac, wake up. You're dreaming. It's not real. Wake up."

A thread of sweat ran down her back as she sat upright on the cot. Her scalp was wet and her eyes burned with salt.

"Acito," she sobbed as the gringo boy held her. "It was going to get Acito."

From within his flat, muscled chest she felt a familiar warmth. A safety. The boy had taken on the burden of her life these last three months as a Maya accepts *cargo*, a responsibility for which there is no reward except the forward movement of time. Chris Joe was five years younger than she was and not any kind of Indian, but he accepted *cargo*. He carried her life. That he also felt for her as a man feels for his woman was something she pretended not to see.

"Acito's fine," he reassured her. "You saw him this morning and he's fine. It was just a dream."

Chac frowned into his pale blue eyes. "*Estúpido!*" she hissed. "*Mi sueño . . .*"

"In English, Chac." He grinned, returning to his work on the blouse. "Remember, pretty soon you're going to have to speak English all the time. Even when you're pissed!"

"A dreeem," she exaggerated the English word angrily, "is sometimes the truth your mind sees and shows it in pictures. These pictures were snakes and a *duende* with backward feet, and Acito was gone from my arms!" Her black eyes grew dull with panic. "I need to go out . . ."

"And get all smacked up over a dream?" he replied without turning to face her. "That sucks, but you know I won't stop you. How long's it been? Two years? You go on out and score some shit off the street, do a nice, big wad. You'll be dead when it hits your heart unless you live long enough to puke to death. But go ahead."

Chac stretched trembling hands at her sides and then clenched them into fists. "I'm so fucking scared," she said quietly.

"I know," he answered. "But in a few days you'll be free as a bird. Soon as you sign that contract, you *fly*, right? And right now I'm making some tea to calm you. Chamomile and ginseng. It settles the nerves."

"And you fly, too, Chris Joe? You stay with me and do the music, just like now, right?"

He turned from the battered hotplate where he was heating water. "I'll stay with you as long as you need me," he said. In his determined look and the set of his jaw Chac saw the man inside the boy, and her terror subsided to a shifting unease.

He would help her. But in her discomfort she sensed a danger the dream had warned her about. The *duende* with its hideous feet was a spirit of something maddened by nature. A person lost in the Guatemalan jungle, wandering in circles for days, would see this *duende* and go insane. It would happen to the lone ones, the ones nobody knew at all.

From beneath a flowered curtain hung over the open door, Chac saw yellow-white sun spill on the dirt alley as light broke through the low clouds. The shadow of someone walking by. Children shouting. The nose of a brown dog, curious and friendly. Everything normal, hiding something too terrible to see. Chris Joe wouldn't understand, but Chac knew it was coming. It had started toward her today.

Chapter Four
The Crossroads

Natalio and Ynéz Cruz were not at home when Bo knocked at the address on Acito's facesheet in the file. In fact, according to a teenage girl who answered but did not open the screen door and spoke English, they might never have been there. They didn't really live there. They were relatives of somebody named Bernardo who also didn't live there. They had been paid to take care of the baby boy, Acito, and they had cared for the baby there sometimes. But now they were gone. Nobody in the sparsely furnished little apartment expected Natalio and Ynéz to return. Ever.

Bo unclipped the plastic Child Protective Services identification badge from the neck of her blouse and cupped it in a raised hand, the way she'd seen cops do on TV shows.

"I'm from CPS," she said, wondering how to look official. "I have to come inside and see where the baby was kept here."

From his seat on a folding chair against the wall, a man in a straw cowboy hat launched into an emotional monologue. In the torrent of Spanish Bo heard the phrase *carta verde* several times. On the chair beside the man, a woman who appeared to be winding colored yarn around plastic drinking straws nodded, her eyes angry and fearful at once. She was making God's Eyes, Bo realized. The compass-shaped wall decorations sold everywhere in Tijuana. Figuring that out did nothing to account for the man's obvious anger.

Carta verde. Bo thought of Carta Blanca, the Mexican beer she didn't like nearly as well as Dos Equis, which meant "Two Xs." And Carta Blanca meant "white card," so *carta verde* would mean what? Surfing through root-word associations, Bo hit on "verdant." Green. The guy was yelling about green cards!

"No INS," she insisted, shaking her head. "CPS is no *la migra*."

Estrella talked about *la migra* all the time—the Mexicans' term for the U.S. Immigration and Naturalization Service, which routinely rounded up and dumped migrant workers found in the U.S. without residency permits back across the border in Tijuana. The practice was akin to emptying the ocean by scooping out buckets of seawater and throwing it on the adjacent sand. But *la migra* was nonetheless a source of continual fear to the thousands of undocumented Latinos who crossed U.S. borders.

The teenage girl opened the door and pointed to a pile of blankets on the floor of an area adjacent to the apartment's kitchen. The blanketed space was enclosed by upended cement blocks, probably, Bo thought, pilfered from a building site. An effective playpen. Bo nodded approval. The sharp corners of the cement blocks had been padded by towels held in place with duct tape. The needs of an eight-month-old had been thoughtfully met.

Bo took the county's Polaroid camera from its strap on her shoulder, and walked self-consciously into the apartment's little kitchen to get a shot of Acito's living quarters. A box of disposable diapers sat on the floor, and a blue plastic baby bottle half full of what looked like apple juice lay among the blankets. Beside the bottle was a small statue of Our Lady of Guadalupe, dressed in starched fabric. In the playpen's corner a glow-in-the-dark plastic crucifix lay atop a chewed prayer card featuring a tonsured saint Bo didn't recognize. The saint looked ecstatically skyward as a rain of flaming arrows pierced his body. Acito's toys had been the religious paraphernalia of his Mexican caretakers.

Get the baby bottle, Bradley. That may be Lysol, not apple juice.

As Bo approached Acito's pen, she noticed that two more people, an elderly woman in a shawl and an expectant mother of indeterminate age, had emerged from a bedroom and were watching her as if she were about to toss them a grenade.

Smiling inanely, she hooked a leg over the cement blocks, leaned to grab the blue bottle, and felt something crunch beneath her sandal. At the sound the old woman's eyes grew large and she hurried to Bo's side. From the blankets she pulled a rosary. Several of its red and black beads were smashed.

"Oh, I'm sorry," Bo began, "I didn't mean to . . ."

But the woman, no longer fearful, was yelling at Bo in nonstop Spanish that, however incomprehensible, left no doubt as to its intent. The man in the straw cowboy hat stood and began to bat at Bo with his hat, creating wafts of hair-oil-scented air. The pregnant woman crossed herself, placed her forehead against the wall, and began to moan. Bo clambered out of Acito's pen and made a dash for the door.

"What the hell . . . ?" she gasped, still clutching the baby bottle.

"That rosary was a gift from my grandmother's mother," the teenager explained, pushing Bo through the screen door and then locking it. "It was, you know, like . . . from her deathbed?"

In the girl's syntax Bo recognized a universal adolescent contempt for the unfathomable stupidity of adults. Beyond the door the old woman kept screaming a word Bo could have sworn was "Tampa."

"Did her mother live in Florida?" Bo asked in spite of herself.

"I dunno," the girl answered. "Her mother's dead."

As initial interviews go, Bo admitted as she tossed the camera and bottle into her car, this one was a disaster. At least she had a snapshot for Es. A snapshot of some cement blocks and a pile of blankets. Not exactly an award-winning document.

At her feet a collection of pigeons rose from pecking at a gum wrapper in the gutter, and flapped southward as if they'd been called. Bo watched the birds swoop over the border and climb the air above Tijuana, only a half mile away. It looked easy.

"Why not?" she asked her right hand as it turned the ignition switch. Acito's mother was over there, somewhere. A nightclub singer named Chac, Madge had said. And most establishments that might qualify, however marginally, as nightclubs were in Tijuana's tourist district. On Avenida Revolución. Only a few blocks from the border.

It would, Bo decided, be ridiculous not to make some casual inquiries regarding the whereabouts of the missing mother. She'd just get the address of the singer's place of employment for the report. Unofficially, of course.

Officially, she reminded herself as she headed toward the border parking lots, the jurisdiction of San Diego County ended where Mexico began. San Diego County Child Protective Services, by international law, could not set foot over that border. But Bo Bradley, U.S. citizen, could. Without a passport, visa, or any form of identification she could walk through two clanging metal turnstiles and into another country. To get back, she needed only to be able to state in unaccented English that she was a U.S. citizen. So much for security at an international border known to see its share of illegal traffic. Too easy to pass up.

Bo found a parking space in an area of packed dirt near the rotary where buses discharged Mexico-bound passengers. A short walk along a fifteen-yard iron fence led into Mexico.

Through the fence Bo watched the Border Patrol drug dogs at work on the U.S. side, happily sniffing cars selected by U.S. border officials for canine scrutiny as they left Mexico. A young German shepherd seemed to smile in her direction, and Bo waved. "Win one for the Gipper!" she yelled at the dog.

After the second turnstile, everything changed. It always did, but today the change seemed portentous. Mexico, whatever it was, began at that turnstile. Impossibly, the air smelled different. Dusty, with an acidic undertone like hot plastic. Bo quickened her pace to avoid two skinny little Indian girls heading toward her with boxes of cellophane-wrapped chiclets.

"*Chiclé?*" the children insisted, their black eyes unreadable as those of birds. "*Chiclé, señorita?*"

On the ground against the wall bordering the main tourist thoroughfare into Tijuana were what appeared to be piles of cloth. These were the mothers of the beggar children, most with babies at the breast. Each draped figure held up one gracefully cupped hand as Bo passed. Yaqui Indians. A Stone Age people living on scraps thrown down by the current century. Acito might be one of these, Bo thought. Except none of the swarming children along the sidewalk had that nose. That oddly bent nose.

Distracted by a pushcart laden with slab-quartz wind chimes cut in the shape of parrots, Bo lost the concentration necessary for running the gauntlet of begging children. A two-year-old boy in a grubby sweater approached her knee and looked up. His nose was running and in his dull eyes Bo recognized exhaustion. Impossible to ignore.

"Here," she sighed, and emptied her coin purse into his sticky hands. It wouldn't do any good, but she'd have nightmares if she did nothing.

"I hate this place," she smiled at a man following her and repeating, "Taxi?" over and over. "I've always hated it and today's even worse. No taxi. Thanks anyway."

The street was a sociology textbook, opened to the chapter on social stratification. Beyond the beggars, Indian women of mixed blood sold woven bracelets and abalone earrings from sheets on the ground. A row of food stands scented the air with roasting cones of meat that, for fifty cents, would be shaved into tortillas and buried in sour cream, fried onions, and mouth-scorching chile peppers. Salivating, Bo chanted "Just say no to fat" and kept walking. The cooked meat was delicious and perfectly safe to eat. The frozen fruit pops further up the street, made with untreated water and named "death on a stick" by San Diego's college students, weren't.

The crush of street vendors ended abruptly at the edge of a large cement plaza boasting a central fountain that had never, in Bo's experience, worked. The plaza sported new, one-story buildings subdivided into shops that catered to the basic needs of border-hopping Americans. Liquor. Mexican-made copies of designer clothing complete with fake labels. And prescription drugs for which no prescription was necessary here.

Indians weren't allowed on the plaza. There were no *churro* vendors with greasy paper bags of sugary stick-donuts. No roasting meat that, on analysis, would turn out to be goat. Bo sighed. The plaza felt like a cumbersome spaceship set down in the midst of biblical Syria. Too clean. Way too quiet. The way Americans liked it.

At the plaza's far side she climbed to an overpass that led into Avenida Revolución. The cement steps, recently completed, were already crumbling. That was just Tijuana, she admitted to herself, wondering if merely noticing constituted a form of criticism. Buildings in Tijuana were invariably half completed and then left that way. Paved streets turned to dirt where least expected. The city's slapdash architecture seemed to grope toward some uncherished goal and then give up halfway there in defiance. A sense of flux. Of things falling apart and being rebuilt endlessly and with no point.

It's just a typical border town, Bradley. For once don't let it get to you.

But it did. It always did. Bo wasn't sure why. Maybe the open acknowledgment of poverty, always guilt-inspiring. More likely the suffocating crush of noise and people and things, the ceaseless clamor. A sensory overload merely tiring to the average American brain, but frightening to Bo's, which was prone to dramatic overreaction even when protected by medication.

"*Kate Harding*, 1892," she pronounced at a canvas-topped stall displaying at least a thousand identical pieces of terra-cotta pottery painted in nightmarish Day-Glo butterflies. "The British schooner *Lily*, 1901," she named a covered alleyway from which two men with gold teeth held out armloads of velour blankets featuring panthers attacking antelopes, an Aztec couple in full ceremonial garb doing something erotic, and the Last Supper. "And you," she remarked to an arcade of glass cases from which gleamed brass knuckles in sizes petite to extra large, enough switchblade knives to arm the entire population of Wyoming, and what looked like a collection of pie plates with razor wire edges, "are the *Jennie French Potter*, 1909."

The litany of Cape Cod shipwrecks was comforting. Her Irish grandmother, whose hobbies ran to the unusual, had often rocked Bo and her little sister, Laurie, on the porch of the family's Wellfleet summer cottage, singing the names of the doomed ships. Having imprinted the list under optimal circumstances, Bo never forgot it and secretly recited its reassuring syllables sometimes, just to calm herself. The names provided a quiet pathway through Avenida Revolución, where you could buy just about anything.

"I don't believe it!" she interrupted a mental retelling of the *Andrea Doria* story as the storefront marquee of a corner drinking establishment came into focus half a block away.

"Shooters, $1.50," the sign said in English. "Dancing Nitely Hear Record Star Singing Sensacion—Chac!"

Too easy. The name was too unusual for there to be more than one bar singer using it. Bo shook off a sense of unease. A sense of moving along some track she couldn't see toward a destination, which, at best, did not seek out her involvement. The feeling was not unfamiliar.

You will have dinner with Dr. Broussard tonight, Bo. You will talk to her about this medication, which seems to be working, but is leaving a few wrinkles. Now, just get the address of this place and then leave.

Nodding at the sensible advice, Bo jotted down the address and then stood looking at the bar's curtained doorway. The black canvas tarp hanging from a wire across the door revealed nothing. Beneath it Bo could see broken maroon asphalt tile, some cigarette butts, a chair leg. An odor of tequila, shots of which were called "shooters" when forced down your throat by costumed waiters, drifted from the tarp. So this was where Acito's mom worked.

Bo remembered promising the baby she'd try to find his mother. How could she just walk away? This Chac might be in the bar right now, unaware that her little son had come close to death. Inside Bo heard voices. A few English words.

"Oh, why not?" She grinned at a burro on the corner, painted in black stripes to approximate a zebra. The burro shook long ears through holes in its flowered sombrero as Bo pulled the black curtain aside and went in.

A passageway running diagonally toward the center of the block between two adjacent storefronts was hung with colored plastic doilies and strands of Christmas tree lights. Eight feet in, a sawhorse over a plastic-draped pile of construction rubble held a sign that said "Peligro." Bo had seen the word on Tijuana's streets. It meant "danger."

"I can't believe you don't know where she is," a male voice spoke in a British accent with overtones Bo couldn't quite identify.

The voice came from just inside a large room at the end of the passageway. The room was half filled with small tables beyond which a bare expanse of soaped concrete served as a dance floor. Into this a wooden ramp supported by oil drums extended about fifteen feet. The oil drums had been painted gold. Along the left wall a long bar rested on forklift pallets, backed by more plastic doilies and yards of hanging metallic strips that looked like limp slices of mirror. Where the two walls would have met was a gaping hole revealing bent concrete reinforcers and more rubble.

"A margarita, *señorita*?" asked the bartender in a white shirt and red satin cummerbund. He seemed genuinely happy to see Bo. Delighted, actually.

"Um, no, just a Coke, please," she answered. For some reason it seemed wise to say nothing, just sit and wonder why a Mexican bartender was radiating joy at her presence. At the end of the bar a man of about thirty with long dark hair pulled back in a ponytail under a leather gaucho hat was working on the wiring of a sound board and bass amplifier.

"The show tomorrow night's critical," he said thoughtfully. "She knows what's at stake."

"*Señorita* Chac, she *never* miss a performance," the bartender said to Bo, as though she had asked. In his hands a perfectly dry bar glass was being dried ferociously with a red paper napkin.

Bo stabbed at the lime wedge in her Coke and let it happen. That wide intensity of awareness that, even when dutifully medicated, she possessed as the dubious gift of an illness that could also destroy her. The bartender, she assessed, was defending Chac, and knew perfectly well where she was. He was afraid of the man in the ponytail, glad to have a customer as a buffer between them.

"I'm a buyer for a little import shop in Idyllwild," she said, noticing an exquisite silver bracelet with a geometric pattern of stone inlay on the wrist of the man with the ponytail. "I'm looking for some quality silver jewelry. Could you recommend a few dealers?"

The question was directed to the bartender as she pulled a pen from her purse and grabbed a paper napkin.

"*Sí*, silver," he answered with enthusiasm. "Lots of good places for silver."

As he named a number of dealers, Bo wrote on the paper napkin. "*Acito in peligro. Donde esta Chac?*" Acito in danger. Where is Chac? The Spanish was pathetic, but the message clear.

"Did I get the street names right?" She smiled, pushing the napkin toward the bartender. Then, "Oh, *that's* what I'm looking for! Something like that." Pretending to notice ponytail for the first time, she strode to his side. "Where *did* you get that incredible bracelet?" she gushed.

"Someplace in Venezuela," he replied. "I'm sorry I really don't remember exactly where." His smile was warm, revealing slightly crooked front teeth in a tanned, outdoorsy face shadowed by the brim of the leather hat pulled low on his brow. And his pronunciation was a dead giveaway. "Some*plyce*," he'd said. "In Venez*wy*la." Australian.

"Well, it's certainly fine work," Bo murmured, retreating.

What did an Australian with expensive taste in jewelry have to do with the poisoned Indian baby who'd drooled his way into her heart only that morning? And why was the bartender afraid of what seemed to be a perfectly nice guy?

"Thanks for your help." Bo smiled over the bar as she gathered her briefcase and the red napkin, and left.

Outside she petted the zebra-striped burro and read the napkin. An address was on it, and the words "*muy peligroso.*" Very dangerous. In the eyes of the burro's owner, hunched on the painted cart where every day he photographed sombreroed tourists, Bo saw something she could only translate as hate.

Chapter Five

"The sun that shows itself is not the real sun."
   —*Popol Vuh*

Dewayne Singleton threw a handful of Tecate cypress cones into the air and listened as they hit the rocky ground. Sometimes you could hear things they said that way. Sometimes almost a real word. This time it was the word "ut-ut," which didn't mean anything. At least not to Dewayne Singleton.

Maybe it was like the sound of feet, somebody with a limp, walking up and down outside his cell at Wade. One of the guards had limped like that. Said he busted his knee playing baseball and the damned state of Louisiana didn't pay him enough to get it fixed. The guard stopped and talked sometimes because he knew nobody ever came on visiting days to the medium-security prison in the Kisatchie National Forest Preserve near the Louisiana/Arkansas border. At least nobody ever came to visit Dewayne Singleton.

"Ut-ut" also sounded a little like the breath catching in the back of the dogs' throats after they ran awhile. Bloodhounds mostly, barking and running right on past Dewayne in a big old pine tree, his socks full of Iodoform. The stuff the prison infirmary dumped into wounds made by knives and axes. He'd put the disinfectant powder in his armpits, too, and in his hair and his crotch, and tied down his shirt and pants cuffs with rubber bands. The dogs couldn't get a scent. An old Choctaw convict taught him that. Said the dogs couldn't smell you unless they were sitting in your lap.

So Dewayne packed himself in Iodoform, went with his crew to clean ditchbanks along the two-lane asphalt road

34

leading to the prison, and waited for his chance. When another convict spotted a water moccasin in the ditch and the freeman guard got off his horse to shoot it, Dewayne sprinted into the dense pine forest and kept going. It was twenty minutes before he heard the dogs behind him, and he climbed the tree.

The Choctaw'd been right, Dewayne nodded as a warm breeze blew up the unpopulated mountain from the Mexican border below. Because the dogs had run on. And Dewayne was far away now, in California.

"Ut-ut," he whispered into the wind, toward Mexico. The syllables blew back, one in each ear. "Al-lah," they said now, and he turned to his left and threw himself facedown on the ground. Left would be east, since Mexico was south. It was easier to figure out which way Mecca was on the outside than it was in Wade, for sure. The prison's narrow, louvered windows set six feet up under the roof overhang kept out the sun, but not Allah's message. The message that he had to tell his wife, down there in Mexico.

As her husband it was his duty to protect her. To tell her what Allah had told him in a prison called Wade Correctional Center sixty miles from Shreveport, Louisiana. To tell her the Angel Jabril, called Gabriel by the infidels, was coming. Coming right here. Because Allah was angry. The Angel Jabril was going to kill a lot of people here because their ways displeased Allah.

With his face pressed to the ground Dewayne prayed and tried to remember this wife he'd married a long time ago. He'd been drunk for weeks in Tijuana then, trying to stop the headaches. She was some foxy lady, he remembered. But she was a whore. The shame of it brought tears to his eyes and he pushed his forehead against a sharp pebble until he smelled blood.

Rising, he crawled to the circle of stones where he'd cooked a squirrel last night, and rubbed ashes into the cut with both hands. The mark, he imagined, would show his devotion to Allah. It would show his wife and everyone else that Allah was the one, the true God. He hoped she'd hear. Because if she didn't, she might have to die.

Chapter Six
The Yellow Road, South

Bo looked at the scribbled address on the red paper napkin in her hand. She couldn't really read it. "Calle something-or-other," it said, with a number. It might have been the address of the Dalai Lama, for all she knew about the city before her. Standing on the corner beside the painted burro, Bo realized that her understanding of Mexico centered entirely on food and fear, nothing more. A cultivated appreciation of fresh salsas, tempered by an uneasy awareness of inexplicable difference.

The address was more than sufficient for Estrella's report. In fact, it would probably earn Es some needed brownie points with Madge, who knew perfectly well what effort an investigator would have to expend to get a parent's Mexican address. Madge might even take Estrella out to lunch, Bo thought. Except that at the moment Estrella's tolerance for lunch wasn't impressive.

It was only 12:30.

"The English vessel *Sparrowhawk*," Bo began the sequence of shipwrecks again. "Aground at Nauset, mid-December 1626." Over Avenida Revolución's thousand purveyors of goods, the sun burned off the last of the haze. Bo thought about the passengers on the *Sparrowhawk*, a tiny ship with room for only about twenty people. They had come all the way from England on an icy dark sea, her grandmother said, courting death from storms, disease, possible starvation once they arrived. And these were mere English. Could an Irishwoman display less courage in obviously safer circumstances?

"Taxi!" she yelled at a rusty 1973 Plymouth cruising Revolución, and handed the red napkin to the driver.

"Sí," he nodded as Bo crawled into the back seat, after which he gunned the car left on Avenida Benito Juárez and headed toward the Ensenada toll road. Bo watched pavement slide by through a hole in the floorboards. Perhaps this had been unwise. Perhaps the address was in Ensenada, some seventy-five miles down the Baja Peninsula. Perhaps it was south of Ensenada, where she couldn't go anyway, without a visa. Where legendary bandidos were still known to prey on unsuspecting gringos.

Stupid gringos who, had they any sense, would be at the outlet mall in San Ysidro right now, looking for bargains. The driver swerved left again over a rocky parkway, and headed south, up into the hills of Tijuana. The road visible through the hole was now dirt. Bo looked out the window and wondered whether to blame this ill-advised adventure on manic impulsivity or a perverse pride that insisted on beating back fear. Either way, it had landed her on what looked like a set for *The Grapes of Wrath*.

"Thanks," she said when the cab stopped, paying the driver and skating through a collection of thin chickens circling her feet. The driver had pointed toward an alleyway between two crumbling walled courtyards. Inside one Bo could see a large, immaculately clean Duroc sow fastened with a long rope to a Model T that seemed to have sunk into the ground. Red geraniums grew in the wheelwells. The alleyway was dim, covered in places by strips of corrugated plastic or boards. The feeling was oddly medieval.

"I'm looking for a woman named Chac," Bo told an old man sitting in a large basket beside a curtained door. He seemed not to hear her, but a middle-aged woman in flip-flops came out and pointed up the alleyway, then showed four fingers. Four doors up that way. Bo headed to the designated door, and stopped. How did you knock on a curtain?

"Is there someone named Chac here?" she yelled into the flowered fabric.

"Who wants to know?" came the answer in a voice that was male, adolescent, and English-speaking. Bo was sure she heard fear in that voice. Why was everybody connected to this case so afraid?

"My name is Bo Bradley," Bo told the shirtless blond boy who now stood in the doorway. "I work for Child Protective Services in San Diego, and I have no official capacity here at all, but I need to see Chac about her baby, Acito. Is she here?"

Bo had given the last three words a deep-voiced emphasis she hoped sounded threatening. Beside the slender boy the curtain moved and a young woman stepped into the alley. A slender young woman with rosy-brown skin, braided hair so black it reflected light in tones of blue, and a classic nose Bo recognized immediately.

"I am Chac," the young woman said. "What did you say about my baby, Acito?"

"This could be a trick," the boy muttered.

"You're Maya," Bo noted with enthusiasm. "The baby's nose . . . I don't know why I didn't think—"

"What about my baby!" Chac's black eyes were filling with tears as she wadded handfuls of the baggy white T-shirt she was wearing into the waistband of tight black jeans.

"He's in the hospital, but he's doing fine," Bo explained. "St. Mary's Hospital for Children in San Diego. He's been poisoned. They haven't figured out the substance yet. Babies get into things sometimes. But he's getting the best care. He's going to be just fine."

"Acito is poisoned?" Chac gasped and grabbed the door frame. "Poisoned by what? I was with him in San Ysidro this morning. He was not poisoned then. I do not believe you."

The singer's English sounded formal. Old-fashioned.

"Your English is beautiful," Bo said, puzzled. "Where did you learn it?"

"I learned in Antigua, at a convent school called Instituto Indígena Nuestra Señora del Socorro," Chac replied as if the school's name were an impressive calling card. "I was trained as a teacher there and I have U.S. residency papers." Her voice was fierce. "My son is a U.S. citizen. You have no right to take away my son! I will go to the U.S. consulate—"

"Wait a minute," Bo interjected. This changed everything, if it were true. And a call from the U.S. consul's office in Tijuana to Madge Aldenhoven might just lose Bo and Estrella both their jobs. "Natalio and Ynéz Cruz brought Acito all the way into San Diego, to St. Mary's, because he was very sick. Since then they've vanished, but the baby's okay. The hospital placed a hold on him and notified my agency because there was no way to reach a parent, but if your child really is a U.S. citizen . . ."

"Come in," Chac sighed. "I will show you."

The blond boy scowled and hitched faded Levi's an inch higher over his gaunt hips. He must still be growing, Bo thought. He had that awkward late-adolescent gangliness that would one day fill out in the body of a tall, attractive man. Holding aside the curtain, he glowered at Bo and then tossed his long hair in a gesture meant to demonstrate aloof contempt. It succeeded only in demonstrating that he was several years short of voting age.

"Thank you," Bo said, stepping into a large room created by fastening sheets of plywood to a stucccoed rear wall. The roof was a canvas tarp. The floor, dirt.

"How'd you get this address?" he asked in a slightly nasal tenor. "Get" was pronounced "git." An American. And a country boy.

"From the bartender at the place on Revolución where Chac sings," Bo answered. "He seemed afraid . . ."

Chac had been searching through a brightly woven backpack pulled from beneath a cot. "Here," she said, tossing the backpack on the bed and handing Bo an envelope. "This is my marriage certificate. My husband is an American, which makes my baby one, too. You must return our baby."

Our baby? "Are you Acito's father?" Bo asked the blond boy, who had picked up a guitar and was tuning it with elaborate care. At the question he turned a key too far, bringing a rising whine from the instrument.

"No, no, Chris Joe is just a friend," Chac answered, pacing. "Read the marriage papers."

Chris Joe's pale cheeks flushed crimson as he began to play "Midnight in Moscow" at a furious tempo never intended, Bo was certain, by its Russian composer. His guitar strings, she noticed, were of silk-wrapped steel. Chac's words had hurt him. Bo was beginning to get the picture. The boy was in love with the woman, hiding his feelings in a tremulous display of musical virtuosity. It was transparently clear to Bo that Chris Joe wished he *were* the father. Chac seemed not to notice.

Bo unfolded the document in her hands slowly, taking time

to memorize the room, the people. A sense of urgency pervaded both. An uneasiness Bo associated with the night before leaving on a long journey. Chac's bag, thrown carelessly on the cot, had spilled makeup, a hairbrush, a plastic coin purse, and a rectangular box onto the blanket. Bo's glance doubled back to the box. Clairol aerosol hair coloring. Black. Why would a healthy young woman whose hair was naturally black need dye?

"Um, yes, I see." Bo nodded at the marriage certificate. It said that someone named María Elena Bolon, a citizen of Guatemala, had married someone named Dewayne L. Singleton, a citizen of the State of Louisiana, United States of America, in a Mexican civil ceremony two and a half years ago. Bo copied the information on a deposit slip torn from her wallet. "And are you María Elena Bolon?" she asked.

"Sí," Chac answered, leaning to pull something else from the bag. "Here are my papers."

Beneath the acorn-colored skin of the woman's inner arm Bo saw fading purplish scars that could only mean one thing. Maybe the reason for the hair dye. Bo had seen heroin addicts whose hair turned prematurely gray, and heroin was the most likely explanation for those collapsed veins. Tracks. The reason most addicts wore long sleeves, even in summer.

On the deposit slip she noted, "Mo IV drug user; check baby for HIV." AIDS. If Chac had shared needles with other drug users before or during her pregnancy, she could have contracted the virus, which could have infected her baby before his birth. The tracks were old, healed. But Chac might have contracted the virus years in the past. Bo thought of the dark-eyed baby in his hospital crib, and sighed. Life was always, she mused, a complete crap shoot.

The identification papers of María Elena Bolon were in order, and included a photograph of the woman now calling herself Chac.

"Why did you change your name?" Bo asked, noticing a shelf of labeled jars over a battered table holding a hotplate and Chris Joe's guitar case. The labels named various herbs. And scratched white stenciled lettering on the guitar case spelled "C.J. Gavin, Henderson, KY, GHOST PONY RULES!"

Chris Joe rolled his eyes at the ceiling tarp, and switched from the Russian song to a plaintive melody that sounded folkloric. He was, Bo realized, creating a musical background for Chac.

"I'm a singer," the young woman said, nodding to the music. "Singers use special names. Mine is a Maya god. What else do you wish to know?"

Bo could think of several hundred questions, but settled on the obvious. "Where's Acito's father, this Dewayne Singleton?"

"I don't know. He left me before Acito was born."

"Do you have any idea where he might be? We need to contact him. Notification of both parents is standard procedure when a child is in custody."

"No," Chac answered flatly.

Chris Joe had placed the guitar in its case and picked up a sort of wooden flute. As he played a haunting refrain that Bo found vaguely familiar, Chac began to sing softly in Spanish. Or at least it was partly Spanish. And the voice filling the dingy room, Bo realized, might be that of an angel. A trained voice, molding invisible fire out of vibrating air. At the song's end Bo heard the phrase "Mi Acito."

"It is the song of my love for my son," Chac whispered. "He is my heart. Do you understand? I cannot lose him!"

Bo felt tears swimming in her eyes. The song was the one she'd heard on the radio. Live, it was mesmerizing. And so was this team of musicians who had her crying in a Mexican hovel in broad daylight. She felt dizzy, as though she were slipping in and out of differing points of view.

Get out of here, Bradley. This is too weird!

"Acito isn't really my case," she stammered, backing toward the door. "You need to contact my co-worker, Estrella Benedict. She'll tell you what to do. Here's the number."

Handing her own CPS business card to Chac, Bo pushed aside the doorway curtain and bolted into the alleyway. The old man in the basket was gone, and so was the Duroc sow. In the mile hike to the nearest paved street where she could catch a bus, Bo saw only a succession of crumbling walls that seemed to hide peculiar and incomprehensible dangers. She hoped if she looked straight ahead, whatever lay behind those baked adobe walls would ignore her as well.

Chapter Seven
Chi Pixab, the Place of Advice

Madge Aldenhoven was characteristically sullen when Bo returned to the CPS offices at 3:00.

"Your new case is on your desk, and where's Estrella?" she called from her office without looking up as Bo passed the door. Amid stacks of manila case files piled on the desk, three chairs, and the floor, the supervisor seemed dwarfed by paper. Bo couldn't help thinking of Poe's "The Cask of Amontillado." Of Madge Aldenhoven sealed forever in her office behind thick walls of case files, eventually becoming a cobwebby skeleton with three Bic pens stuck in its spun-sugar hair. The skeleton, Bo fantasized, would be found centuries in the future by archaeologists excavating San Diego after an earthquake separated the city from the continental U.S. The archaeologists would think Madge had been the priestess of a cult that worshipped paper.

"I don't know, but I'm sure she'll be back soon." Bo smiled at Madge's door frame. "Why?"

"Dr. LaMarche called an hour ago," Madge said into a box of tissues on her desk. "The Mexican baby poisoning was not accidental. Estrella needs to pick up those lab reports before filing the case."

"I'll call St. Mary's and have them faxed over." Bo stated the obvious, turning the corner into her own office. Once inside, she pressed her head against the wall for a moment, picturing the little Indian baby in her mind. He was so strong and eloquent in his preverbal way. How could anyone deliberately hurt him?

The news was sickening, but then so was most of the news useful to San Diego County's Child Protective Services. People sometimes murdered children, who could be an intolerable nuisance, or burden. But why Acito? And who? One of the paid caretakers in the little San Ysidro apartment? Bo thought it unlikely. Acito had been a source of desperately needed income to them, and besides, why would they then have taken him to a hospital?

Chac said she'd visited Acito only this morning. Had Chris Joe accompanied her? Could the mother or the strange expatriate hillbilly have wanted a burdensome baby out of the way? Bo didn't like the picture framing itself in her mind. The picture San Diego's police would be sure to see as well. A struggling singer with a history of drug abuse, clawing her way to stardom in the Tijuana music scene. A talented young accompanist, angry at the world and devoted to Chac in a way that could easily become distorted. The police would assume that either one of them could have done it, Bo admitted. The thought made her teeth taste like varnish.

Pulling a pack of cigarettes out of her purse, she began stacking them individually in a crisscross pattern bordering her desk blotter. From the bulletin board above, fifteen faces looked down in sympathy. William Faulkner frowned. Ernest Hemingway scowled. "Monstrous," Mary Shelley mused into the air over Bo's head.

"You're all crazy," Bo told the photographs as Estrella opened the door with a swoosh.

"Oh, great. You're building cigarette fences and talking to those damn pictures again. Did you find out anything about this Indian baby, or have you been sitting here all day conversing with dead people?"

Estrella's mood, Bo noted, had not measurably improved.

"He's a Maya baby," Bo answered, "and I've got vast documentation for you, including a baby bottle and Mom's Tijuana address, but none of it points to infanticide, which is what the lab reports are indicating."

The word hung in the little room, an anachronism.

"Infanticide," Bo thought, had something to do with

European kings. Or with Greek folklore. *Oedipus Rex,* maybe. Not with Indian babies from cities with dirt streets.

Estrella's reaction to the word was less cerebral. "Oh, *sheet!*" she began crying, her fists knotted on Acito's case file Bo had tossed on her desk. "I *can't.* I just can't do it!"

"Can't do what?" Bo asked, puzzled. "I'll run the petition over to court for you, if you'll just fill out the forms. No problem."

Estrella's face seemed composed of fragments, like a mosaic. The friend Bo had known for years was visibly going to pieces.

"I had decided," Estrella began in a whisper, "that I wasn't going to have this baby. I thought about it all day, sitting at home. No matter what Henry and my family and everybody would think, I decided. But I can't do it." She was sobbing. "I just can't have an abortion."

Bo opened her mouth and then closed it when she realized that everything she could think to say was either inappropriate or idiotic. Instead she sat on her friend's desk and draped an arm over the heaving shoulders.

"Walls for the wind," she crooned the first Irish blessing that came to mind into Estrella's upswept coif, and distractedly looked out the window. "And a roof for the rain." A black and white bird dropped from the bright, glassy air and paced in the shade of a peeling eucalyptus. "And tea beside the fire . . ." Bo trailed off. The bird couldn't be a magpie, could it? Were there magpies in Southern California? Bridget Mairead O'Reilly had taught her granddaughters well the things the presence of magpies could mean.

"Do you know," Estrella straightened her back and sobbed at the wall, "that my father's parents raised six kids in a *truck,* picking crops all over the West? And my mother is deaf in one ear because there was no money for a doctor when she was a child, and her eardrum burst from an infection?"

"I didn't know," Bo murmured, watching the bird.

"Do you know that I'm the first person in my entire family to go to college, to have a job like this? I *like* my job, Bo. It's important; it helps people sometimes. I like helping." Tears were leaving dark splotches on Estrella's wine-red silk blouse. "I don't want to have to quit working."

The black and white bird cocked its smooth head at the sky.

"One for sorrow," Bo whispered the first line of the magpie rhyme her grandmother had recited at every piebald bird summering at Cape Cod with Bo's family.

"Can you believe I really don't want an excuse to quit this underpaid job?" Estrella giggled into a Kleenex, her eyes wild.

A second magpie locked tiny feet over a low-hanging branch of the eucalyptus. "Two is for mirth."

"And Henry will make the best father a kid could want . . ."

"Three is for marriage." Bo smiled as a third bird joined the first on the ground and began preening its feathers. If a fourth magpie showed up, this whole conversation would be moot.

"I just wish . . ." Estrella snuffled, toying with Acito's case file, "it wasn't so damned complicated."

"And four for a birth!" Bo grinned to herself as one more black and white form rustled the menthol-scented leaves. "I know you're gonna work it out," she said to Estrella while shaking a congratulatory fist toward the window. "You're one smart woman; you can cope!"

Pleased, Estrella opened the case file and pulled a handful of legal forms from her desk drawer. "Why are you waving at the yard?" she asked as though the behavior were perfectly ordinary.

"Magpies." Bo blushed. "I think they're leaving."

"There are no magpies in San Diego, Bo."

"Not usually," Bo agreed.

An hour later Bo slipped Bach's Toccata and Fugue in D into her dashboard stereo and turned it up. Her new case had been one of the hundreds of crack babies born to mothers who abused the powerfully addictive drug. She'd been to the small, south-county hospital, interviewed the mother, seen the baby. Crack baby cases were all alike. And all sad. A petition filed in juvenile court would remove the child from its mother while she entered a drug treatment program, but nothing could repair the damage already done.

Crack babies were growing up to demonstrate impaired

intellectual functioning even as toddlers and preschoolers. Bo would file the petition tomorrow, but her mind was on Acito and her own behavior in Tijuana.

"My best friend is a Latina, and yet Mexico feels like a house of horrors to me," she remarked to the vinyl sun visor shielding her eyes from the late afternoon glare. "Nonetheless I manage to burst into tears over a tune by some bar singer who may have tried to poison her own baby only this morning. Is it safe to say that my response to this situation leaves something to be desired?"

On the passenger's seat Mildred, Bo's aging fox terrier, chewed on a slab of rawhide cut to resemble a gingerbread man, and said nothing. Bo had gone home to pick up the dog before heading by the hospital and then out eastbound 94 toward the little high-desert community called Jamul.

"Hah-mool," she sang the Spanish syllables over blasting organ chords, and wondered what the word meant. Maybe Dr. Broussard would know. The transplanted French-Canadian psychiatrist had settled into San Diego's melting-pot culture with a verve, and at sixty was learning both Spanish and rock-carving while continuing her research with a community of people who believed in extraterrestrial landings.

Compared to Eva Broussard's life, Bo mused, her own was an encyclopedia of boredom. On the other hand, for a manic-depressive, boredom was probably okay. Sort of.

Only twenty-five miles from downtown San Diego, Jamul rose dramatically from the spaghetti-tangle of freeways below, a sparsely populated backcountry of hilly dirt roads and bleached boulders not one of which was smaller than a single-engine Cessna. Bo could understand why Eva and her group had chosen to buy a hundred and sixty acres of mountaintop privacy up here. The views were spectacular, the air cool and clean.

Turning off 94 to begin the climb toward the shrink's airy compound, Bo slowed to admire the late afternoon sun gilding a thousand white boulders in a color like lemonade. Beside the road leaves of scrub oak and chamise reflected the light in flashes, while on the hillsides yuccas stretched creamy blooms skyward. Nothing moved but a red-tailed hawk circling on the horizon.

Bo sighed and replaced the Bach tape with Vivaldi's Concerto for Two Flutes, Strings and Basso in C Major. The music, ecstatic in its major key, spoke of landscapes in which no rheumy-eyed children begged, no raven-haired babies lay poisoned and lonely in hospital cribs.

"It isn't right!" Bo remarked to Mildred, surprised at her own outburst. "Everything about this case, and everything that goes on at this border isn't right. I don't understand it, but it's out of balance. It's wrong."

Mildred looked up in concern and nudged the rawhide gingerbread man toward Bo with her nose. One leathery arm had been reduced to slick white pulp.

"Ycchh," Bo said. "Thanks anyway."

On a dirt road named Mother Grundy by nineteenth-century settlers who couldn't pronounce "Madre Grande," Bo engaged the four-wheel drive and revved the little vehicle uphill with abandon. A gate halfway to the first ridge stood open to a rocky jeep trail leading further upward through boulders and chaparral.

Bo turned the flute duet even louder and imagined the delicate notes rising like liquid crystal over lemon-colored hills. The jeep trail would lead to a half-Iroquois psychiatrist whom many would write off as eccentric, Bo smiled, but whom she trusted more than anyone since her first doctor, the long-dead Lois Bittner.

"Happiness for some of us," she told Mildred, "involves finding a decent shrink."

The dog merely nodded.

"I heard you coming," Eva Blindhawk Broussard called from the porch of a crumbling adobe hacienda. "So did everyone for twenty miles. What lovely music!"

In moccasins and jeans the older woman looked as lithe as a greyhound despite the halo of stiff white hair framing her copper-colored face. She might have been thirty instead of sixty. Bo made a mental vow to get to the gym more often than twice a year.

"The place is shaping up!" she noted after a long hug from a woman she regarded more as a sister than a doctor. "The floor looks terrific."

"Mexican quarry tile," Eva Broussard explained. "It's quite inexpensive over the border in Tecate, and I enjoy driving down there. What's truly amazing, though, is that I have a steady supply of craftsmen walking through the property every day."

The hills, Bo knew, were laced with pathways created by thousands of undocumented laborers walking to destinations that might be hundreds of miles away.

"A group of Guatemalan refugees did most of this tile work," Eva went on. "But I know you didn't come to talk about tile. You said on the phone that you're having some concern about the new medication?"

"I saw a woman from Guatemala today," Bo said, interested. "A Maya Indian. She sings in a club in Tijuana. Her baby's been poisoned, and LaMarche is convinced that the poisoning was deliberate, but I don't know . . ."

To the west, nested layers of hillside were mantled in early shadow. Beiges and grays with fleeting fringes of purple. Eva sat beside Bo on the porch's tiled floor and sighed at the view.

"The Maya," she pronounced in deep, Canadian-French-accented syllables that invited close attention, "are a most fascinating people. Very different from northern native peoples, like my own tribe. Very special. And being brutalized to near-extinction as a culture even as we speak. Tell me, what is this baby's name?"

"Acito," Bo answered. "And the mother calls herself Chac. Does his name mean anything? She said hers was a god."

" 'Ac' is the Maya word for turtle. And the suffix 'ito' is the Spanish diminutive. 'Acito' would mean 'Little Turtle.' Have you met him?"

"At St. Mary's today," Bo answered.

"And is he a Little Turtle?"

Bo remembered small hands clutching her hair, a soft, coal-black cowlick. "Absolutely," she said. That was Acito, all right. Hard-shelled enough to survive. Looking for something in that loopy way a turtle looks. Looking for his mother.

"The Maya understand that a person may have a *nagual*, an

animal co-spirit," Eva went on, squinting as the sun dropped lower, bathing the porch in sudden gold. "Acito's mother, this Chac, knows and respects her son's heart, to have named him so well."

"Chac is one of the prime suspects in Acito's poisoning," Bo whispered, running both hands through her windblown red-silver curls.

Eva shook her head and stood. "No," she said. "That's not possible. We cannot harm another whose true name we know. Not without doing identical harm to ourselves. Chac did not harm Acito."

"I knew that," Bo said. "I just didn't know how I knew it."

"Why do you constantly question your intuition?" Eva asked, throwing a stick for Mildred.

"Because I'm crazy," Bo answered softly, using the pejorative term she would allow no one else to use. "I never quite know, even with the medication, what's absolutely true and what my mind is exaggerating all out of proportion. I was spooked down there, just being in Tijuana, and then Chac sang a song about Acito that brought me to tears. It was embarrassing, and I just left."

"Nothing is absolutely true," Eva said, pulling Bo to her feet with both large hands. "And just because your perception is more extreme than others doesn't mean that what you're perceiving isn't really there. It is."

Everything was coated in sparkling gilt fifteen minutes later as Bo drove Eva, holding Mildred, back down the main road and a red-painted plywood restaurant named El Coyote.

"The *chile verde* is exceptional," Eva mentioned while herding both Bo and Mildred to the restaurant's candlelit back patio of white chairs and green tablecloths. "And they use a low-alcohol tequila in the margaritas. Now, what's this about your medication? Are you unable to sleep, irritable, grandiose, paranoid? I can prescribe something to go with the Depakote."

"No symptoms, really," Bo said, relaxing as a faint moon materialized in the summer sky. "But I just can't seem to react to things like everybody else. Estrella's pregnant and upset. LaMarche keeps acting like something out of a Fred Astaire movie. And a song I can't understand makes me cry. Nothing seems, well, normal."

"Perhaps you need simply to accept your own reactions, Bo. 'Normal' is such a relative term. You know the symptoms to watch out for. If they're not there, then what is?"

Bo lit a cigarette and pondered the question, grinning. "Just me," she answered. "Whoever that is." It occurred to her that a bronze-skinned baby with an animal's name might just help her figure that out.

From the restaurant's radio a familiar song drifted across the patio and out over the mountains. A woman's voice, trained and powerful, accompanied by a wooden flute.

"*Mi Acito*," the voice whispered. "My Little Turtle."

Chapter Eight
Hunahpu Monkey, a Tune

Hell had broken out in patches when Bo arrived at the office on Thursday. She hadn't even pried the squeaking plastic lid off the lukewarm fluid called "coffee" by the Department of Social Services cafeteria, before Madge was at the door doing a sort of jitterbug while juggling case files. Bo slumped in her chair and tried to focus on the scene. It was hopeless before coffee.

"A distressing incident at the hospital last night . . ." Madge said. "In the department's judgment it will be better if Estrella doesn't handle it, so . . ."

The muted thudding of Bo's phone interrupted the supervisor's narrative. It was for just such moments as this, Bo smiled sleepily, that she'd covered the little bell inside her desk phone with a layer of adhesive tape. The clanging of an unmuted bell before noon was intolerable. "Child Protective Services, Bo Bradley speaking," she yawned.

"Dr. LaMarche says you don't think the mother poisoned the kid," Detective Dar Reinert boomed amicably and without preamble. "Had a real nasty mess with her last night at the hospital. Wound up letting her go, but my bet is, we'll never see her on this side of the border again. Whaddaya think?"

Dar Reinert was the San Diego P.D. child abuse detective who'd found Bo the car of her dreams. A fact that did nothing whatever to make what he was saying any more comprehensible.

"You must be talking about Estrella's case, the little Maya baby . . ." Bo answered, watching Madge push up the sleeves of a gold ramie hip-length sweater that made her look as if she were about to join a bicycle tour in France.

51

"It's not Estrella's case now," the supervisor insisted, pointedly placing Acito's case file on Bo's desk while placing the file of the crack baby on Estrella's. "I've been trying to tell you . . ."

"I'll have to call you back, Dar," Bo said into the phone as Madge crossed her arms over a necklace of carved wooden beads that precisely matched the dead-leaf brown of her cashmere slacks. "In the meantime can you run a check for me on . . ." Bo fumbled in Acito's case file for the names she'd heard yesterday. ". . . Dewayne Singleton from someplace in Louisiana, and a minor called Chris Joe Gavin, Henderson, Kentucky. Thanks, Dar." To Madge she said, "Are you trying to give me a Spanish-speaking case? Where's Estrella?"

"Estrella is sick this *morning*," Madge emphasized the key word, "and as it turns out the mother speaks English. Estrella did a superb initial investigation yesterday, but I'm afraid this case has just become too demanding for her current, well . . . resources."

"Her *resources?*"

"Any woman who's ever been pregnant could identify Estrella's condition immediately, Bo. It's hardly a secret. And after what happened at the hospital last night, we've decided that it would be more appropriate for you to continue the investigation."

"Because I'm not pregnant?" Bo had to ask. "I'll bet Nick Paratore's not pregnant, either. He's in our unit, too. I just saw him in the cafeteria. He wasn't barfing or anything. Why don't you give the case to him? And what happened at the hospital last night?" She widened green eyes and let them go glassy. "Let me guess. The baby turned out to be a tiny werewolf and ate the entire night staff, right?"

Madge stared at the floor as if it were about to slip away, and clenched her teeth. "The mother showed up at St. Mary's last night, demanding the release of the baby. There was a row when staff explained that he had to remain in the hospital for an HIV test, and then go into foster care pending the outcome of our investigation. The police were called. I think the mother actually assaulted Detective Reinert, but he allowed her to return to Tijuana in spite of that. Doubtless a mistake, not that it matters. We're probably looking at a 'freed for adoption' here unless the father can be located. That's what I want you to do. Either find the father or let's file for termination of parental rights. If the baby's HIV positive, transfer him to medically fragile long-term foster care. If not, transfer him to adoptions, assuming you don't find the father, or he forfeits his right to the child. Meanwhile, Estrella will handle your case from yesterday. Any questions?"

"No," Bo answered. "No questions."

Except why wasn't I invited to your installation as God, Madge? And how inspiring that you haven't let it go to your head.

"Good." Aldenhoven sighed and stalked into the hall.

Bo pushed the heels of her hands against her knees under an African print skirt featuring ragged black suns on rust-colored homespun, and grimaced. The Maya mother and baby, she thought, had wandered too close to a nation made of systems. Bureaucratic systems like the one she worked for, which weren't real, which were nothing but interlocking grids of rules. Which could never, ever hear a mother's song or touch a baby's soft black hair.

"I'm overreacting," she said to a photograph of the poet Anne Sexton on her bulletin board, "as usual. But then, you'd understand, wouldn't you?"

The system was going to take Chac's baby away, unless somebody stopped it.

"CPS, Bo Bradley," Bo snarled into the phone when it rang again. "Oh, hi, Andy . . . yes, I heard." The sleeveless black turtleneck she'd chosen to complement the woodblock-printed skirt felt as though it were alive and slowly choking her. "Sure, I can come right over," she agreed, pulling the fabric away from her throat. Proximity to the dry, mechanical heart of injustice, Bo realized, made even her own clothes feel threatening.

"I'm going over to St. Mary's," she yelled at Madge's door, "for a technical explanation of the substance that poisoned Acito."

"That will be good in the court report," the supervisor answered with a disinterested calm typical of strangers at bus stops discussing pleasant weather. A calm that Bo Bradley, carefully medicated and stabilized manic-depressive, would never feel. Or, she admitted, ever want to feel.

Andrew LaMarche was waiting for her in the carpeted lobby of St. Mary's Hospital for Children, holding Acito's medical records and a nosegay of white violets. Beneath his starched lab coat an oxford cloth shirt in eggshell and a surprising silk tie painted in taupe and cream asters made his gray eyes seem almost blue.

"For you," he said, proffering the nosegay. "My lady."

"Oh, God, Andy," Bo replied, pleased but aware that everyone in the lobby might be watching, "thank you. They're lovely, really, but . . ."

"It's a summer day," he insisted, ushering her toward the hospital's glass-walled cafeteria. "Flowers before business. I'd like to see you tonight, Bo." Beneath a graying brown mustache his smile was confident, almost impish.

Not for the first time Bo experienced a familiar conceptual lurch at the warmth of that smile. The warmth of the man, who had proven to be a stalwart friend as well as a tantalizing potential lover. Except that he insisted on muddying the situation with archaic references to love and marriage.

"Andy, we just don't have the same agenda," Bo said as he paid for two coffees and accompanied her to a cement table in the cafeteria's outdoor courtyard. "I'm not the marrying kind. My attention span's too short."

"Nonsense," he murmured.

"Andy, that was a *joke*. Now, tell me about this poison."

He opened the record file and handed Bo duplicates of several pages. "It's a substance called abrin, derived from a tropical plant. It has no known use in any commercially produced product either here or in Mexico, and in fact would be very difficult to acquire. One would almost have to grow, harvest, and store it deliberately. It's quite unusual, Bo. There's simply no way a baby could accidentally ingest it."

Bo ran her right hand through her hair and pursed her lips. An image of jars full of herbs rose in her mind and refused to vanish. Chris Joe Gavin, boy-guitarist, had a thing for dried plants.

"As the mother is a native of Guatemala, it may be possible that she has some knowledge of tropical plants, perhaps even of primitive medicine . . ." Andrew LaMarche suggested somberly and then stopped as Bo's green eyes turned pine-dark at his words.

"Why would Chac want to poison Acito?" she demanded. "She adores that baby. She even wrote a song for him. And what, exactly, do you mean by 'primitive'? Surely not the thousand herbal remedies drug companies are scrambling to document and produce synthetically?" Bo rummaged in her purse for a cigarette, lit it, and blew smoke in an eloquent column over her right shoulder.

"My sister, Elizabeth, quit smoking a couple of years ago," LaMarche mentioned to a cement bowl of pink lantana on the table. "She said it was like having to learn to talk all over again."

"Please give your sister my regards when you speak to her," Bo muttered, letting the cigarette hang from the corner of her mouth in a manner reminiscent of Humphrey Bogart. A trench coat, she realized, would be a big help.

"Actually, I'll be seeing her on Monday," he said, inspecting immaculate, buffed nails. "I'm flying down to Louisiana to be an expert witness in a New Orleans case. Lafayette's only a short drive from there. I thought you might like to join me."

"I have a job, Andy. That precludes almost all impromptu jet-setting. And why would you want me to go, anyway?"

"To meet my family." His smile was a cross between a sort of mannered lechery and something deeper. "I'd like you to meet my sister and her husband, and their children."

The desire in his eyes created an instant movie in Bo's brain. A balconied New Orleans hotel room with plush furniture, magnolia petals falling slowly through warm, moist air. A single blues sax echoing in narrow streets while on the bed . . . She could run by Victoria's Secret over the weekend and pick up something tantalizing yet demure. Something to match the magnolias, whatever in hell color magnolias were.

Bo felt a flush escaping her turtleneck and rising to stain her cheeks, if not her freckles, which would now be splatters of beige putty. Her hand around the now empty coffee cup was trembling.

The hell with demure, Bradley. Demure is not what you have in mind here. By the way, what do you have in mind here?

"Perhaps this is somewhat premature," he offered.

"No," Bo answered thoughtfully. "Not exactly."

Accustomed to occasional manic episodes with their predictable sexual surges, Bo assessed her feeling for Andrew LaMarche and found it to be something slightly different. The usual compelling inclination was there, trailed by a cloud that seemed full of lightning and half-lit corridors. The unknown. But so what? This was just something that happened. A gift from a universe probably created in the same yearning away from aloneness.

"I can't go to visit your family, Andy," Bo began, "and I'm not going to marry you, but I do have an idea."

"Bo, I want to have a life with you, not just—"

"I'm only talking about *tonight*, Andy. I'm saying yes, let's do something tonight. I'd like to go down to Tijuana to see Chac's show, maybe talk to her about the legal hurdles ahead in getting Acito back. Will you go with me?"

Something in the atmosphere switched gears. In reversing their roles she'd seized the reins of a situation that had gone on for too long. If people wanted to make love, they should just do it and get it over with, Bo reasoned. And wasn't it the prerogative of the woman to set the terms of that experience?

Andrew LaMarche stood and shot his cuffs. "I'll be happy to go, but do you really think it's wise?"

"Absolutely," Bo said, crushing her cigarette in the Styrofoam coffee cup before throwing the whole mess into the trash. "And now I've got work to do. I'll just check in on Acito before going back to the office." She waved the violet nosegay. "See you tonight."

"Oui," Andrew LaMarche said, reverting to the language of his Cajun childhood as he invariably did when under stress.

Bo found Acito untrammeled by IV lines, happily banging on a Fisher-Price drum in the fourth-floor playroom. He shared a playpen with a black baby girl whose exquisitely cornrowed and beaded hair, Bo assessed with admiration, must have taken somebody hours to do. Acito ignored his companion, focusing exclusively on his drum.

"You cad." Bo knelt and smiled through the pen's mesh side. "You're going to tell her nothing matters but your music, right?"

"Dogwuggg," Acito said as Bo stood and gathered him into her arms. "Wugggeee."

"Dogwood *is* woody." Bo nodded, hugging him.

His companion immediately dropped to her diapered rump and began banging on the drum with both hands. Acito turned in Bo's arms to watch, and a glassine string of saliva fell from a pool at the corner of his mouth.

"Still teething, I see," she said with approval. "You're doing a fine job."

In profile his classic Maya nose seemed more pronounced. Bo imagined him in quetzal feathers and embroidered loincloth, standing atop a limestone pyramid in some jungle as yet unscathed by Spanish invaders. And maybe he'd have that flattened forehead Eva said the ancient Maya created by binding infants' skulls between boards. A desirable deformity that made the child godlike.

Any deformity, Eva said, was considered a blessing by the ancient Maya. A cleft palate or clubfoot, an extra finger or crossed eyes—any departure from the physical norm was evidence of the gods' favor. Bo placed the baby back in the pen, hoping no hidden virus was creating its own deformity within his cells. The HIV test results wouldn't be back until Monday.

Instead of going straight back to the office, Bo turned onto San Diego's central artery, the old Cabrillo Highway, and grinned. Taking charge of the Andrew LaMarche problem entailed certain responsibilities.

In five minutes she was in the artsy, upscale little community called Hillcrest, home to coffeehouses, restaurants, counterculture music emporiums, several specialty bookstores, and a shop catering to the sexually active.

"I'm looking for something conservative," she told the

young man behind an impressive display of condoms. "Maybe a pinstripe, or a foulard pattern. Nothing splashy."

"Wow," the boy answered. "I don't know. We've got, you know, your basics. Stars and stripes. Rainbow, of course. A glow-in-the-dark green. And this new one—a Navajo blanket design. That's our best-seller right now. But you know these novelty ones are just for show, don't you? Guys'll wear one of these over the real one. Kind of a layered look."

"I think not," Bo said, trying to imagine Andrew's likely response to a layered look. "Just one will have to do."

"We have a Japanese model that's very popular—incredibly thin and embossed with tiny white roses, but as strong as the heavier ones."

The embossed roses sounded intriguing. Bo was certain she could find something in rose-embroidered silk to match.

"I'll take three," she decided, and tucked the parcel in her purse.

On the way back to the office she found Radio Romántico on the dial, and listened to both "Unchained Melody" and an old Dolly Parton hit redone in Spanish. What this wholesale piracy of dated music might mean, Bo couldn't guess. But it was fun to sing along.

"Es, can you tell me why Mexican studios are recutting every top ten hit from 1955 on in Spanish?" she asked when she returned.

Estrella looked, Bo thought, like death in a biscuit tin. Bo's grandmother had frequently used the phrase to describe pale, gaunt people. It fit Estrella perfectly.

"Who knows?" Estrella answered. Unspoken was the codicil, ". . . and who cares?"

Bo had not seen Estrella at work before in less than full makeup. She had also never seen Estrella at work in jeans and a faded sweater. Time for a different approach.

"Okay," Bo began, "you're depressed. You feel like dirty paint on the walls of a dark room where nobody ever goes. You don't blame them. You wouldn't go there, either. You think you might prefer being dead, but it's such a hassle it's not worth it. Am I right?"

"You're right," Estrella sighed. "Every time I think I've got on top of this, it falls apart. I don't know what to do."

"First, remind yourself that it won't last. Your chemistry will stabilize in a while. In the meantime, you need something to distract you. Like a good time."

Estrella's eyelids remained at half-mast. "Hah," she muttered.

"I'm serious," Bo went on, warming to an idea. "Andy's going with me down to T.J. tonight. I want to talk to Chac again, and the easiest way's to see her show at this bar on Revolución. How about you and Henry coming along?"

"You're going out with him again?" Faint color was returning to Estrella's face. "But I thought . . ."

Estrella's approval of Andrew LaMarche knew no boundaries. To further escalate her friend's mood, Bo showed her ace.

"Not just going out." She grinned, displaying the little foil-wrapped items she had just purchased in Hillcrest.

"Wow! What made you change your mind about him? Oh, Bo, that's terrific. And of course I'd love to go along, but shouldn't you two be alone?"

"We will be," Bo vamped dramatically over the top of a report on welfare fraud she grabbed from her desk and held like a Japanese fan, "later."

Chapter Nine

"As they looked, their knowledge became intense."

—*Popol Vuh*

A sadness overcame Dewayne Singleton as he stood watching people hurry back and forth across the border. They looked like mice in clothes. But that wasn't why he felt sad. At his feet swirls of dust puffed up and then fell to nothing with every step.

It almost made him cry, but he couldn't stop walking just to stop the little puffs of dust, which would have to die. Maybe, he thought, this was how Allah felt. How Allah couldn't stop walking just to stop creating people with every step. Maybe people were just dust kicked up by something walking by. Something big, not paying attention to its feet.

The sadness of that made his bones vibrate and feel sick, although he didn't know why. Allah could do whatever He wanted without Dewayne Singleton feeling one way or the other about it.

Even from a quarter-mile distance the problem in Mexico seemed to rattle in the air like somebody's radio on to something you can't really hear, but you can't not hear. The whore, his wife. She might not still be there, but he thought she probably was. Unless she was dead from shooting up. That might be. But then why was he here? Allah would know, as long at Dewayne prayed five times a day. That was the important thing.

Dewayne flung himself upon the cluttered dust beside the border and faced Mecca. Five Japanese tourists from a guided group took snapshots of him before being led to the metal turnstiles where no one asked to see their passports.

The dust in Dewayne's nose smelled like cooking *poule d'eau*, he thought. Water chicken. Like the black, swimming chickens on Bayou Teche with their little pod claws. His family lived on *poule d'eau*, and the baitfish called *chou picque*. It was pretty good. But his family didn't worship Allah.

Tears filled Dewayne's eyes again as he rose and brushed himself off. His family would die in Allah's wrath, too, if the curse rising from this place wasn't stopped.

Overhead the sun wobbled a little, like a rolling egg, and then stopped. Dewayne watched it and thought about Papa and Buster, the day they ran him off.

"You're nuthin' but trouble," Papa said. "Go on outta here an' don' come back!"

His younger brother, Buster, didn't say anything, just whomped him with a board until his nose bled. Dewayne knew Mama was back at the house cryin' and prayin'. Mama always loved Dewayne best. No matter what. He'd have to save Mama, at least.

Beyond the border turnstiles a man held a rack of stone wind chimes that clinked in the breeze. Dewayne felt his mind ride the sound as he headed into Mexico.

Chapter Ten
Bone Flute, Bird Whistle

By nine o'clock Avenida Revolución reminded Bo of the bar scene from *Blade Runner*. A festival of nations in a boozy neon-lit haze pouring from a hundred open doorways. "Free Margaritas for the ladies!" yelled a man in one doorway, countered by another yelling, "Your first shooter only fifty cents!"

Groups of foreign tourists bused down from San Diego's hotels walked expectantly through streams of colored light, their plastic name badges reflecting magenta, then greenish yellow. Five pale college boys, already very drunk and wearing newly purchased ponchos and sombreros, stood on a bus bench singing "Hava Nagila." Bo didn't miss the look of hate crossing the face of a Mexican busboy working an adjacent sidewalk café.

She hoped the young revelers would stay on Revolución, where it was safe. But they probably wouldn't. The darker side streets only blocks away offered other, sometimes deadly, attractions. Drugs, prostitution, live pornography in floor shows rumored to include women enjoying the sexual prowess of German shepherds.

San Diego's abundance of collegiate and military adolescent males learned through folklore passed from generation to generation how to "do" Tijuana. Out-of-town boys sometimes found themselves drugged, beaten, robbed, and left to wake up the next morning in rancid alleys. Occasionally one of them didn't wake up.

"An interesting environment," Andrew LaMarche said, steering Bo around an ancient woman begging in the middle of the sidewalk. "One scarcely knows what to make of it."

Bo slid her right arm around his waist and found the gesture comfortable. "I love it when you don't have an opinion." She grinned, enjoying the warmth of his hand cupping her shoulder. In June, nights were still cool, but she'd worn a clingy cowl-necked shell in black silk that had no sleeves and weighed about as much as a wooden match. With black lamé gaucho pants and dramatic gold earrings, the dark silk would, she calculated, create an aura of sensual worldliness. If only Estrella could bring herself to stop beaming.

"How much further is this bar?" Lieutenant Commander Henry Benedict, Estrella's husband, asked. "You know, Tijuana's off-limits to navy personnel. And I've already forgotten where we parked the car."

Gangly in a sport coat and tie instead of his usual navy uniform, he bent his tall frame over Estrella protectively. The colored lights made his short blond hair look like shaved tinsel.

"You're not in uniform, and it's in the lot on Benito Juárez," Estrella grinned. "Only four blocks from here. How on earth do you keep from getting lost when you're running around underwater in submarines?"

"Fortunately my field's communication, not navigation." Henry grinned back as Estrella wrapped both arms around his waist.

Bo looked approvingly at her friend, carefully made-up and dressed in a chic peach satin peacoat over caramel brown slacks that as yet gave no hint of the debatably blessed event. Es was, Bo thought, resplendent. In fact they were all resplendent, and it was nice to be one of them. Nice to be part of a couple out with another couple to do something interesting. Nice just to be normal.

Too nice.

Watch it, Bradley. You're falling into a trap that has been known to involve Tupperware and loss of identity. You did take your medication today, didn't you?

Bo remembered the vitamin-sized pink pills, tossed back with tomato juice morning and evening. No problem.

"This must be the place." LaMarche nodded at the corner doorway ahead, above which the name "Chac" was spelled in twinkling Christmas tree lights Bo had not seen earlier. In the dark the little club seemed sophisticated, devil-may-care.

"Hey!" Estrella whispered as they traversed the long hall and entered the club's main room. "If that's Chac, she's good!"

Every table was filled, and Bo's party leaned against the bar as the singer finished the lyrics to a traditional Mexican polka, prancing on the narrow runway stage like a wiry pony. Her black hair hung thick and straight, flashing blue sparks as she moved gracefully despite three-inch spike heels and white satin toreador pants so tight her abdominal muscles could be seen. Flat abdominal muscles, like brickwork. Bo sucked in her own stomach and made another vow to get to the gym soon. Maybe this week. Maybe tomorrow.

Andrew ordered a pitcher of margaritas and a Coke for Estrella, and toasted Bo as Chac began another song. A photographer with a Polaroid camera was snapping shots of couples for a dollar apiece.

At the end of the bar Bo noticed the Australian she'd met yesterday, still wearing the unusual inlaid-stone bracelet. He seemed to be controlling the sound mix for Chac's accompanying taped music. Without the gaucho hat he was less theatrical, more ruggedly handsome with a patch of white hair curling over the right side of his forehead amid the mass of dark waves pulled back in a ponytail. Beside him a slender woman whose profile reminded Bo of Nefertiti smiled and leaned to say something in his ear.

Where the stage intersected the missing far wall, Bo noted, Chris Joe Gavin sat on a stool, his Martin six-string in his hands. As Chac completed the song's introductory bars, he began a thrumming counterpoint to her melody.

The song's words were Spanish, but Bo was sure she could name the theme. Some things transcended mere language. As the music escalated, Chac's clear voice grew husky, then hoarse. A single pin spotlight framed her head and shoulders against smoky darkness, and the guitar's notes seemed to move through her like electricity.

It was a wail of longing barely confined by the music. Erotic longing. The near-obsessive need of one person to join wholly with one another. Alone. Bo noticed that her knees felt like gauze, and carefully set her drink on the bar behind her to avoid simply dropping it on her feet. At her right shoulder the presence of Andrew LaMarche's chest had created a magnetic field that made it impossible to move. Or breathe.

As the music crescendoed, Chac dropped to her knees and threw her head back. Her hair was a cascade of sleek blackness, damp at the temples. Her eyes were closed as she held the last, long note, then doubled forward over the hand-held mike to breathless silence and then thunderous applause.

Bo let her head fall back against the man at her side, and felt his lips brush her temple and remain there as he pressed his skull against hers.

"It's good that you went shopping today," Estrella whispered happily into her Coke. "Hey, people are leaving. We'd better grab a table before you collapse."

"Let me get Chac," Bo said, forcing herself to move. "I have to talk to her."

In the shuffle of people leaving to barhop elsewhere or just milling around between musical sets, Bo gestured toward the young singer. "Chac!" she yelled. "It's Bo Bradley, remember? Could you join us between sets? There are some important things we need to discuss."

The singer was signing tape cassettes at the end of the bar, flanked by Chris Joe, the Australian, and his companion, who in the light looked as though she'd know her way around Hollywood. That attitude. Open, self-assured, expensively dressed. Not the usual habitué of Tijuana nightspots. Bo found a ten dollar bill in her purse and bought one of Chac's tapes.

"*Sí, un momento,*" Chac answered, and then jumped in fear as an altercation broke out in the hallway. Over a cacophony of Spanish as leather-jacketed bouncers flung themselves into the dim passageway, Bo heard a voice bellowing something in English. Something about Allah and a curse on infidels. The speaker was invisible, the Mideastern words weirdly out of place among the hanging plastic doilies and omnipresent Christmas tree lights of Tijuana.

"What's that all about?" she asked Estrella over the din after pushing her way to their table.

"Just some nut," Es answered, immediately wincing at the choice of words. "I mean, it's probably a Saudi tourist who's had too much to drink. You know how it is down here."

Bo frowned. "You mean a Muslim? They don't drink."

"Well, this one's a backslider then." Es laughed as the offender was hauled into the street, his words fading.

LaMarche had succeeded in securing a table in the front, and as Bo, Estrella, and Henry took their seats, Chac approached.

"Why are you keeping Acito from me?" she asked, slamming an oversize shot glass of tequila on the table. The full sleeves of her white blouse were covered with thousands of flashing sequins, and the front and back of the garment fell to points.

The blouse was made, Bo realized, by folding a square of fabric corner-to-corner. The traditional Maya woman's costume with the addition of sleeves. There had been an exhibit of these *huipiles* at a San Diego museum only a few months ago.

"You can't take him away. You have no right!"

"Please sit down for a moment," Bo said. "And let me introduce Estrella Benedict and her husband, Henry, and Dr. Andrew LaMarche, the director of the Child Abuse Unit at St. Mary's Hospital."

"Child abuse!" Chac bristled, nearly overturning her drink as she shook a trembling fist at Bo. She was unconsciously squashing a wedge of lime cupped in her hand. Estrella caught the shot glass before it tipped, and pushed a salt shaker toward the distraught singer.

"We'd like to help you," Estrella said in Spanish.

"To Little Turtle," Bo toasted, holding up her margarita.

Chac's black eyes softened momentarily as she squeezed lime juice on the back of her left wrist, sprinkled salt on it, licked her wrist, and then downed the tequila.

"You know his name," she said, shuddering at the high-proof alcohol. "How did you . . . ?"

"I have a friend," Bo explained, "who's an Iroquois, among other things, and she's read a lot about the Maya . . ."

"Then she has read that a Maya mother does not hurt her

baby," Chac finished the sentence for Bo, demonstrating impressive fluency in English. "And why are they doing this AIDS test on my son, on a *baby*?"

In theatrical makeup and her sequined costume the young woman was exquisitely beautiful. Bo wished there were a way to avoid shattering that illusion, but there wasn't.

"When I saw you yesterday, I noticed the tracks on your arms," she said. "They were old and healed, but Acito is eight months old now. You could have been using while you were pregnant with him. If you shared needles with other addicts while you were using IV drugs, you and Acito could have been exposed to the AIDS virus."

"We have to test the children of IV drug-using mothers," Andrew LaMarche interjected sadly. "It's standard procedure." He shifted uncomfortably in his chair. "And I'd also like to ask if you know anything about poisonous plants. Do you know what I'm talking about, Chac?"

"Andy!" Bo interjected. "She doesn't know anything about—"

"What is he talking about?" Chac asked Bo. "What plant?"

Over Chac's shoulder Bo could see Chris Joe and the Australian discussing a piece of paper and stacking cassettes beside the tape deck feeding four speakers flanking the narrow stage. Chac's program for the second set, Bo assumed. As Chac's accompanist, Chris Joe would need to know the order of music. But who was this cowboy Australian with his stripe of white hair and easygoing grin?

"The substance that harmed Acito," Bo explained, "was from a plant. A tropical plant."

"I don't know anything about a plant," Chac said, frowning.

Bo lowered her voice. "Do you think Chris Joe might know something about it?"

"Chris Joe? Do you mean you think . . . ?" Chac looked uneasily over her shoulder. "Chris Joe is like a . . . a *curandero*." She glanced at Estrella. "With the herbs. Many people here use herbs. There are shops on the streets . . . to buy herbs."

Estrella nodded. "A *curandero* is a sort of folk healer, Bo. Among poor people this is still the practice. Few have money for doctors. And there are *farmacias* everywhere that sell herbs. Right outside on Revolución, as well as in every village in Mexico. I'm surprised you haven't noticed."

"I just assumed '*farmacia*' meant pharmacy." Bo plowed through her own cultural failing and pursued the original goal. "Was Chris Joe with you when you visited Acito in San Ysidro yesterday morning, Chac?"

"*Sí*, yes, he brought fresh apple juice. He strain it for, you know, the bottle, and boil it so there was no germs."

Nervous, the young woman was losing facility in what Bo realized was probably a third language.

"When you were a child in Guatemala, did you speak Spanish?" Bo asked, changing the subject.

"No, we spoke Tzutuhil. That is the language of the Maya in my region near Atitlán. My village was San Juan la Laguna. Why? What does Tzutuhil have to do with this plant that poisoned Acito?"

"I don't know," Bo admitted. "I'm just really impressed with all you've done, all the languages you speak, your singing career. How did you get here, Chac, all the way from Guatemala to stardom in Tijuana? I hear your songs on the radio in San Diego. You're going places! But the journey from there to here must have been difficult. Was it?"

Beneath her tawny skin a flush crept up the young woman's cheeks. She glanced toward both men at the table, and a hard smile, almost a sneer, distorted her mouth. "Tell your friend," she said to Estrella in Spanish, "she asks too many questions."

"Never mind," Bo went on miserably, having seen the ugly truth on Chac's face. "We just need to tell you about the hearing in court on Monday."

Bradley, as a diplomat you'd make a terrific sideshow barker. How in hell do you think she got this far? How does any young woman with nothing get anything? You need to listen to more country and western music or else shut up!

The house lights, such as they were, were dimming.

"I have to go," Chac said, standing. "What is this hearing?"

Bo handed her a card with the address of San Diego County's Juvenile Court embossed on it, as well as her own number at CPS. "Nine o'clock Monday," Bo said. "Dress conservatively, like you were going to church. You won't get Acito back at this hearing, but if you're not there it'll only make things worse."

"I'm going to get my baby back!" Chac insisted, heading for the stage. "I am!"

"Do you think we should leave?" Henry Benedict suggested. "God, Strell, I don't know how you deal with this every day."

The Australian was onstage, apparently introducing Chac. Even in his Spanish Bo could hear the characteristic accent. In a sweeping spotlight he exuded confidence and an articulate excitement that might have been genuine and might, Bo thought, have been blown up his nose through a straw. His companion was nowhere in sight.

"Let's stay just a little longer," she said. "Es, what's he saying?"

"That he's Munson Terrell, Chac's manager, and that he's proud to introduce the Maya singing sensation who's about to sign a contract with a Hollywood music producer. A contract that's going to make Chac a star."

Under the applause generated by Terrell's introduction, Chris Joe began a traditional rock 'n' roll guitar accompaniment, backed by acoustical guitar and drums on a tape. Chac jumped into the song at a chorus, full out, no slow build up. The audience loved it. Bo, frustrated, could only make out one word, "*libertad*."

"What's she singing?" she asked Estrella.

"About freedom. She's saying, 'You can't have my freedom, set me free.' That kind of thing."

"No, no, no!" Chac ended the brief number, already sweating.

"I want to get Estrella home," Henry suggested again. "She shouldn't overdo it tonight."

"*Madre de dios*." Estrella sighed. "I'm sitting right here, Henry. Stop talking about me as if I were a child. I can't stand it when you get like this, and if it's going to be this way for seven more months . . ."

"I'd like to get on the road, too," LaMarche mentioned, looking at Bo. "There may be a wait at the border."

"You're right," Estrella agreed in an about-face that made up in enthusiasm what it lacked in subtlety, standing and smoothing her jacket.

"Wait. Bo Bradley!"

It was Chac's voice, from the stage. "This song . . . you must hear this song."

After a whispered consultation with Chris Joe, the young musician unfastened his guitar strap and picked up the wooden flute Bo had seen the day before. During the melodic introduction Chac merely stood, head bowed, one hand pressed against her stomach.

In a blue spotlight she seemed pale, although Bo could see perspiration still beading on her forehead. Odd, Bo thought, for her to be sweating so profusely only one song into the set.

"She's going to do Acito's song," she whispered. "Es, can you translate it for me?"

LaMarche handed Estrella a pen, and she grabbed one of the club's red napkins for use as a notepad.

The melody was as evocative as before, enhanced by lighting and a sense of desperation emanating from the slight figure singing on the stage. Bo couldn't help thinking of the French chanteuse, Edith Piaf, called "The Little Sparrow" in her time. A picture of Chac as a little bird drifted up in Bo's mind. A white bird with huge, black eyes.

Signaling the photographer, she dug a dollar from her purse and said, "A photograph of Chac, *por favor*." In seconds the damp, developing snapshot was in her hands.

On stage Chac had stopped between verses and was speaking in English over the haunting flute.

"The Maya believe that the *huipil*," she tugged at her blouse, "is the symbol of woman, who is like the caves and the surface of water. The woman is the passageway," she whispered breathlessly, "between the underworld and this life. The Maya live to keep time going. That is our task."

Her rapid, shallow breathing suggested great feeling. Her face was contorted as if from pain. "And at the center of time," she went on, "is a woman birthing a child. No one may interfere with that. No one."

Estrella, Bo noticed, was crying. And Chac actually was

pale under the blue light. Deathly pale. Her voice as she began the last verse of the song was too high and strangely off-key. Her black eyes seemed polished, and then suddenly empty. The microphone slipped from her hand.

"*Mi corazón*," she whispered, her eyes rolling back in her head. "*Mi Acito*."

Bo watched as a white bird simply slid from the air and crumpled on a plywood stage held up by oil drums. Chac's arms stiffened for a moment, as though she were reaching for something far away, and then she was still. A bubbling foam at her lips continued to reflect the light in blue sparkles.

In the pandemonium that followed, people yelled, "Doctor! *Médico!*" and Andrew LaMarche flung a khakied knee onto the narrow stage and crawled to the white form lying in the pool of blue light. In less than a minute he turned and found Bo's eyes in the panicked crowd.

"She's dead," he mouthed. "Call the police."

The Australian named Munson Terrell, Bo noticed, was on the stage cradling Chac's head. At the back of the room a skinny, long-haired boy with a guitar pulled aside the plastic tarp where a wall should have been, and vanished into the rubble-strewn darkness on the other side.

Chapter Eleven
The Moth Gatherer

Bo woke from an uncomfortable sleep and for moments wasn't sure where she was. Checking her darkened surroundings, she recognized an open closet door revealing a familiar clutter of clothes. Mildred asleep and snoring in her basket beside the bed. And outside, the endless surging of the Pacific Ocean against Sunset Cliffs. Home. Relentlessly accurate, her digital clock radio announced in green numbers that dawn was a thing of the future: "4:23 A.M.," it said.

"Shit," Bo remarked, noting that her beige pinstriped sheets were knotted in ropes and three of the four pillows with which she liked to bank herself against potential things that go bump in the night were on the floor. The fourth was squeezed to a damp wad against her chest. In the dark beyond the end of the bed the scene in Tijuana seemed to be just out of sight. A small white bird, fallen and still. Bo rubbed at her eyes with the edge of a rumpled pillowcase, flung long legs over the side of the bed, and stumbled onto the little balcony facing the sea.

"It's okay to cry," she told the foggy breeze blowing up from the beach. "Healthy, even. Who wouldn't?" Wrapping her arms around her ribs under one of the old T-shirts she always slept in, she allowed herself the experience popularly termed a good cry. Except in Bo's experience, crying invariably caused nothing but a lingering headache, sore throat, and burning eyes. Sniffling, she wondered why everyone else in the world waxed so rhapsodic about crying. It just wasn't her thing, she acknowledged, popular wisdom notwithstanding.

Wandering back into the apartment, she pulled on a pair of sweat pants and her most closely guarded secret, armadillo houseslippers. The stuffed-toy footwear boasted washable vinyl plating and cute suedecloth faces, one of which was missing its nose after an early encounter with Mildred. Bo had found the slippers at a swap meet only weeks ago, and decided to allow herself the eccentricity of owning them. Pretending *not* to be eccentric all the time was so draining. Andrew, she thought with amusement, would undoubtedly abandon his suit for her hand if he could, at the moment, see her feet.

But he couldn't. He'd stayed at the Avenida Revolución club with Chac's lifeless body, urging Henry to take Estrella and Bo home. Determined to stay, Bo had only begun a tirade against patronizing men who think women swoon at unpleasantness, when Estrella obliterated Bo's thesis by actually swooning. Or almost swooning. She'd been caught in the crush of people trying either to leave or to gawk at the singer's body, turned pale under her makeup, and slumped to a chair in which she quickly placed her head between her knees. Bo had recognized no option but to accompany her friend to the street as Henry ran to retrieve the car. When he returned, Estrella had recovered but Henry seemed to be hyperventilating. Needed, Bo gave up hope of immediate information regarding Chac's death, and climbed into the Benedicts' car. Andrew would have to walk back over the border, she'd assessed ruefully. The cab fare back to his Del Mar condo would rival minor aspects of the space program in cost.

Brewing a cup of instant mocha decaf cappuccino in the microwave, Bo rubbed her temples and considered the night's terminal event. Acito's mother, dead. But why? Had the stress of her baby's seizure by San Diego County authorities caused Chac to relapse? To start using drugs again? On either side of the border, drugs were a fixture of nightclub life. Chac would have had no trouble scoring any drug she wanted without leaving the bar. Bo felt a clammy, metallic weight on her chest. Guilt.

Maybe their presence at the club had driven the marginal young woman over the edge. Maybe if they'd just stayed home like nice anglos and reinforced their cultural imperative by watching reruns of old Andy Griffith shows on TV, Chac would still be alive. Acito would still have a mother.

"You screwed up," Bo said to her reflection in the microwave's door. "Got up to your neck in a situation you didn't understand, and made it worse. Now a little boy will grow up among strangers. He'll know nothing of his mother or what she might have taught him about being what he is, a Maya Indian. Now there's nothing left of his history but a lullaby. You're an arrogant, ignorant, meddling imperialist. You might as well be Madge Aldenhoven."

Bo held the hot coffee in both hands and wiggled her ears. The scalp movement sometimes helped the throbbing tension headaches that could descend out of thin air and felt like sock-cymbals thudding in her skull. That dull reverberation. But it wasn't working.

"Mildred," she called softly into the bedroom. "How about a little ride?"

The dog placed one paw over a furry head and pretended not to hear.

"There will be treats," Bo mentioned, grabbing a paint-smudged sweatshirt that had once been avocado green from a pile of clothes on the closet floor. "Among them your favorite peanut-butter bones and the ever-popular desiccated liver jerky."

Stiffly the old dog capitulated to bribery, and got up. After providing one of the promised bones, Bo massaged the fox terrier's arthritic joints and dressed her in a warm parka Bo had made out of an old down vest. In the red nylon garment Mildred might have modeled, Bo thought, for an L.L. Bean catalogue.

"We're going to Jamul," she told the dog. "To talk our way through this before it gets any worse."

Eva Broussard was already awake when Bo arrived at the high-desert property about 5:00. Up and dressed, sipping coffee. Lug-soled boots and a thermos peeking from her backpack suggested that Bo had interrupted the prelude to one of the doctor's lengthy hikes into the mountains.

"No, just a last chance to be alone with the hills before the first group from New York arrives this afternoon," Eva explained. "There will be quite a bit of construction, all environmentally sensitive, of course. But noisy. I have to admit, I've loved the solitude. You know, Bo, when my research with the Seekers is finished, I'm thinking of moving further out. Someplace really isolated. But you haven't come here at dawn to discuss my love of the desert, nor to go hiking, judging by your shoes."

After watching Mildred chase something reptilian to safety under a rock, Bo stared at the toy armadillos on her feet and sighed. "Chac died last night on the stage at the club where she worked," she told Eva Broussard. "Probably a drug overdose. She had some old, healed tracks. She'd obviously stopped using. But then something set her off again. Es and Henry and LaMarche and I were there. It was awful."

"If she injected an amount similar to what she used when she was addicted, it could kill her," Eva agreed, leading Bo and Mildred into the adobe house and throwing a small log on the remains of last night's fire. "But you don't know that's what happened. You're only guessing. And you're quite upset."

"Well, no kidding!" Bo exploded. "I promise a baby I'll find his mother, and then what do I do? I scare her so much with threats from CPS and the courts that she accidentally overdoses and dies. I should have just taken Acito down there and handed him to her. We don't have any business imposing our values and rules on people like Chac and Acito. Do you have any idea what her life must have been like before now . . . ?" Bo was pacing in front of the fireplace, the armadillos making shuffle-flap sounds with every step.

"I have agreed to an unorthodox professional relationship with you, Bo," Eva said from where she was seated cross-legged on the tile floor. "As a psychiatrist I can prescribe medications and monitor your mental status. But it's your task to put the necessary boundaries around your own experience. You're overreacting to this death and dramatizing aspects of it that are as yet sheer speculation. Internalizing responsibility for this woman's death may seem noble to you, but in fact is—"

"Grandiose?" Bo concluded the sentence. "I knew you'd say that. It's why I drove up here."

"But I didn't say it." Eva Broussard smiled, revealing straight, healthy teeth. "You did."

By eight o'clock Bo was at the office dressed in a tailored suit and lacy white cotton blouse whose ruffle had taken three quarters of an hour to iron. With expensive black pumps and matching bag, the ensemble suggested a chic competence she was determined to feel.

"I didn't know you were scheduled for court today," Madge noted from her office as Bo entered.

"I'm not. I'm auditioning for the lead in *Auntie Mame*. Do you think these pearl earrings are too conservative?"

A simmering silence followed Bo to her office door. She switched on the desk lamp and settled in to begin the arduous sequence of phone calls necessary to find the man who was Acito's father. Or not find him. With Chac dead, Acito was already half orphaned. If, after every avenue had been explored, a father could not be found, she would inform the court and proceedings freeing the baby for adoption could begin. But first she had to document "due diligence." No stone could be left unturned in a parent search, especially when there was only one parent left. The first call was to Dar Reinert.

"Bradley," the detective roared genially, "Dr. LaMarche informed me about the death of our suspect in that baby poisoning. I called the Tijuana police. They put it down to a drug overdose. Must have been some scene over there."

"Yeah, a scene," Bo replied. "Listen, Dar, the reason I'm calling is I'm starting the parent search for the baby's father. Did you dig up anything on this Dewayne Singleton?"

"We're both in luck on this one," he answered. "I get to close the case on the baby, and you get—"

"Close the case? How can you close it?"

"No motive, no witnesses, no suspects. The kid's okay. He's in your agency's hands now."

Bo made a face at the telephone.

"But there *is* still a suspect, Dar. This kid, Chris Joe Gavin.

The mother's been living with him. And he's into herbs. He could have poisoned Acito."

The delicate glen plaid of her suit was beginning to annoy Bo. Its interesting black lines created a grid that seemed to be closing in. If somebody had tried to poison a baby, how could the police just look the other way?

Dar Reinert sighed. "I checked with the Henderson, Kentucky, P.D.," he went on. "This Gavin's listed as a missing person. Ran away from a foster home last year when he was sixteen. You can get the skivvy on him through CPS in Henderson, if you want to, but he's got no juvenile record. We'd have to extradite him out of Mexico just to talk to him, *if* we could find him. The Mexican cops went to his digs last night, looking for drugs. He's cleared out, Bo. Probably gone on down to Mexico City or something. For all practical purposes, he doesn't exist. Now, about Singleton—"

"Wait a minute," Bo interjected. "Do you mean to tell me you're just forgetting about this case?"

"Look, Bo," Reinert continued as if explaining quantum physics to a kindergartener, "we don't know that a crime was actually committed. When my kids were little they were into everything. One of 'em even ate the dog's worm pills. Besides which, we don't know which country this alleged crime took place in. Sorting it out would take time and manpower we just don't have, and neither do the cops in Mexico. It's a loser. It can't go anywhere. It's dead."

Estrella came in and Bo nodded, then continued doodling pictures of police badges on a notepad. Limp badges, like Dali's clocks, draped over baby bottles.

"So tell me about Singleton," she sighed.

"You're gonna love this," Reinert said, regaining his characteristic buoyancy. "The guy's got a record in Louisiana. Most recently a felony theft conviction. And guess what he stole!"

"Pralines," Bo countered. "Somebody's crawfish pie?"

"Stop talking about crawfish!" Estrella stage-whispered from her desk.

"Locusts," Reinert chortled. "The guy stole three thousand genetically altered bugs called *Pachytylus pardalina* from a

New Orleans university lab. He was working there as a janitor. But wait'll you hear—"

Bo flipped her notepad to a clean page. "Let me get this straight. Chac's husband has been convicted of a felony in Louisiana. Does that mean he's in jail? Why would he steal bugs? And how can stealing bugs amount to a felony charge? Bugs are cheap, especially in that climate."

"Not these babies," Reinert went on. "These were experimental bugs, meant for release in agricultural areas. They were supposed to breed with the regular bugs and produce offspring that won't eat rice plants or something. But the best part is what he did with them. Are you ready for this?"

"Probably not," Bo answered.

Reinert was clearly enjoying himself. "Got to be some kind of nut. Get this. He fried the little suckers, coated 'em in caramelized honey, and sold 'em to voodoo shops in the French Quarter as vitamins! Can you believe it?"

Bo stared at the photographs pinned to the bulletin board over her desk. Every face seemed to share with her an uneasy perception of what voodoo bug-vitamins might mean. "Uh, Dar, do you know if he had a name for these . . . vitamins?"

"Funny you should ask." He was audibly rummaging through paper. "It was in this report they faxed . . . here it is. 'Jean Baptiste.' Called 'em 'Jean Baptiste Vitamins.' Musta named 'em after his girlfriend, huh?"

Uh-oh.

"Not exactly, Dar," Bo concluded the conversation. "Did you get a current address?"

"Sure. Home address, R.R. 3, Franklin, Louisiana. Current address, Wade Correctional Center, Haynesville, Louisiana. Except he's not there."

"What do you mean he's not there?"

"Walked off a work crew eight days ago. They sent dogs after him, of course, but the dogs came back empty-handed. The guy flew the coop."

Bo couldn't help smiling at the image of empty-handed dogs.

"Thanks, Dar," she sighed, turning her own hands up in a gesture of futility. "I'm back at square one."

A brief phone call to Henderson, Kentucky's, Department of Child Welfare netted Bo the name of the social worker who'd supervised Chris Joe Gavin's last foster care placement.

"Mexico?" the gravely voice of a woman named Gracie Belker exclaimed after Bo informed her of Chris Joe's whereabouts. "What in hell's he doin' in Mexico?"

Gracie Belker was friendly and informative. Christopher Joseph Gavin, she told Bo, had been placed in foster care at the age of two on the occasion of his mother's first incarceration for accessory to auto theft. She had since graduated to more serious offenses and was never out of prison long enough to reclaim her son, although she refused to free the boy for adoption. Chris Joe, Belker said, had been in no fewer than twenty-three foster homes in fifteen years. The last, a particularly big-hearted family named Springer, had gone to enormous lengths to keep the boy with them when they had to move out of state. Chris Joe and their older son were like real brothers, and had formed a garage band called Ghost Pony. In Belker's view, the loss of the Springers' love and support when their legal appeal failed and they had to leave without him broke Chris Joe Gavin's heart. The night before he was to go to his twenty-fourth foster home, he ran away.

"He's a good kid," Gracie Belker informed Bo. "Did well in school in spite of being changed every whipstitch, never in any real trouble. Five or six of the foster families wanted to adopt him along the way, including the Springers, but Mom wouldn't let go. Guess he just couldn't take any more, huh?"

Bo thanked the Kentucky social worker and sighed. At seventeen, Chris Joe Gavin had been about to lose someone else he loved. Was the pain so great that he'd been driven to kill what he was about to lose? The thought was troubling.

Several carefully documented calls to Louisiana later, Bo knew nothing more definitive than she'd learned in Kentucky. The authorities at Wade Correctional Center had no idea where Dewayne Singleton might be, but would be delighted to mail copies of pertinent files just as soon as their copier got fixed. The sheriff responsible for Franklin, Louisiana, was visiting his sister down in Cocodrie, but two deputies, both named Fontenot and distantly related, were certain Dewayne Singleton hadn't come home to his family because his family ran him off in the first place. Besides, everybody in town knew he'd escaped from Wade. Any one of the townspeople would call the sheriff's office if he showed up. And no, his family didn't have a phone. The Franklin Public Schools had no record at all of a Dewayne Singleton, but then their available records only went back four years. And the secretary of every church in Franklin professed much too forcefully her certainty that nobody by that name had ever been a member.

By 11:15 Bo was dropping Gs randomly and using "y'all" as a generic nominative of address. When the phone rang almost as soon as she replaced it in its cradle, she answered "Gud mawnin' " without missing a beat.

"Bo?" It was Andrew LaMarche. "I'm in the reception area of your building. Mrs. Aldenhoven has refused permission for me to come to your office even though your line's been busy for hours. I need to talk to you, and Estrella. Are you free for lunch?"

His voice seemed unusually edgy, even under the circumstances.

"We'll be right there," Bo agreed. "But what's wrong?"

"I have some rather disturbing news," he said softly. "Just meet me in front of the building."

Chapter Twelve
Fox and Coyote

Rombo Perry paced the length of the new living room, turned, and skated back to the Dutch door. His socks, he noted, remained immaculate. The recently stripped, sanded, and refinished floor reflected dappled sunlight filtering through a superb deodar cedar that filled the front yard and obviated any need for grass. The dwarf periwinkle Martin had planted would soon cover any bare spots.

"What time do you have to be at the hospital?" Martin St. John inquired from a hall office where he lay on the floor surrounded by open cookbooks. His tone suggested casual, almost careless interest.

Rombo peered through black wire-framed glasses at the street for the twelfth time in fifteen minutes. "Twelve thirty. You know perfectly well it's twelve thirty. But I wanted to be here when they brought it. I can't believe we've bought an entertainment center, Martin. It's so seventies. What if it overwhelms the couch?"

"The couch will survive, Rom," Martin grinned, ambling into the room barefooted. "But you won't if you don't get out of here before that truck arrives." He flung long arms above his curly dark hair in a rough approximation of a ballet position, then bowed clumsily to the floor. "They're going to have shoes on." His hands caressed the surface of the floor as he cocked his head and smiled impishly upward. "Our floor's virginity will be sacrificed to hobnailed ruffians, uncouth deliverymen groaning beneath the weight of handcrafted cabinetry designed to disguise the fact that the Industrial Revolution has already happened." He stood and straightened the hem of a gray sweatshirt as if it were a military tunic.

"You can't handle it, Rom. Your patients are waiting. Go on to the hospital."

"Social workers use the term 'clients,' not 'patients,' even psychiatric social workers, and we've been working on this floor for two solid weeks." Rombo sighed. "It's perfect. Do you really think these ballet classes you've been taking are helping your back?"

"Yep," Martin replied, "best thing for baker's back. That's what Madame Anouchka said. I can't wait to get the CD player in so I can listen to *Les Sylphides* while the rolls rise. It'll be good for Watson, too. We want him to have musical taste, right?"

Watson, the golden retriever puppy for whom Rombo and Martin had bartered a three-year supply of St. John Catering's popular whole wheat yeast rolls, was scheduled to leave his mother in less than two weeks.

"What's baker's back?" Rombo's crooked nose, broken by somebody named Billy Beloit on the Midwest boxing circuit in another life, flared in disbelief. He'd been trying to interest Martin in physical fitness for years, but the lanky caterer had, until now, shown total disinterest.

"Occupational hazard of kneading, lifting trays in and out of the ovens. Overworks minor muscle groups while the rest of my classically well-proportioned body atrophies into something approximating string cheese. I'm trying to talk Bo into joining the class. She'd like the music."

Rombo glanced out the window again. "I think that's the truck. Are she and Andy coming for dinner on Sunday? Or did we decide to wait for them to 'define their relationship'?" He shook his head fondly. "With all the encouragement straight people get, you'd think they'd have the drill down by now, wouldn't you?"

"It *is* the truck." Martin nodded as the hall phone rang. "I'll get that. Go to work."

Rombo opened the top of the Dutch door and caught a dried bougainvillea bract blowing in from the spectacular plant trellised to the Spanish cottage next door. "I'm not leaving until I see it against the wall," he said. "What if the doors won't close over the TV? What if they didn't put the speaker-cord holes where we told them?"

"It's for you," Martin called from the Berber-carpeted hall. "It's the ER."

"What's up?" Rombo said into a replica of a 1920s wall phone friends had provided as a housewarming gift. "Sure. I guess so."

Outside a gleaming van embossed with the name "Pickwick Furniture" in heavily serifed lettering backed into the driveway.

"I don't believe it," Rombo fumed, hopping while tying polished black Italian dress shoes. "The cops have brought over some guy they picked up at the border last night, stopping cars on the U.S. side and warning people about a curse. They kept him in county jail all night, can you believe? Then they bring him over to the hospital, where he should have been from the beginning, at *noon*, when of course the duty intake worker's gone to lunch. I've got to get over there to do the intake. Guy's name is Dee-wayne something-or-other. Sounds Southern. The desk clerk says he looks like he's been beaten pretty badly, too, but he's in no shape to tell anybody what happened."

"Have I told you lately that you're about the most exceptional guy I've ever met?" Martin asked, opening the lower half of the door for Rombo.

"I hate it when you get emotional." Rombo blushed as he pulled a lightweight gray blazer over his polo shirt and grabbed his keys.

"No you don't, you love it." Martin nodded, hugging the muscular social worker. "Call Bo and check on Sunday, okay?"

From the furniture van two women in tennis shoes deftly maneuvered the first section of a hand-rubbed cypress wall unit onto a rubber-wheeled dolly.

"Don't worry," one beamed at Rombo. "We won't scratch your floor."

Chapter Thirteen

"No cleanly blotted blood . . ."

—*Popol Vuh*

"Unquestionably, Chac was poisoned. I knew from the almond smell when I leaned over her," Andrew LaMarche told Bo and Estrella over a plate of kung pao squid at one of the many Vietnamese restaurants in the neighborhood surrounding CPS headquarters. "But in the excitement I couldn't quite recall what that odor meant, just that it meant poison."

"So you grabbed Chac's glass off our table when you left, and then had the residue tested this morning. Andy, you're a genius! If it weren't for you, nobody would ever have known. I mean, I just assumed it was a drug overdose, and so did the Mexican police."

Estrella was using her chopsticks to push a plateful of barbecued pork fried rice into a landscape of small hills. "I keep seeing that foam bubbling out of her mouth," she whispered. "That's what smelled like almonds, isn't it?"

"Probably," LaMarche answered. "The odor is characteristic of cyanide poisoning. But the foaming would have been caused by a second poison, also found in the shot glass. It's an alcohol called cicutoxin. Comes from a wild herb that, according to the chief toxicologist at the Poison Control Center, doesn't grow naturally in this climate. Some kind of hemlock. Looks like parsley, he said. Grows wild near streams or in wet meadows."

"There isn't a wet meadow within five hundred miles of here," Bo told a serving of ground shrimp on sugarcane she'd ordered to impress Andrew LaMarche with the sophistication of her palate. The dish, while odd, wasn't half bad. From the determination with which he was chewing his squid, Bo feared the same could not be said of Andrew LaMarche's own attempt at culinary broadmindedness. Estrella appeared to have discovered some troubling message beneath her fried rice, and was frowning at it.

"So there were two poisons in Chac's shot of tequila," Bo went on. "But why two? Wouldn't either one of them have been enough to kill her?"

"It's quite strange," LaMarche continued. "Almost as if her murderer particularly wanted the cyanide to be present, but didn't trust its efficacy." He leaned forward and poked with a chopstick at the red plastic dragon topping their table lamp. "Cyanide's volatile, a gas. Even in a suspension, the molecules won't stay put. And this particular cyanogenic glycoside appears to have been extracted from a fruit. The lab thinks it was probably apple."

Bo registered disbelief. "A cyanide apple? Come on, Andy. The groceries haven't run a special on those in ages."

"Oh, the fleshy part of apples is, obviously, perfectly safe to eat. But the seeds contain cyanide, Bo. A few won't hurt you, but a couple of handfuls would be lethal."

"Kind of ruins the Johnny Appleseed story, doesn't it?" Bo mused, eyeing the rice paper on her plate.

"Bo?" It was Estrella, her face a mask of dismay.

"Are you okay, Es? You haven't eaten much. Want to go walk around outside for a minute?"

"No. It's not that." Estrella's dark eyes were troubled. "Chac's death is my fault, Bo. If it weren't for me, she'd still be alive."

"Oh, Es," Bo said with sympathy. "I felt that way, too. Like we never should have opened this investigation. We should just have left Chac and Acito alone. But—"

Estrella took a deep breath. "The poisons were in her drink, right?" she asked. "Well, she almost knocked her drink over when she was yelling at you. If I hadn't caught the glass, it would have spilled, and she wouldn't have drunk it, and . . ."

Bo placed her hand over Estrella's trembling one as LaMarche shook his head. "Estrella," he insisted, "somebody wanted Chac dead. If that drink had spilled, there would have been another one. What it looks like to me," he scowled, "is that both the baby and his mother were targeted for death by someone well versed in natural poisons. It's really quite peculiar."

"Peculiar," Estrella repeated, shuddering.

"It's out of our hands now, Es," Bo said, recognizing the response as rational and sane. "It's a criminal case. I'm sure the police will find Chac's killer. In the meantime, I'm going to request a confidential foster care placement for Acito. What did the police say when you told them about the lab report on Chac's glass, Andy?"

The waiter had brought the check and LaMarche made a production out of figuring the tip, then getting a doggy bag for Estrella's fried rice. Once outside the restaurant he launched into a monologue about the very shopping center in which they now stood. "It's the first in the nation," he expounded, "built in the forties when—"

"Andy!" Bo interrupted. "What did the police say?"

"The San Diego Police said," Estrella answered, climbing into the passenger's side of Bo's vehicle, "that the crime took place in Tijuana and its investigation is therefore the responsibility of the Mexican police."

"So?" Bo asked, looking quizzically at LaMarche, who was elaborately adjusting a windshield wiper on his maroon Jaguar, parked next to Bo's Pathfinder under a coral tree. On the sidewalk beyond the tree an ancient woman in traditional loose black trousers held a flowered umbrella over her head as she carried a baby in a shawl on her back. Bo thought the baby could win a Buddha look-alike contest, if only one of the three Oriental supermarkets in the shopping center would sponsor one.

"Um," Andrew LaMarche said, watching the progress of the baby Buddha. "The San Diego Police have contacted the Mexican authorities, and will send both the glass and the toxicology report to Tijuana by courier this afternoon." His tone attempted businesslike closure on the subject, a ploy Bo hadn't fallen for since the last time her mother tried it when Bo was about five.

"And then what?" she insisted, standing on the Pathfinder's narrow runningboard and tossing her hair.

Andrew LaMarche seemed miserable. "An investigation of some sort, I assume," he said, pulling at a corner of his mustache. "Probably not right away . . ."

"What do you mean, 'not right away'? A woman's been murdered! Detective Reinert told me they went to Chris Joe's last night, looking for drugs when they thought Chac died of an overdose. Chris Joe's gone. Won't they search for him, interview us and everybody else they can find who was at the bar last night? What's an investigation of 'some sort'? What are you saying, Andy?"

Estrella sighed and pulled the door on her side of Bo's car closed. "Mexican police procedures are different," she said. "We need to get back to the office, Bo."

Andrew LaMarche nodded at Estrella's words as if they contained profound and immutable wisdom. "Dinner tonight, Bo?" he suggested with abrupt lightheartedness. "I'm cooking."

"Sure, Andy, dinner." Bo scowled from her perch on the runningboard. "We've just witnessed the gruesome murder of an innocent woman. A woman about whom I think you're telling me the police in Mexico don't really give a damn. I think you're telling me they're not even going to *try* to find her killer. Her orphaned baby, also poisoned, now gives new meaning to the phrase 'stranger in a strange land,' and has the double misfortune to be trapped in the hands of an agency made up of people like Madge Aldenhoven. So of course we have nothing to think about except dinner."

"Chac was not a Mexican citizen," he said, picking invisible lint from the Jaguar's gleaming roof. "And her, uh, occupational history prior to the success of her singing career had brought her to the attention of the Tijuana police. I learned this morning that she'd been arrested for prostitution, Bo, more than once. A dangerous way to make a living. And I'm afraid it's a fact of life that police on either side of the border—"

Bo felt a snap behind her eyes, and a rush of anger that writhed in her shoulders. What good did it do to take your medication and behave at all times with overweening rationality, when the world itself was devoid of reason?

"So it's just okay to murder prostitutes?" she yelled, more at the coral tree than at Andrew LaMarche, who was gesturing helplessly to Estrella. "Chac exchanged sex for money in a world structured entirely around the hormonal habits of men, and because of that she *and* her baby ceased to be human, right? They became animals. Humans are allowed to kill animals anytime they damn well please. That's it, isn't it?"

A small crowd was gathering, drifting toward Bo from the parking lot and the doorways of several establishments selling jewelry, live eels, and videos whose titles were spelled in Oriental pictograms. Bo hit the top of the Pathfinder with a fist, then climbed inside.

"Okay, okay," she breathed before Estrella could say anything. "But I'm not being crazy, Es. If I hadn't been born in Boston to a fairly wealthy family, if I hadn't been educated, if I hadn't found psychiatrists who could teach me how to keep going with an illness that leaves thousands of women on the streets every year, I could be Chac! I've never even been hungry, Es. But I know perfectly well I'd sell my body if I were starving and there were no other way to get food."

"I know," Estrella sighed. "Every woman knows. We just don't talk about it."

As Bo backed into the parking lot, she and Estrella stared at Andrew LaMarche, still standing beside his car. In some ways the distance between herself and Estrella and this perfectly nice man, Bo thought, surpassed that between earth and the furthest star in the Milky Way. The reality of prostitution was a factor in that distance. "I'm not going to forget about this," she told Estrella. "I'm going to find out who killed Chac."

"Count me in," Es replied, straightening under her seatbelt and patting her stomach. "After all, this baby might be a little girl, my daughter. What would she think if her mom just looked the other way?"

"All right!" Bo yelled, and gunned the Pathfinder into the street.

Chapter Fourteen
The Red Road

Bo dropped Estrella at the front of the CPS building, closer by a city block to the cafeteria refrigerator than their office. The carton of fried rice, if preserved, would provide dinner for Henry Benedict. Estrella was committed to that possibility.

"You have several phone calls," Madge said as Bo entered the building through the back parking lot door. "And St. Mary's can release the Indian baby to a foster home just as soon as you make the arrangements. I'd like you to do that right now, Bo. Let's free that hospital bed for the weekend."

What Madge really meant, Bo knew, was "Let's free our budget of two more days' worth of hospital bills." A month of foster care cost less than a day in St. Mary's Hospital.

"There are some problems," Bo said, sitting on a pile of case files stacked on the chair next to the supervisor's desk. "For one, Acito's AIDS test results won't be available until Monday. I won't know until then whether he can go to a regular foster home, or he has to go to a medically fragile placement." She had attended the training for foster parents willing to take in babies with AIDS. Disposable diapers had to be used, and these had to be discarded in special red plastic trash bags provided by the county. The foster parents were supposed to wear rubber gloves for changes. Chicken pox and other childhood skin diseases presented serious obstacles to needed cuddling. The training had been so upsetting that Bo lost an entire night's sleep just thinking about the reality it addressed.

"I'd forgotten about that," Aldenhoven noted sadly. In the moment of silence shared with Bo, the usual antagonism was absent.

"And I haven't thought through the issue of ethnicity," Bo went on. "He's a Maya Indian, but don't the Indian Child Welfare rules only apply to tribes in the U.S.? And even though his mother lived in Mexico, she wasn't Mexican, she was from Guatemala, and the presumed father is a U.S. citizen. And she was married to him. That would make Acito a citizen on two counts. So what kind of foster home is appropriate?"

As Bo had expected, Madge grabbed the four-pound Department of Social Services Procedures Manual from its place of prominence on her desk, and knit her brow. "Let me check on this," she said, nodding. "We can probably cover our bases with a Hispanic home, but the Indian thing's touchy. I'll have to check with Legal. Don't do anything yet. And keep trying to find that father."

In the strategic war that comprised their working relationship, Bo thought as she headed into her own office, Madge Aldenhoven had just lost a skirmish. Not much, but enough to allow Bo to think about the enormity of her responsibility to Acito, whose future now lay in her hands.

An argument that he was Native American would take him out of San Diego County's supervision, and place him with one of the local tribes. In the event that his father could not be found, Acito would automatically remain in the care of the Indian Child Welfare Council until his eighteenth birthday or until his adoption by an Indian family. But, Bo pondered while rifling through her phone messages, would Chac want that for Acito? Had she come all the way from Guatemala and married an American so that her baby would grow up on a reservation?

You have no idea what Chac would have wanted, Bradley. Just try to keep your dismally elitist opinions out of it. Be objective.

Finding Acito's father would eliminate the need for any official decisions regarding the baby's future. Bo looked at her "due diligence" documentation, and sighed. Dewayne Singleton, whoever he was, did not appear anxious to be found. An escaped convict with a bizarre criminal record Bo suspected wasn't criminal at all.

"How many of you picked up on the 'Jean Baptiste'

business?" she asked the faces on her bulletin board. "Anybody here ever been tempted to find a cure in the Bible? Maybe tried eating locusts and honey like *John the Baptist*? Didn't work, did it? But where else could you turn? There was no lithium in your time, no clozapine, no Prozac, Zoloft, *or* Paxil. No Thorazine, no Haldol, no Tegretol, or imipramine, even. Nothing to harness your chemical demons. If you'd tried Bible bugs for medication, it would have made sense. But this guy has better options. Why would he be thinking like that?"

The face of Virginia Woolf stared out from between Cole Porter and Mark Twain. "We do not know our own souls, let alone the souls of others," her words from *The Moment and Other Essays* echoed in Bo's brain.

"So true," Bo nodded to the writer who had at the end waded into a deep stream, her pockets full of stones. "But I need to know if I'm right. I need to know if Dewayne Singleton's crazy."

Estrella's entrance caused a draft of air from the hall that rustled the pictures above Bo's desk. Tchaikovsky and Edna St. Vincent Millay appeared to nod vigorously.

"Stop talking to the dead and start figuring out who killed Chac," Estrella said. "I've been thinking. Chris Joe seems the most likely candidate, but we can't overlook other possibilities. What do we know about her manager, this Munson Terrell? And wasn't there a woman with him? Who's she?"

"And the bartender," Bo added. "After all, he made the drinks. The woman was probably Terrell's wife or whatever. And the bartender's name is Jorge, I think. When I went there the first time on Wednesday, he seemed nervous. Terrell was asking where Chac was, and Jorge wasn't telling him, but he told me. He seemed afraid of Terrell."

"It's pronounced 'Hor-hay,' " Estrella grinned. "So how can we talk to this Jorge without Terrell knowing he's a suspect?"

Bo nudged off her shoes under the desk and searched for a rubber band with which to corral her hair. "He isn't a suspect," she said into a drawer containing pens, pushpins, a stapler, a staple remover, Post-its in five colors, at least eight hundred paper clips, and no rubber bands. "Nobody's a suspect in any real sense, because there's no police investigation. Do you have a rubber band?"

Estrella tossed one to Bo. "You need a haircut," she noted. "So what do we do?"

"Jorge doesn't speak much English." Bo smiled pointedly at her friend. "Didn't I hear you say you needed a velvet painting of Elvis when he weighed less than a refrigerator? You could just run down to T.J. . . ."

"I'll do it, Bo, but it's not the Mexican people who buy that junk, you know. They just make it for American tourists who have bad taste. *Lots* of American tourists with *lots* of bad taste."

Bo cringed. "Sorry," she said, snapping the rubber band around a wad of hair at the base of her neck. "Guess I just don't want to deal with much of anything about that border. Es . . ." She turned to face a woman whose name had been Sánchez before Henry Benedict joined her life. "What's going to happen down there, with NAFTA and everything? What's going to happen to the Yaqui Indians and all the refugees like Chac, pouring into Mexico from Guatemala and El Salvador and Nicaragua? Are we going to turn Mexico into one huge border town, catering to our sleaziest inclinations?"

"You think I can answer that because my grandparents were born there and I speak Spanish?" Estrella answered, wide-eyed. "And no matter what happens to people like Chac in the future, it can't be any worse than what's really happened to Chac right now! We can't save Mexico from its future, but we can make sure somebody doesn't get away with murder *in* Mexico *this* week. *Comprende?*"

"*Sí.*" Bo smiled across the little office and a cultural gap Estrella had just bridged with her heartfelt pragmatism. "I just wish we knew how we were going to do that—"

The muffled thud of the phone interrupted Bo's train of thought.

"Child Protective Services, Bo Bradley speaking," she answered.

"Hey Bo," Rombo Perry's voice greeted her fondly, "I hear Martin's trying to talk you into ballet classes. You can practice pas de deux after dinner on Sunday, if you'd like. How about it? Would you and Andrew like to join us for something high-carb, low-fat at about . . ."

Someone was talking in the background. Bo couldn't quite make out the words, but the soft male voice sounded agitated. Not surprising, given Rombo's place of employment. County Psychiatric was the last safe haven left for thousands whose faulty brain chemistry brought them to the attention of the police. One of these obviously wanted to talk to his social worker.

"Sure. I'll be with you in just a moment," Rombo said to the man. "At about six, Bo. Martin's experimenting with an orange salsa and—"

"The Angel Jabril," said the voice in the background. "Y'all don' know, but the curse of Allah . . ."

"I need to talk with a client," Rombo told Bo. "Could you call me back about Sunday?"

"Wait a minute, Rom," Bo said, clutching the phone and staring into the wild eyes of Victor Hugo glaring down from the bulletin board above. "Who's the guy talking about Allah?"

"A client, Bo. You know we observe confidentiality, and—"

"Rom, there was somebody in Tijuana last night, in the hallway of a bar where the mother of *my* client was murdered. Somebody yelling about Allah and a curse. I can't believe it, but what if this is that guy?"

From the muffled exchange Bo could hear, it was clear that Rombo Perry had covered the phone with his hand. But even though the conversation was unintelligible, the cadences of speech were distinct. Rombo's Chicago accent with its Midwestern, rapid twang. And the other man, a drawl, broad vowels, blurred consonants. As if the edges of his speech had been worn away, leaving what sounded like a spoken song. Southern. Like the voices Bo had heard in the morning's calls to Louisiana.

"Rom," she spoke loudly enough to be heard over the ongoing conversation, "is the man you're talking to named Dewayne Singleton? If he is, he's the father of a baby on my caseload. A baby who's orphaned and will be freed for adoption if I can't find the father. Just tell me no if that's not his name, okay? You won't be violating confidentiality that way."

An intake of breath and then a sigh told Bo everything she needed to know before Rombo Perry answered. "Oh, boy," he breathed. "This is too weird."

"I'm coming right over there, Rom," Bo told the social worker. "Will they let me in?"

"Your agency can subpoena our records, Bo, but you can't just barge into a locked facility to interview one of our clients. This man is in no condition to—"

"Oh come on, Rom, remember whom you're talking to. I've been *in* psychiatric hospitals." Bo noticed that her hand was shaking as she unconsciously drew a series of barred windows on the margin of her desk calendar. "Nobody's going to be more compassionate, gentle, and nonintrusive. But this is really important, Rom. There's an eight-month-old baby boy with *nobody* . . ."

"Come on over," Rombo Perry acceded. "I'll talk with you about this, but I can't guarantee you access to my client."

Bo grabbed Acito's case file and her keys, her breath shallow.

"I'm afraid we've got another suspect," she told Estrella. "Acito's father is in County Psychiatric, yelling about Allah."

Estrella's mouth formed an O. "*Madre de dios,*" she whispered.

Chapter Fifteen
Rattling House

From the front, San Diego County's new psychiatric hospital looked like what it had once been, the corporate headquarters of a grocery chain. Nestled in an old industrial development between two freeways, the sprawling one-story building could have been a Kmart. No resemblance to Bedlam whatsoever.

"Pretty nice," Bo told the building as she minced her way through the expansive parking lot on pinched feet. The black pumps might be terrific for sitting around in board rooms, she acknowledged, but for treks across large cement parking lots sneakers were without peer.

"Uh, you're talking to the hospital," a soft male voice mentioned from a sidewalk leading to tinted glass doors. The speaker, whose long gray hair and beard shone in the sunlight, was holding a clipboard.

"Yeah," Bo admitted, blushing. "It looks so pleasant."

The eyes gazing from under bushy eyebrows took Bo's measure in one sweeping glance. "It is," the man said, straightening a flowered tie worn over a blue satin bowling shirt. "But as you may know, this is only a short-term facility. Many who need a long-term supportive environment have nowhere to go after they leave here. Are you registered to vote in San Diego County?" The man's eyes, reflecting the blue in his shirt, were sparkling.

Bo had been waylaid for worse causes by fake ministers at airports in several major cities. "Yes," she said, "but—"

"Would you sign a petition urging the county council to allocate funds for subacute psychiatric care in—"

"Hold it!" Bo grinned. "Let me read this thing, and I'll sign it. You're preaching to the choir here. I know all about it."

"You'll forgive me," he said after Bo's signature was on the petition, "but have you just spent twenty years smoking cigarettes and watching daytime television in a board-and-care where nobody talks to you except when they pass out the pills?"

"No, I haven't," Bo answered, entertaining the thought that her presence here might just possibly be ill-advised.

"Then you don't know all about it. I do."

"But you're not watching TV in a board-and-care now," she pointed out. "What happened?"

"Technology's finally catching up to schizophrenia," the man beamed. "Cops picked me up talking to the candy machine at the bus station three months ago, brought me here. New medication, new man. I can't hold down a job yet, but I can help the folks who're still lost out there, right?"

"Absolutely!" Bo grinned, entertaining the thought that she ought to come down here more often. Maybe volunteer or something. Except she'd have to marry Andrew LaMarche and quit her job in order to have the time. Probably not the best idea. "Keep up the good work." She waved and walked under the hospital's freshly painted entrance overhang.

At the guards' cage Bo showed her CPS badge and was given a red plastic visitor's tag before the locked door was opened to a paved courtyard where Rombo Perry balanced a twirling volleyball on his index finger. The courtyard, she noted with approval, was immaculate and equipped with the same modern cement tables and benches that graced St. Mary's Hospital's outdoor dining area. Rombo seemed, as usual, to just have come from posing for a fitness magazine. The deltoid muscles beneath his polo shirt moved like silk as he tossed the ball in the air and spun for an impressive catch.

"How *do* you keep in such good shape?" Bo asked. "I'd kill to have just one award-winning muscle."

"How about going to Martin's ballet class?" Rombo suggested. "That'd do it."

"Rom, get real. Can you see me in a tutu?"

"Martin was worried about that, too. He has his limits, it seems. But the class wears sweats, Bo. Only the more daring have moved up to the dashing tights-and-legwarmers look.

And they don't really dance; they just work out at the barre. From Martin's progress, I'd estimate about a year and a half before they attempt the opening steps to 'Itsy-Bitsy Spider.' He's sure you'll love it."

"I don't have time." Bo sighed. "This job eats my life, and I like to work on my paintings in what's left. So what's going on with Dewayne Singleton? Are you going to let me interview him?"

"He's in B Unit," Rombo said, nodding toward a glass wall behind which the traditional central nurses' station was topped by an attractive tiered skylight. "You can talk to him, but he's pretty psychotic, Bo. No upsetting topics, okay?"

Of course not. Just a few questions about poisons and murder. Bradley, this is unconscionable.

Rombo unlocked the B Unit door and escorted Bo into a carpeted lobby area. "In here," he indicated an airy dayroom containing upholstered chairs and the ubiquitous TV, which was not on. There was nobody in the dayroom but a wiry black man looking out the far window. Bo noticed without wanting to that all the pictures adorning the walls were fastened in place with screws through the frames, and glazed with sheet plastic in place of glass. But the pictures were nice. Her own hospitalizations, she remembered, had not included pictures.

"In where?" she asked.

"Right there. That's Mr. Singleton."

Bo touched Rombo's arm. "No. It can't be. The baby's father isn't black. I'm sure of it."

"Well, Mr. Singleton obviously is. If you don't want to talk to him, I'll take him on back to his group."

"No, I need to interview him."

Bo took Acito's case file from her briefcase and walked across the pale teal green carpeting with trepidation. This couldn't be the Little Turtle's dad, or could it?

"Mr. Singleton?" she said, and then reeled with recognition as the man turned swiftly to face her. The look in his eyes was one Bo had seen in mirrors. A fanatic certainty frustrated by the inability of everyone else to comprehend it. "I'm Bo

Bradley, an investigator from Child Protective Services. I'd like to talk to you about—"

"Beau a man's name," Dewayne Singleton interrupted. From his demeanor it was clear that he felt pride in having recognized an obvious attempt at deception. "Why you want to call yourself that?"

At about five foot seven, he looked taller than that in new Levi's and a plaid shirt with sleeves rolled halfway up his chocolate-colored arms. A healing cut on his forehead was the only flaw on an otherwise attractive, clean-shaven face.

"In the South it *is* usually a man's name," she agreed. There was no point in elaborate explanation. "Mr. Singleton, did you marry a woman named María Elena Bolon in Mexico?"

"Yeah, that the ho." He scowled. "Got to warn the woman, that woman my *wife*! Man's job to shield his woman under a wing, even if she a ho." He nodded his head with conviction.

"Hoe?" Bo thought, and then recognized the reference. Whore. Same song, different lyric. But at least Chac's husband surpassed the Mexican police in his definition of himself relative to her. He wanted to warn and protect her. Maybe.

"What did you want to warn your wife about?"

Dewayne Singleton began to walk the length of the windowed wall, alternately hunching his shoulders and then straightening them. "There be a curse," he said, staring ahead. "Allah send his angel Jabril to punish the infidel!"

"What infidel?" Bo asked before she could catch herself. Difficult to avoid falling into the irrational conversation. The need to believe sense could be made of it if only one paid close attention.

Dewayne Singleton's brown eyes grew wide in a reaction Bo could replicate from memory. The manicky reaction to a world of dense, sluggish robots who seemed too stupid to merit the designation "human."

"Some gon' die," he said, causing Bo to wince. "Angel Jabril like a hammer sent down. Everybody know the law in they heart, but ain't nobody here *obey* the law no way. This be California." He emphasized the fact as though it reflected a widely accepted body of knowledge.

Bo wondered if he'd next point out that the Indian deity named Kali, called Caillech in Gaelic traditions, had worn her necklace of skulls centuries before a Western state would be named in her honor. "Evil root here," he went on rapidly, gesturing out the window. "Look at them trees. Ain't normal trees. Look like *pineapples*, you ask me. Ole, ugly trees."

Palm trees never having been a personal favorite, Bo couldn't argue. "Did you know that Elena has a baby?" she asked. "A baby boy?"

"Don' know about no baby." Dewayne sighed. "But she my wife, that my baby." A weight seemed to fall on the thin figure pacing beside the glass wall. Bo watched as he moved puppetlike, up and down beyond a row of chairs. An ache at the back of her nose made her sniff.

Don't start crying, Bradley. Just don't.

"In order to establish your paternity," she began, masking the outrageous request in clipped syllables, "we'll need to do a comparative analysis of blood types." She took a standard release of medical information form from her briefcase. "Will you sign a release authorizing my agency to contract for such a test on your blood?"

"I don't care," Dewayne answered, reaching for the pen Bo offered. "Allah be the one, the true God."

"Just a minute." It was Rombo Perry, striding across the pastel carpeting in a manner reminiscent of his younger days as a boxer. "What are you asking Mr. Singleton to sign?" He might have been a mother bear eyeing an intruder threatening her cub. Seriously not to be messed with.

"Just a release for a blood match, Rom," Bo said, admiring her friend's devotion to his client.

"I'd like to strike out access to all other information," the social worker noted, taking the form from Bo. In a moment he handed it back. "You can sign now, if you choose to," he told Dewayne.

"Yeah, yeah, *Rambo*." Dewayne nodded, signing the form. "Big white ape, that dude. Saw his movie one time. He don' talk, jus' grunt. You talk. Why you got that name?"

Rombo wrapped a muscular arm around Dewayne's shoulders and steered him toward the hall. "I think that's enough, Bo," he said. "I'll see Mr. Singleton to his group and be right back."

Bo sat in a nubby blue tweed chair and whispered names of shipwrecks. "The *Job H. Jackson, Jr.*," she sighed. "The *Hannah E. Schubert*, the *Jason*, the *Ethel Maude*." Dewayne Singleton was at the moment so lost in a forest of misfiring brain synapses that what she had just done was probably a mortal sin. Something like shooting an albatross, or a mockingbird. Except it had to be done. A lonely, black-eyed baby was waiting.

"Did you know he escaped from a prison in Louisiana?" Bo asked Rombo Perry when he returned and pulled a chair near hers.

Rombo looked at his shoes. "No, and I don't know it now. I want to keep him here for a while, Bo. We've got a good doctor. His tentative diagnosis on Dewayne is bipolar disorder, as you've undoubtedly guessed from the symptoms. From what Dewayne says, he's never been diagnosed before, never had meds. Hard to tell if that's true right now. But my guess is, it is."

"Shit," Bo said softly. "How old is he?"

"Just turned thirty. He's on Haldol with Klonopin now, to calm him down. But the bloodwork's done and he'll be started on lithium tomorrow. If lithium helps, we'll know the diagnosis is the right one. But we need some time."

"His life will have been a total mess if nobody ever knew what was wrong," Bo said, drawing turtles on Acito's case file. "I don't see any reason for me to call Louisiana. You'll do it when he's stabilized, right?"

Rombo nodded. "Yeah. You'll remember to tell me then, and we'll let them come and get him. By the way, what'd he do that landed him in prison?"

"Stole a bunch of bugs."

Rombo helped Bo from her chair and pulled a keyring from his pocket. "Bugs?"

In an unbreakable Lexan wall mirror Bo noticed that the businesslike look she'd attempted that morning had gone bankrupt. "Locusts," she said. "He fried and honeycoated them, and then sold them to New Orleans voodoo shops as 'John the Baptist Vitamins.' "

"Pretty enterprising use of the religiosity problem." Rombo smiled. "Wonder how he got off John the Baptist and into the Islamic stuff, not that it matters."

"What I wonder is whether or not he poisoned his wife," Bo mentioned at the door. "He could have done it, you know, Rom. And maybe Acito, too. Maybe he thinks he's this Angel Jabril and Chac was an infidel."

"We'll know more in ten days or so," Rombo said, letting Bo out.

The guards were busy and didn't look up after buzzing Bo through the wire cage separating the courtyard from the administrative section of San Diego County's Mental Health Services. Against the pale mauve corridor wall her shadow was a reminder of what might have been. What still might be if she weren't careful. A blurry, faceless figure in a mental hospital. She'd lived with that shadow for two decades. Weird to see it right there in the real setting.

"Hey," Bo whispered to that ephemeral twin. "Let's get out of here!"

Chapter Sixteen
Dance of the Weasel

Estrella was sitting on the edge of her desk, deep in Spanish conversation when Bo returned from the hospital. "*Gracias, Jorge,*" she said as Bo closed the door.

"Jorge? The bartender? You just called him on the phone?"

"Sure." Estrella shrugged. "I called the club to see if he was there, and he answered. I let him think we're convinced Chac died of an overdose, that we're just looking for her relatives. He knew her pretty well, Bo. He cried the whole time I was talking to him."

"Unlike Americans, Latin men aren't afraid to cry. It doesn't mean he didn't poison her. What did he tell you?"

Estrella smiled and shook her head. "What do you know about Latin men?" she asked.

Bo slumped in her desk chair. "Don't you remember Paolo, that surveyor I met at a rally for endangered desert plants? He wasn't afraid to cry."

"It was a rally to end animal experimentation in the cosmetic industry; everybody was crying. Besides, he was Italian. By the way, Andrew phoned. He said just show up for dinner, you don't need to call. So what did you find out at the hospital?"

Bo kicked off her shoes and propped her feet on the desk. "A man named Dewayne Singleton is in County Psychiatric Hospital," she began. "He's Chac's husband. But he's not Acito's father." In spite of herself Bo felt two enormous tears spill over the edges of her lower eyelashes. "He's really disoriented, Es. I'm sure it's a manic episode. Pretty hard to see."

"Oh, Bo," Estrella said, hurrying to wrap her arms around

her friend. "You shouldn't have gone there. Of course it was hard on you. But just because he's ill doesn't mean he's not Acito's dad."

"It's not that," Bo snuffled. "It's that he's black. And there's absolutely nothing about Acito to suggest a black parent. We'll do a blood match. Dewayne signed a permission, and I'll sign one for Acito, but I already know what it's going to show."

A knot behind Bo's eyes dissolved in more tears. "This man has never had any kind of treatment, Es. Nobody ever helped him and he's thirty and that probably means he won't respond as well to medication now and it's just so damn *rotten*, why didn't anybody get him into treatment when he was young, before—"

"Bo!" Estrella spoke sharply, tightening her embrace. "You're getting carried away. Slow down. You can cry, but breathe. And don't talk."

Obeying, Bo breathed as Estrella walked to the window, scratched the back of one ear, and took a deep breath. "Is there any real chance that Singleton poisoned Chac?" she asked quietly.

"What do you think?" Bo answered. "We know he was at the bar; we heard him in the hall, even though we didn't see him. How many Muslims with Southern accents traditionally hang around Tijuana bars yelling about curses from Allah?"

She banged her head softly on the desk, then stood and grimaced at her reflection in the mirror on the back of the door. The glen plaid suit looked like the before picture in an ad for steam irons. "And he's got a classic motive. Acito's not his baby, Es. He might have found out somehow, and . . ."

"And decided to kill both of them," Estrella finished the sentence, running a polished nail down the dusty miniblinds at the window. "I'm so sorry, Bo. This has got to be horrible for you."

"No, horrible for Chac," Bo answered dismally. "Pretty horrible for Acito, too. I'm going to go outside and smoke an entire pack of cigarettes. If the Heart Association calls, tell them I'm an android. Wash-and-wear organs. No sweat."

"I'll tell them," Estrella agreed, betraying by no more than a raised eyebrow her concern over Bo's bare feet.

In the parking lot Bo lit a cigarette, opened the Pathfinder, turned the ignition switch to power, and crammed a random tape into the deck. Albinoni's Adagio in G, top of twentieth-century tear-jerker charts. The piece, Bo's violinist mother had loved to explain, was actually written by the Baroque composer's biographer, Remo Giazotto, almost two centuries after Albinoni's death.

Bo turned up the throbbing, sentimental violin music, paced beside the car and sobbed, envisioning a bleak and bedraggled procession of the world's mentally ill, herself and Dewayne Singleton included. Some few in the desperate parade had done violence to loved ones. Millions more had done violence to themselves.

"It isn't fair," Bo told the ascending chromatic chords against which a violin wept threads of sound. "This shouldn't have happened."

In her office window overlooking the parking lot, Bo saw the silhouette of Madge Aldenhoven, watching. But Madge would think nothing of a worker crying. Crying was, in fact, encouraged. CPS workers who never cried would eventually either crack up or become hardened automatons. But Madge wouldn't know Bo was crying over a perpetrator, not a victim. Madge would make assumptions, Bo acknowledged as the violin dropped to a deep intermezzo, in the same way the world of music assumed this Italian Baroque piece was written by an Italian Baroque composer. Reality, Bo thought as she exhaled, could be described as a system of interlocking erroneous assumptions. The thought made her eyes grow wide.

Bradley, you idiot! You don't have a clue about what actually happened to Chac. Dewayne Singleton isn't automatically guilty of murder because he has a psychiatric illness. You're supposed to know better. You do know better.

Minutes later Bo padded back into the office on shredded stockings, grinning. "Giazotto wrote Albinoni's Adagio, not Albinoni," she mentioned to Estrella. "And Dewayne didn't necessarily kill Chac."

"I know. So what do you think about the name Basil if the baby's a boy?" Estrella asked without looking up. "Henry had an uncle named Basil."

"Basil Benedict? Sounds like an herbed egg dish in a restaurant with no view and pea green napkins. Cloth, of course. You're doing this to demonstrate how little my outbursts affect you, right?"

"Right." Estrella handed Bo a slip of paper. "Jorge told me Chac's manager, this Munson Terrell, has a business in San Diego. While you were out flirting with cancer, emphysema, and early death, I called the county recorder's office. This is it."

"Outback Odyssey, Incorporated?" Bo read aloud. "What's that?"

"I called the number and got a tape. Apparently Munson and his wife, Kee, do motivational workshops out in the desert. He's doing one for men this weekend. They're going to define their masculinity."

Bo envied her friend's ability at dramatic eye-rolling. "What's to define?" she asked.

"Who knows? But these men's things are in right now. My brother-in-law went to one sponsored by his church. Male bonding for Christ or something. From the tape I think the Terrells' workshops have an Australian flavor. Lot of stuff about Aboriginal dreamtime and lost fathers."

Bo remembered Munson Terrell with his ponytail, cradling the head of a dead singer on a flimsy stage in blue light. What had that relationship been?

"He must be upset about Chac's death," she mused. "How can he run off to the desert to do boomerang workshops before she's even buried? And who will bury her?"

"I asked Jorge that." Estrella sighed. "The club's soliciting contributions to cover expenses. She'll be buried in Tijuana. Jorge said they all wanted a nice grave in consecrated ground for Acito to visit, not just a pauper's grave."

Bo paused to consider the cultural differences that had promoted this particular concern, and gave up. She would never have thought of it. But it was nice. "So everybody who worked with her at the club knew about Acito?" she asked.

"Yeah. She used to bring him with her for rehearsals. Why?"

"I wonder why she boarded him across the border in San Ysidro. Why did she start doing that three months ago instead of keeping him with her?"

"Maybe the boyfriend didn't want a baby around?"

"You mean Chris Joe?" Bo frowned. "I don't think he was exactly a boyfriend. And he cared about Acito, even made fresh apple juice for him . . ."

Bo trailed off as the implications of what she'd just said filled the little office.

"Apples," Estrella said, nodding. "Cyanide in the seeds."

"Did we get the lab report back on the baby bottle I picked up in San Ysidro?" Bo gnawed her lip, thinking.

"Yeah. It was just apple juice. But Bo . . ." Estrella's voice slid higher. "Didn't Andy say cyanide molecules evaporate or something? That they don't stay put?"

"It wasn't cyanide that poisoned Acito," Bo thought aloud. "But then why did Chris Joe run when Chac died?"

Late afternoon sun streaked the walls with blurred bars of light as Estrella glanced at her watch. "Three o'clock," she noted. "I've got to pick up a psychological evaluation for court on Monday. I won't be back in the office today. Is there anything we should do over the weekend?"

Bo clicked a pen against her front teeth. "There's nothing I can think of, unless . . . Es, what's Henry doing tomorrow?"

"Henry? He's on duty at the base. Why?"

"Damn," Bo said, dropping the pen. "We need a man."

Estrella's grin was rueful as she patted her stomach. "A girl can get into trouble that way," she warned.

"I mean to infiltrate Terrell's masculinity workshop tomorrow, Es. They're bound to talk about women. If we had a spy there, we might find out something about Terrell's relationship with Chac. Surely he'll talk about her death as he's bonding with the other guys and playing didgeridoos in the desert."

"What about Andy?"

"Oh, right. Andrew LaMarche beating drums beneath the

moon in a poignant search for the meaning of manhood? Not in this life."

"Well, call me if you need me," Estrella called over her shoulder as she left. "And seduce that doctor!"

"I will." Bo nodded, scrolling mentally through a list of male acquaintances who might be willing to go undercover to a masculinity workshop. An image of Dar Reinert rose in her mind and then crumbled. The chunky detective, she realized, chuckling, would regard the whole endeavor as an unwholesome joke. Like men dressing up in tights to catch women leaping across stages in toe shoes. Dar wouldn't do. But then who?

It had to be somebody younger than Andrew and less hidebound than Dar Reinert. Somebody trendy and upscale enough to fit in with men in ponytails and exquisite jewelry. Somebody likable, open to the impulsive confidences that might emerge in such a context. Bo hummed the opening bars of the minuet from *Swan Lake*, and conducted an imaginary orchestra with her pen until a broad smile lit her face.

Bingo! You're a genius, Bradley. This will work!

Punching numbers on the phone with her pen, Bo beamed and waited for an answer. "Martin!" she gushed, "you know those ballet classes you've been wanting me to take with you? Well, I'm willing to try it, but there's something I want you to do for me, okay?"

The sales job would take a while, but it was going to work.

Chapter Seventeen
White Sparkstriker

Madge Aldenhoven was talking on the phone and slamming her Procedures Manual repeatedly against the desk when Bo returned.

"There's a new worker in foster care," she said over her shoulder as Bo stood in the doorway. The words were weighted with a significance that seemed just out of reach. Into the phone she said, "Ms. Bradley will have to do a visit immediately, thanks to your incompetence. And this will be written up as a performance review. Your supervisor will have a copy by Monday morning."

The reference was to one of the infamous "purple poison" DSS review forms, so named for the lavender paper on which they were printed. A bad performance review could guarantee a worker an assignment to an undesirable job forever. Apparently the new worker in foster care was going to get one from Madge Aldenhoven. Bo waited to hear why her name had been brought into it.

"The Indian baby," Madge explained after banging the phone into its cradle, "has been removed from St. Mary's and placed in foster care. The hospital social worker phoned our foster care unit to confirm the need for AIDS precautions at least until the test results come back. The new worker, apparently unaware of standard procedures, went ahead and made arrangements for a couple named Dooley to pick up the baby. Here's their address in La Jolla."

"Dooley?" Bo shook her head, taking the slip of paper from Madge. "That's not an Indian name, or a Mexican name. It's Irish. What about the ethnicity business? Why do we have seven thousand pages of rules about who can care for black, white, red, brown, and plaid kids if nobody's going to follow them? And what are these people doing in La Jolla? Most of our foster parents couldn't afford to rent a *garage* out there, much less a house."

The news was only one more straw on the back of an arthritic camel. Exhausted from the emotional drain of visiting County Psychiatric, Bo decided to give the current administrative crisis minimal attention. Acito would be safe in the licensed foster home, regardless of the ethnic heritage possessed by the foster parents, or the fact that they were obviously wealthy enough to live in one of San Diego's oldest and priciest communities.

"They're supposed to be Hispanic," Madge sighed. "They said they were Hispanic when licensing did the original interviews and home evaluation."

Bo tried to imagine somebody named Juan Dooley, and succeeded only in mentally resurrecting a song, the lyrics to which would now be "Hang down your head, Juan Dooley . . ." Accompanied by penny whistle and flamenco guitar.

You're tired, Bradley. Go home and eat fudge. This can all wait until tomorrow, when you'll be less likely to break into song.

"I'll do the visit tonight or tomorrow." Bo nodded. "You'll have to okay the overtime."

"You use too much overtime," Madge said. "If you'd budget your time more efficiently—"

"If I'd budgeted my *life* more efficiently, I'd be painting in New Mexico right now. Yes or no on the overtime?"

Madge found a blank phone memo on her desk and tore it carefully into strips. "Yes," she answered.

On the drive home Bo located Radio Romántico on her FM dial. Beneath the seatbelt she swayed to a sultry tango whose words, if they meant anything close to her translation, told the tale of a small wig and a dog named Cho who had not paid his taxes. San Diego County would pay the community college tuition of any CPS worker wishing to study Spanish. Bo thought it might be time to take advantage of that perk. Too late to help with this case, but she might at least learn what "*corazón*" meant. The word seemed central to every song. Including Chac's song.

As someone who sounded remarkably like Elvis Presley sang "Heartbreak Hotel" in Spanish, Bo reached into the dash compartment for the tape she'd bought in Tijuana. Its cover showed Chac in a strapless black gown at a table adorned with a blazing candelabra.

"I'll bet she was pregnant with Acito when this picture was taken," Bo mused aloud. "That's why they had to pose her seated behind a table." The eyes looking out from the cassette case were a lifetime older than the young face. A skillfully draped length of sparkling chiffon covered Chac's inner arms at the joints, where purple needle tracks would have ruined the image. With one hand Bo took the cassette from its case and put it in the deck. Fast-forwarding the tape to the end, she listened to Acito's song until I-8 reached its terminus at Ocean Beach and the final miles before North America dropped into saltwater.

After parking near her apartment on Narragansett, Bo walked back to Ocean Beach's shopping district on Newport. The used bookstore had exactly what she wanted. A paperback English/Spanish dictionary. Before leaving the store she opened it to the Cs. "*Corazón*," it turned out, meant "heart."

"I should have known that," she told the store's owner, who had been a shrimper until the fleet folded, and merely nodded while staring out to sea.

At home Bo gathered Mildred from the elderly neighbor with whom the elderly dog watched soap operas all day, and gratefully unlocked her own door. Crisp business suits, she acknowledged, removing the failed glen plaid, were clearly meant only for crisp businesses. A category from which child abuse investigating could be excluded handily.

Wandering to the deck doors in bra and half slip, Bo opened the apartment to a salty breeze and let it blow through her hair. It was time to plan the evening. Scrupulously.

In the bathroom she ran a warm bath and threw in a cheesecloth bag of dried citrus peel and cloves. In the pharmacopoeia of the venerable Bridget Mairead O'Reilly, the combined scents were an unbeatable aphrodisiac. Bo sank into the water, grinning at the possibility of Andrew LaMarche breathing the flavor of her skin and wondering why she smelled like a pomander ball. How to tell a Cajun doctor there are things known only to Irish grandmothers, who are never wrong. Allowing her head to submerge, Bo tried to recite her grandmother's favorite, Yeats's "The Lake Isle of Innisfree," in its entirety underwater. Hopeless. By the cricket singing in the sixth line she was gasping for air. Time to cut back on the cigarettes, probably. Or else develop an obsessive interest in Martin's ballet class. Maybe both.

But the familiar poem had called up another. One of Yeats's bleak ones recited by Grandma Bridget on dark days.

"I dreamed that one had died in a strange place," Bo whispered, lathering her tangle of curls with an imported shampoo guaranteed to make auburn hair flash like aged claret in candlelight. "Near no accustomed hand . . ." The poem was called "A Dream of Death," and might have, Bo thought, been written about Chac. The singer had died far from her home in Guatemala. And there had been no familiar hand to close her eyes. That tender task was performed by Andrew LaMarche. Bo felt a wave of deep affection for him that made her hands shake as she rinsed her hair under the tub's chrome faucet.

But his life wasn't over. Chac's was. Bo sighed as she realized that her planned dalliance among the living would be haunted by the young mother's ghost if she didn't check on the Little Turtle's well-being.

"Ye were born in the night," her grandmother had insisted, causing Bo's mother to clench her teeth and call Bo's father to intervene, "so ye'll have the power to see ghosts, ye will."

Bo's understanding of ghosts lay more in the realm of psychiatry than folklore, but why take chances?

"We're going to visit a baby before we go to Andy's," she told Mildred. The dog was busy dragging underwear from the bathroom floor into the living room, and showed no interest in the information.

Bo dried her hair with a round brush that encouraged graceful waves over the ever-threatening Orphan Annie curls. From her closet she pulled a series of blouses that wouldn't do, and finally settled on an off-white scoop-necked cotton sweater with dramatic sleeves she'd bought months ago on a shopping trip to Laguna Beach with Estrella, and forgotten about. With a gold torque and sand-colored knit slacks, the look would either be casually elegant or understatedly boring. Bo held one ornate earring to her ear and then hung it back on its wooden rack on the bathroom counter. Under harsh scrutiny, she realized, the earrings looked like chandeliers for a dollhouse. Better to stick with simple gold hoops. No perfume. A class act.

On the way out Bo packed clean unmentionables and a plastic Baggie of Science Diet Senior dry dog food in her briefcase, and loaded Mildred's sheepskin-lined bed in the car before returning to phone the Dooleys. They would be happy to see her, Mr. Dooley said. They were just bathing the baby for bed, but would keep him up for his social worker's visit.

Checking her purse for the purchases made yesterday in anticipation of an erotic interlude made impossible by Chac's death, Bo tucked one small foil package in the pocket of her slacks. The remaining two fit inconspicuously in a small outer compartment of her leather bag. Within easy reach. The Boy Scouts, Bo smiled, would be in awe of her devotion to preparation.

The Dooleys, Davy and Constanzia, who preferred to be called Connie, were Hispanic after all. Bo had found their house with some difficulty, nestled in a grove of eucalyptus beside a seacliff mansion whose every room had at one time or another been featured in the local newspaper's Sunday supplement. Its guest bathroom, Bo recalled, had actually won an award in a juried art competition. The room's floor, walls, and ceiling were covered in a mosaic of exotic glass and stone chips designed to re-create a nocturnal desert landscape. The Dooleys lived in the property's coach house.

"We're the caretakers," Davy Dooley told Bo jovially, limping as he crossed the room to offer her a selection of homemade cookies from a painted tray. "I make a little money as a paid bass in two church choirs, and Connie does the billing for several charter fishing outfits and a couple of restaurants from her computer here at home, but keeping this place up is our main job for the moment. Would you like to see the baby's room? Connie's changing the little guy so he'll be socially acceptable."

Davy Dooley looked about forty, with graying dark hair worn

in a long braid over the back of a denim shirt. With the exception of the limp, he exuded an outdoorsy athletic vigor Bo associated with forest rangers and tour guides. "On your foster care application your said you were Hispanic?" she mentioned.

"Yep," he answered. "Born in Mexico City. My dad was an Irish missionary priest." His blue eyes crinkled at the edges with laughter. "Guess Mom was a knockout in those days. Still is, for that matter. The church sent Dad back to Ireland and gave Mom a job cooking at an orphanage. When I was three she married an American architectural restoration specialist she met when he was restoring the cathedral reredos, and moved here. But my real father's family wanted me to keep the name, and that's how the world got Davy Dooley, the Mexican stuntman."

"Stuntman?" Bo said, recording the information in Acito's case file.

"Hollywood," Acito's foster father answered, stretching to throw another stick on a small fire in the craftsman bungalow's tiled fireplace. "Indian parts mostly, because I'm dark-skinned. Can't tell you how many horses, cliffs, and waterfalls I've been shot off of. But after I busted my leg up good in the first shoot of the buffalo hunt scene in *Dances with Wolves*, I knew my stunt days were over. Connie and I have a nice nest egg in some blue-chip investments, but we don't need to touch any of it right now. It's there, though, if we ever get a kid."

Bo watched fog drifting through an open window from the sea. The little summer fire was pleasant, she thought. Just enough to burn off the damp without appreciably heating the room. "What do you mean, 'get a kid'?" she asked.

"I had endometrial cancer when I was only twenty-two," Connie Dooley answered, entering with a sleepy Acito and taking a seat in a rocker beside her husband. "Had to have a hysterectomy. We can't have children, and want to adopt, but it's not easy. We're too old, they say."

"And too unconventional," Davy added. "We don't like nine-to-five jobs, I'm seen as a cripple, and to top it off, Connie's Buddhist."

Bo glanced at the woman, who looked a great deal like her

husband except for brown eyes and two braids instead of one. "Wow," she said.

Connie grinned mischievously over the Little Turtle's freshly washed and electric hair. "It's okay," she said. "I chose Buddhism over a PR career in Hollywood that involved years of lying to the press about the sexual and substance-abuse hobbies of beautiful people. Got out just before I made so much money I'd have had to become one of them. Kept the Porsche, though. Nobody's perfect."

Bo laughed, realizing that she liked these people. Backlit by firelight, they looked like an odd version of Rembrandt's *The Holy Family*.

"I'll just have a look at the baby's room, and then go," she said, accepting the cooing Turtle from Connie's arms. He looked adorable in new pajamas with snaps at the waist and a conga line of ducks in baseball caps across the chest. Bo buried her face in soft black hair and offered a silent prayer to any deity who might be listening that no deadly virus lurked in his blood.

"You can just go ahead and put him down," Connie Dooley told Bo as Davy turned on the bright overhead light in the nursery. A crib was made up, soft coverlet waiting. In a corner of the room the edges of a red plastic "contaminated waste" bag were visible under the lid of a diaper pail.

"We understand about the precautions." Davy nodded somberly. "Until we find out the test results."

Bo lay Chac's Little Turtle on his back in the crib, and admired his Maya nose and coal-black hair. Except something was wrong with his hair. Standing back, Bo tilted her head from side to side, looking. It wasn't just the light. A tuft of hair above his right eye was lighter than the rest, gray-looking. Leaning to examine the anomaly, she brushed back his thick hair. At the scalp the barely visible new growth was white!

Bo gasped and felt her eyes widen.

"What is it?" Connie asked. "Is something wrong?"

"No," Bo attempted a recovery. "I just remembered I left my iron on at home. Gosh, I'd better run."

The Dooleys would think she was flaky, Bo thought as she hurried to the car. But the likelihood paled in comparison to what she'd discovered. Nothing less than the identity of Acito's father!

Chapter Eighteen
Cutting Ant

Dewayne Singleton saw the red plastic visitor's tag fall from the black sweater of a nun who'd come to the hospital to teach the evening crafts class. She'd taken the sweater off in the hall by the nurses' station, and in folding it to fit over her arm she'd pulled loose the spring-loaded clip that fastened the tag to the sweater's neck. It fell to the floor beneath the wooden extension that kept patients from reaching objects on the circular work surface inside the open station. The wooden ledge, Dewayne observed, also prevented the staff from seeing the floor beneath it.

Prison life had taught him to betray no interest in events taking place nearby. To fasten his gaze on an imaginary horizon hanging always twenty feet ahead of him. The pills they'd given him made it easier, although they made the muscles in his legs hurt, too. Looking straight ahead he approached the nurses' station and stepped on the tag. Through the hospital slipper he could feel its metal clip.

"Muscles in my legs and arms be hurtin'," he told one of the people behind the desk. "That normal?"

"Haldol does that," a beefy white psych tech in a Pearl Jam T-shirt answered sympathetically. "Doctor's ordered you to start on lithium tomorrow. Soon as it gets up to blood levels, we can take down the Haldol. Meanwhile, you can have a couple Tylenol if you want."

"Sure," Dewayne said.

The psych tech asked a nurse to unlock the medication safe, and went to fill a small paper cup with water.

"Whoa," Dewayne groaned, leaning to rub his ankles. "Sure do hurt down here in my ankle." While bent over, he retrieved the plastic tag from beneath his foot, stood, and jammed his hands into the pockets of his jeans.

"Here, this should help a little," the psych tech said, handing Dewayne two gelcaps and the cup of water. "You can have some more later if you need it."

"Thanks, man," Dewayne answered, swallowing the pills.

He didn't know what he'd do with the red plastic tag, but it might help him get out. The message from Allah about the curse wasn't so clear now. Just a sort of memory, like you'd remember a dream and not be sure whether or not it really happened. But it must have happened or he wouldn't be here. Allah must have sent him to warn the woman, his wife. Get her out of California. Her and this baby she had. They had to go away.

Dewayne paced beside the dayroom wall, and wondered why the idea sounded so familiar. It had nothing to do with Allah and the Muslim leader at Wade, the Imam who'd showed Dewayne the true way. It was older than that, like from his childhood when Mama would read from the infidels' Bible and tell Dewayne he was a blessing-child sent to warm her heart. The thought of Mama made him cry.

The duty nurse noticed and wrote in Dewayne's chart, "Patient discussing religion all day, agitated and tearful at 7:30 P.M. Rule out manic-depressive illness."

Chapter Nineteen

"A heart sacrifice"

—*Popol Vub*

Bo parked the Pathfinder near Andrew LaMarche's Del Mar condo, and sat staring at a Torrey pine bending seaward from a sandy bluff behind the shake-shingled buildings. The ancient trees, she remembered from a seminar on San Diego's native plants, grew nowhere but here and one small island off the coast further north. Slipping an extended version of Pachelbel's Canon into the tape deck, she allowed her head to rest against the seatback and fixed her attention on the tree.

The Canon had been used for everything from TV commercials to background at a memorial service held by a local animal rights group for dolphins enslaved by a Chicago aquarium, but Bo still loved its simplistic theme. The music, if languorously orchestrated, made her think of the Sidhe, the fairy people. In her mind it was a lullaby for the Little Folk, now asleep unseen in Irish glades where no sound but dripping rain might disturb their vanished story.

Relaxed, Bo watched as from beneath the horizon the sun sent red-orange fire that bathed the Torrey pine briefly, then slid away. "The tree remains, but not the hand that planted it." She repeated one of her grandmother's many and frequently quoted aphorisms. Chac's ghost, she hoped, would rest tonight. Maybe find its way to some mythical realm where fairies slept in ferny shadows, and lie down with them. The Little Turtle was safe.

But someone else was not. Chac's murderer, who had also tried to kill a handsome baby boy, could not know how dogged one certifiably mad Irishwoman could be. If the police

117

in two countries chose to do nothing, an underpaid DSS investigator could make life miserable for someone who liked to play with poison. Someone either smart or careless enough to muddy jurisdictional legalities by playing criminal in marginal contexts with people about whom the world doesn't care. A drug-abusing Indian prostitute and her ugly little bastard. That's how it was. But not, Bo smiled at the Torrey pine, for long.

If Andrew LaMarche, surprisingly dressed in an oversized washable silk shirt that made him look more like Lord Byron than an urban pediatrician, was unnerved when Bo arrived at his door with a dog bed and a dog, he quickly recovered. "Ah, hello, Mildred." He smiled, bowing slightly. "How good of you to bring your mistress, on whose clamoring wing rides my faint but willing heart."

"Willing, huh?" Bo grinned against his freshly shaven cheek in an embrace at once sweet and oddly alarming. A foghorn's vibrato, played by a harpsichord. "You've been reading Romantic poets again, haven't you?" The flippant remark did little to assuage the dizzying minor chord thrumming in her chest. Flippancy wasn't going to work in this context.

"Shall we put the dowager's pillow near the hearth?" he suggested, pushing a button on a slate-topped coffee table that caused the gas logs in a small fireplace to ignite with a whoosh.

Bo watched as Mildred sniffed a large black crackleware vase full of sanded tree limbs near the door, and then strolled regally to her bed near the fire. Despite a decorator's rather artsy insignia, Andrew's living quarters were comfortable, Bo thought. Mildred seemed to agree and settled into her bed, one white foreleg stretched possessively toward the gas logs. Or maybe it was just the scent of something simmering in an herb sauce that made the elegantly masculine rooms feel welcoming, even cozy.

"I didn't know you were interested in folk art, Andy," Bo said, admiring a New England glass painting of a wintry country churchyard framed in twigs against the creamy wall over the mantel.

He'd crouched behind a bleached birchwood bar to extract several bottles of wine from a storage rack. "My sister, Elizabeth, sent me that," he said. "Would you prefer the Pouilly-Fuissé, the Chardonnay, the Geisenheimer, or something unusual? I have a ginger, a plum, and a hawthorn, as well as—"

Bo couldn't help herself. "I don't suppose you have a flagon of mead down there, do you? I've a taste for honey. Can't think why, really." Nobody west of Boston's Back Bay would believe mead was anything but an aspect of Norse mythology, she was sure.

He didn't miss a beat. "Mead? Of course. Not a flagon's worth, I'm afraid, but I can offer you both the traditional and a raspberry . . ." He pulled two small bottles from beneath the bar.

"You win." Bo laughed, shaking her head. "I'll have the Chardonnay. Just tell me how it's possible that you actually have mead in Southern California."

"Ordered three cases last year at Christmas from a meadery in New York State. Gifts for the staff at the hospital. Happen to have a few left." His wide smile was triumphant as he opened and poured the Chardonnay, and then lifted his glass to Bo. "It's about time I had the upper hand." He beamed.

Bo tasted the wine. "It's the last time," she whispered.

"Probably," he agreed, rounding the bar to take her in his arms and kiss her at first tentatively, and then with an intensity she freely returned. Beneath the silk shirt she felt his heart, and a loneliness that pulled her to him more wildly than the eagerness of his lips, sending tympanic echoes of desire deep in her belly. And something else. That same sad keening, felt rather than heard, in the air.

"Bo," he said huskily, pulling her to the twig-framed picture, "my sister is a psychologist."

The remark, she thought, would unquestionably win any awards given for lack of reference. "I know," she said, waiting to hear what his sister had to do with the fact that she wanted to kiss him again. Now. From speakers in a candlelit dining room to the left of the bar Bo heard a muted jazz piano doing "St. James Infirmary." A baritone sax picked up the melody as Andrew took a deep breath and continued.

"She thought I was spending my life compensating for the death of my daughter, so she sent this strange old picture and said if I imagined Sylvie there, in one of those quiet churchyard graves, I might . . . what she said was 'draw a boundary creating the past.' Elizabeth said if I could do that, separate the past and keep it apart, I'd be 'more present' on this side of the boundary."

"Unorthodox, but brilliant," Bo replied, kissing the back of his hand. "Elizabeth loves you, Andy, to try so hard to bring you back from that pain."

He'd told her earlier of a little daughter who drowned while washing toys in a bathtub in New Orleans while he was in Vietnam. The child's mother, his high school girlfriend, had simply vanished after that. In some ways so had he.

"It worked, Bo," he said, turning intense gray eyes to gaze into hers. "I came out of it and I wasn't unhappy. But something was missing. I don't know how to explain it," he whispered, wrapping her in his arms again, "but what was missing was you. I knew almost from the beginning that you were half my heart, and the rest of my life."

In the fervent kiss that followed, Bo did not try to make sense of his story, but let him know she wasn't missing, or absent, or anything but present against his pounding heart. After a while she pulled away. "Did you say something about dinner?" she gasped. "Or shall we save that for later?"

His eyes were soft as he stroked her hair with the back of his fingers. "No. I'd hoped this would be a celebratory dinner for us, Bo. I intend to ask you to marry me again, sometime between the vichyssoise and the green chile sorbet."

"Green chile sorbet!"

"Touché." He grinned, heading for the kitchen. "Better stay on your toes if you want to duck this old Cajun. Do you realize you still haven't said 'Andy, don't start that again'? So how about honeymooning in Spain?"

"Why Spain?" Bo asked, wondering why she had to fall for this strange anachronism of a man who was giving her a headache the like of which she hadn't experienced since she was a virginal teenager determined to stay that way.

"Always admired El Greco," he answered. "Does that mean yes?"

"No. But Spain sounds like fun. Andy, how much do you know about genetics?"

"It's nothing unusual," he said over cold soup in museum-quality champlevé bowls, "but you've lost me." The warm gray eyes showed no concern over being lost.

"You have beautiful eyes," Bo said. "But this is important. I think I know who Acito's father is. At the foster home tonight I noticed that the hair growing in over his right temple is white. That's hereditary, isn't it?"

"Usually, yes. It's called piebaldism. A chromosomal anomaly occurring in furry mammals, including the human variety. Odd that we didn't notice it when he was in the hospital. And how does that—"

"Don't you remember Chac's manager, the Australian? *He's* got a hunk of white hair on the right side of his forehead! He's the daddy, Andy."

In the candlelight a chafing dish produced wafts of savory aroma as Andrew removed the lid. "I'm afraid I was captivated by someone else, Bo," he said. "I only remember that his name was Terrell and that he seemed devastated by Chac's death."

"Maybe that was an act. Andy, maybe he wanted to get rid of both Chac and Acito before his wife found out what he'd been up to. Maybe Chac was blackmailing him. Why else would he be down in Tijuana managing the career of a bar singer with an unsavory history? She couldn't have made it this far in the music business without a lot of financial backing. It fits, Andy."

"There was a woman with Terrell in the bar the night Chac died." Andrew frowned. "May have been the wife. The *jealous* wife, angry enough to poison her rival. Stay out of it, Bo. I don't want you stirring up danger."

"Umm," she answered. The Irish stew he'd prepared with Italian sausage was delicious. The fact was also celebrated by Mildred's quivering stub of a tail as she devoured morsels of the stew's meat from a bowl Andrew placed next to another containing imported water on the kitchen's limestone-tiled floor.

After dinner Bo walked Mildred beneath the Torrey pine and admired the moon through its branches. "He's not like the others, is he?" she remarked to the dog. "None of them noticed you, or remembered that you might like some water. I'm not even sure he's real."

The question was resolved a half hour later as Andrew led Bo up the steeply curving road of the nature preserve across from his condo, and onto a sandy path. "I wanted you to see this," he said. "*Au fond du mon coeur,* until you, this place has been my heart of hearts. It is lovely, *n'est-ce pas?*"

Bo watched the moon's rippled trail narrow and fall over the Pacific horizon. Behind them, the scent of sage mingled with pine drifted from a darkened grove of the silent Torrey pines. Below the promontory where they stood a wrinkled badland of young sandstone fell seven stories to the moonlit beach below, where a solitary beachcomber seemed fragile and lost. "Oh, Andy," she sighed against his mouth, understanding that the odd vibration she felt in his arms was not a psychiatric symptom, but something ancient and beyond comprehension. "It is."

Andrew LaMarche, it turned out, was magnificently real.

Sometime later from a sandy hollow in the grove, Bo saw a pair of mule deer dart through a tattered patch of moonlight. "Andy, look!" she whispered.

His eyes never left the curve of her hip, curled against him in the dark. "I am," he said, tucking his silk shirt over her garmentless body for warmth. She noticed that the tucking stopped just short of her breasts.

It was only the following morning when she dragged herself from his bed toward the promise of coffee brewing in the kitchen that she noticed one of her gold earrings was missing.

"I'll see if I can find it later," he blushed, "if you'll tell me where on earth you found condoms with rosebuds on them."

"Hillcrest," she answered, admiring the fact that he managed to appear elegant in the morning, even wearing nothing but a towel.

And the coffee was the best she'd ever tasted.

Chapter Twenty
One Fox

"I don't believe I said I'd do this," Martin St. John lamented for the fourth time since rising at six on Saturday morning for a last rehearsal. Rombo was bent over eggs Benedict, laughing.

"Don't pick up your coffee cup as if it were Meissen, Marty, just grab it," he chortled.

"You know perfectly well it *is* Meissen," Martin answered. "This is never going to work. I'm going to get out there in the desert and be *sacrificed*. Tied to an anthill with starving young wolves inside my shirt. Probably trussed with cactus spines and cooked over a mesquite fire. Bo will never forgive herself, but then she couldn't have known what might happen to a gay man at a masculinity workshop, right?"

Rombo wiped tears of laughter on his cuff before going to the kitchen for fresh coffee and dessert croissants. The hilarity had begun the night before when seven of their friends arrived to coach Martin in macho behavior for his undercover assignment in the desert. By the evening's end, Martin had been given a hard hat, a roll of stick-on tattoos, three pairs of Fruit of the Loom briefs, a pack of unfiltered Camels, and a 1954 publicity photo of Marlon Brando leaning on a motorcycle, sneering. At the end their friends serenaded Martin with several choruses of "Stout-Hearted Men." Rombo couldn't resist carrying the evening's spirit over into breakfast.

"Don't forget to destroy as many irreplaceable desert plants as you can for no apparent reason, and talk about your plan to produce a line of targets featuring the young of endangered species. These guys'll love ya, Marty. Trust old Rom. I know my men!"

Martin sighed. "Look, this is serious. Bo wants the inside story on Terrell. She thinks I'll fit in with the group at least enough so he won't think I'm a spy. That's all that matters. I'm just supposed to participate in whatever they do, and try to get a sense of this guy."

"You'll do fine," Rombo said, inhaling the steam from his coffee appreciatively. "I'm proud of you for helping Bo, and in that outfit nobody will dream you don't even own an automatic weapon!"

Martin stood and struck a bodybuilder's pose in his khaki shorts and denim shirt. "Dr. Livingstone, I presume?" he intoned, as a car's horn honked outside. "Oh, God, it's them. My carpool to our rendezvous with the four-wheel at the edge of Canyon Sin Nombre. Terrell said we'd go in two or three groups, set up camp, and then go off alone on individual 'symbol quests,' whatever that means. Then we're going to do a sweat lodge. I can't believe I let Bo talk me into this. Rom, if I don't return, tell the puppy about me, okay? Tell him I died fighting for truth, justice, and the American way."

Rombo hugged his partner and handed him a duffel bag full of bottled water and fresh fruit. "It's only one night, Martin. And it *is* a good cause. See you tomorrow afternoon!"

Martin squared his shoulders, adopted what he imagined would be the attitude of a French Legionnaire about to be shot, and stomped out the door in borrowed hiking boots that were too big even with three pairs of socks.

"Try to avoid teenage rattlesnakes," Rombo called a last warning. "They haven't learned to control the venom yet, you know. They just shoot all they've got. Certain death. You can recognize them because they'll be the ones listening to rap music."

"Of course." Martin sighed, and hurried to the waiting car.

Chapter Twenty-one
Skull Owl, the Messenger

After a casual Saturday morning breakfast Bo drove down to the sea from Andrew's condo, pondering what to do next. She'd begged off on spending the day with him, claiming a need to work on a nonexistent case. Probably wise not to let the relationship take on trappings of something it could never be, she thought. Wise not to wallow in those first heady days when intimacy might form the remembered core of something more serious. To her surprise and to his credit, he'd merely nodded and said, "Of course."

In the morning light the beach was a ribbon of clean white sand, scalloped at its edge by blue-green waves. A few beachcombers strolled the littoral, their heads bent toward tangles of kelp. Knee-deep in water and spaced widely along the shore, three fishermen cast lines into the sparkling surf. A postcard picture. Irresistible. Bo parked the car along California's Old Highway One, secured Mildred's leash to her collar, and clambered down the seawall rocks. Beneath her bare feet the sand felt cool, as though the night before still hid there.

She'd taken her morning medication with Andrew's coffee, and its initial effect made her feel, as usual, somewhat dull. Comfortably sluggish. Like an overfed goldfish in warm tap water. A light breeze suggested that the day might be well spent doing nothing. Maybe a hike in the hills behind Eva's, or a new painting roughed out on the gessoed canvas waiting at home. The painting felt right.

Bo picked up a stick and scratched in the wet sand where foam from a receding wave hissed and evaporated. Squiggles at first. Then a face with a bent nose and huge, wild eyes staring into Bo's. From her memory came stretched, long ears with pegs in the lobes. Pegs made of bone. A headdress of quetzal feathers. A Maya face, drawn from some museum visit filed in her brain, trying to speak from the sand.

"What can I really do?" she asked, staring into its grainy eyes. "Munson Terrell, or his wife, or Dewayne Singleton, or Chris Joe Gavin, or somebody else I don't even know about has murdered one of your people in a Mexican bar. Poisoned her and the Little Turtle as well. But I'm not a cop. I don't know how to track a murderer, and even if I did, I have no authority to do anything about it."

The wind, blowing sand in swirls over the Maya face, made a sound like a wooden flute. Distant and eerie behind the sunlit air. The fierce eyes seemed to fade.

"All I can do is make sure Acito has the best chance for a future. I think that's what Chac . . . "

But the face was gone, smoothed away by a small wave. Where it had been was only wet sand now, pocked with the airholes of submerged bean clams. As Bo watched, a seagull feather tumbling in the breeze rested briefly on the faceless sand. Then the feather blew into the surf and was swallowed. The whole scenario took less than three minutes and left Bo breathless.

"We'll keep this to ourselves," she told Mildred, "but medication or not, I know what that meant. I have to do something, stay with this thing and not drift off into my meds *or* the arms of pediatricians. They're counting on me."

Mildred did not ask who "they" might be, and Bo wasn't sure she could have answered, anyway. The Maya, maybe. About whom Bo knew practically nothing.

In the car she ran a brush through her windblown hair and searched in her purse for the slip of paper Estrella had provided yesterday. The slip containing an address for Munson and Kee Terrell, the former of whom would at this moment be en route to the desert with his band of merry men. "Let's go see how much the missus knows about a Maya baby with her husband's hair," she said.

The Terrells' house, built at the top of a winding hill street in the upscale San Diego community called Rancho Sante Fe, made Bo salivate. In weathered natural cedar, it nestled against the hill in unassuming levels that seemed to have sprung up by themselves. In its facade a two-story paned window topped by an arch of glass revealed gray-washed vaulted ceilings beamed with twisted wood milled to look as though it had been found in some desert wash. To the left of a curved and cobbled driveway, the edge of a cantilevered deck could be seen stretching over the wooded canyon beyond. Bo sighed as she approached and rang the doorbell. The house, with its light and solitude, was, so far, a dream.

The woman who answered the door did nothing to dispel the illusion.

"Yes?" She smiled in the open, self-assured way Bo remembered from the Tijuana bar. Barefoot in 501s and a black silk tank top, she looked like an Italian model. Emaciated and waiflike. Bo acknowledged privately that with luck she could probably fit both arms into jeans as slim as Kee Terrell's, but not a leg. At least not an entire leg.

"I'm Bo Bradley, from Child Protective Services," she sighed, showing her badge to a woman who at thirty-something could still play Beth in *Little Women* without foundation garments. "I need to speak with Mrs. Terrell about the death of a singer in Mexico Thursday night."

"I'm Kee Terrell," the woman said, inspecting Bo's badge. "But I don't understand what your agency has to do with Chac's death."

Bo scanned the response, the woman's face, and overall presentation for nuance. There was a zinging nervousness, a tendency to shallow breathing, a hollowness around the eyes. But these, Bo sensed, were always there. Her words hadn't brought them up.

"Chac was the mother of an eight-month-old boy," she went on, casting about for something official-sounding to say next. "Of course we're anxious to locate any relatives who may be willing to assume custody of the baby, and thought that Mr. Terrell, as Chac's manager, might know if such relatives exist."

Close, Bradley. You're shaving it to the bone here. But if she knows, it may show.

"Please, come in." Kee Terrell nodded. "I remember something about a baby, I think. But then Mundy's done all the work with Chac. He handles the music promotions. It's a separate business entirely. We were both so upset by her death, you know. Mundy had such hopes for her career, which was booming, and then this drug thing . . ."

Her voice trailed off as she showed Bo into a living area tastefully strewn with a dazzling array of primitive art and handcrafted mission furniture. "Please, just have a seat and let me get you some tea," she offered. "I'll be right back."

There was *something* about Kee Terrell, Bo admitted. Something caged and pacing beneath the unruffled surface. But it was old and lived-with, like a secret handicap to which the woman had long ago adjusted. And from her response, it seemed that Kee Terrell had little contact with a young Maya singer named Chac, and no awareness at all of her husband's role in the conception of a Little Turtle. The response was superficial, but then, Bo suspected, so was Kee Terrell.

Bo admired what she suspected was a real Santero George Lopez table beside a stone fireplace over which hung a Pop Chalee painting of saguaro cacti in fanciful colors. The desert plants were rendered with such graceful delicacy and joy that they seemed to dance beneath a stylized, almost Oriental moon. On both sides of the fireplace, mission doors led to the deck. The entire west wall was glass, overlooking the canyon and half filled by a towering live oak. Before it sat a bronze life-size painted sculpture of an aged Indian woman holding a basket of rabbits. Bo tried to imagine what it would be like to live in such a house, own such exquisite things, and failed.

"It's my own blend," Kee mentioned, placing pottery cups and teapot on a glass-topped coffee table. "I mix it with fresh mint from the canyon." Beneath the glass was a shelf displaying tiny fetish animals, mostly bears.

"Had to put them someplace," Kee went on, nodding at the fetishes. "Mundy and I are anticipating the arrival of an heir, as he puts it, so we're child-proofing the house. Everything breakable or edible out of reach." Her smile was sweet, even gleeful.

Bo felt momentarily like the only woman alive and under

seventy who wasn't pregnant. A marvelous feeling. "So you're expecting the heir early next year?" she smiled, mentally calculating how long it should take somebody as flat-bellied as Kee Terrell to produce a baby. And calculating how uncomfortably information about the existence of a previous "heir" might be received at the moment. Or any moment.

"Oh, I'm not pregnant!" Kee explained with enthusiasm. "Mundy and I feel strongly that an atavistic attachment to one's own DNA is arrogant and pathetic. There are so many beautiful children orphaned by mindless violence, especially in Third World countries. So we're adopting!"

"That's wonderful," Bo said, wondering why she felt like a guest at a high school symposium on world problems. "And I know you must be busy, so I'll just leave my card in case you or Mr. Terrell think of any familial connections to Chac that we might explore." The spicy tea in her cup reminded Bo of Christmas with its scent.

"I'll ask Mundy when he gets home tomorrow. He's running one of our workshops this weekend. Motivational seminars, really, with a spiritual dimension for which so many are seeking these days. I do the workshops for women, and we both do the mixed groups. Here, let me get you one of our fliers. You might enjoy coming to one."

Bo glanced at the slick brochure. The front was decorated with a Mimbres Indian turtle design that seemed fraught with meaning. Had Munson Terrell designed a business brochure to honor his unacknowledged son? An inside page outlined the benefits of a women's workshop called "Spirit Colour."

"You use British spellings?" Bo asked as Kee showed her out.

"Mundy's Australian." Kee nodded. "We use some Australian Aboriginal themes in the seminars, and he thinks the spellings give our print materials a certain panache."

"He's probably right," Bo agreed. "And please call if you think of anything that may help us."

On the way home Bo stopped at the Ocean Beach Library and took out its only book on Maya hieroglyphics. Back at her apartment she changed into jeans and a T-shirt, and went downstairs to get her mail before drifting into the familiar trance-state from which a painting would be born.

The Mimbres turtle floated before her eyes, its cross-hatched shell obscuring something. A face. Chac's face, staring out from behind the spidery lines. The Mimbres turtle wouldn't do, Bo realized. There would be a turtle in this painting, but it would have to be Maya. And the painting itself would be a portrait of Chac, a gift for Acito to take with him into his new life when the adoptive parents were chosen.

Deep in thought, Bo gave only surface attention to the mail stuffed in its metal rectangle. Bills. Fliers from a local carpet-cleaning outfit and a place that did something with brakes and mufflers. A museum catalogue from Boston. And an envelope, hand-addressed to "Barbara J. Bradley," the name on her CPS business card, used nowhere else except tax forms. The envelope bore a San Diego postmark from the day before and no return address.

Bo tore it open, still framing Chac's portrait in her mind. Inside were a Wells Fargo Bank statement for an account in the name Elena Rother, and a note written in blue ballpoint on a sheet of spiral notebook paper.

"Chac names her murderer in music," it said. "Listen."

The note was signed with the initials "G.P."

Bounding up the steps of the apartment building, Bo opened her door and dashed to the phone. Elena had been Chac's real name! The bank had a twenty-four-hour service line. And the account held $3,246.29, with an available ATM withdrawal limit of $250. Bo waited on the line for one of the service operators who unaccountably worked on weekends. A lure for customers in San Diego's endless banking wars, Bo assumed.

"San Diego County Department of Conservatorship," Bo lied when the operator answered. "Calling to confirm Acito Singleton as minor co-signatory on this account." There was no such thing as a county department of conservatorship, and babies undoubtedly couldn't co-sign on bank accounts, but it sounded official.

"We list a Tomás Acito Bolon on that account," the woman told Bo, "in addition to Elena Rother and Christopher J. Gavin. But no Singleton."

"Thank you," Bo said, and hung up.

So Chac had a San Diego bank account under an assumed name, set up so that Acito, under her maiden name, could have access to the money without probate in the event of Chac's absence or death. But of course it would be Acito's caretaker who would access the money. Bo noted the Tijuana address on the bank statement. It was the same one she had visited on Monday. Chris Joe Gavin's address in the dirt-paved alleyway. But why would he sign with the initials "G.P."?

Bo stood in her living room and stared into a blank canvas on its easel near a southern window. The G could stand for Gavin, but what was the P? Or maybe the bartender, Jorge, had sent the note. Jorge in English would be George. But what was his last name, and if he had access to Chac's money, wouldn't he have used it for her burial expenses in Tijuana instead of taking a collection from the impoverished staff at the bar? Or wouldn't he simply have taken the money for himself? But Jorge had no way of knowing her name, Bo thought. And maybe the note's author was Munson Terrell, who might have established the account secretly for Chac and Acito, and who now wanted the resources used for the son he couldn't claim.

Bo paced through the pool of light admitted by the window, and cleared her mind. A trick learned to diminish sensory overload, the constant bane of minds prone to mania. Breathing from her diaphragm, she imagined a single pinlight at arm's length before her, and stretched her mind toward it. The welter of questions subsided, leaving only a cool silence. In it an image rose, seen on a battered guitar case beneath a shelf of jars. "C.J. Gavin," it said. "Henderson, KY, GHOST PONY RULES!"

"Ghost Pony," she said aloud. "G.P."

Chapter Twenty-two

"Calm Snake," a lineage god

— *Popol Vuh*

Bo phoned Estrella, describing the contents of the mysterious envelope and asking her to complete the promised translation of Acito's lullaby as quickly as possible.

"I'll do it right now," Es answered, sniffling. Her voice was an octave lower than usual and bore a suspicious huskiness.

"Es, are you crying?" Bo asked. "What's the matter?"

"My sister's here," Estrella whispered. "She blew up when I told her I wasn't going to quit work when the baby's born. She says I'm unnatural and the baby will grow up to be a mass murderer."

Bo felt her face conform to what she liked to call "the homicidal maniac smile." "Put your sister on the phone, will you, Es? I just want to . . ."

"Never mind, Bo." Estrella laughed. "She wouldn't survive. But it's good to hear a voice from the real world. You understand, it's our *mother* who's agreed to be the paid nanny while I work. Mom says she'd love to earn enough for a trip to Lourdes her altar society's planning for two years from now, and she wants a wide-screen TV. She even mentioned a facelift. She's thrilled, but my sister . . ."

"Your sister's jealous," Bo named the obvious, "because your life is more interesting than hers. By the way, I'm going out to the desert this afternoon. Canyon Sin Nombre. You know the drill. I'll call you about those lyrics when I get back, okay?"

Bo had years ago begun the habit of informing Estrella and Henry of her desert trips, her intended destination. In the event that she failed to return, her friends could tell the sheriff's department where to look. As an additional precaution she always took along a plain white king-sized flat sheet, purchased at a thrift store for this purpose. Aerial searchers could easily see the sheet stretched out on the desert floor, where they might miss a person or even a vehicle.

"Are you going to camp?" Estrella asked.

"I don't think so. I just want to brood about a painting I'm working on. It's for Acito. But I might be back late. Don't worry unless I don't call you tomorrow morning."

"Roger," Es agreed. "And Bo, if Chris Joe really is the one who mailed that stuff to you, then he's in San Diego, right?"

"He was yesterday, anyway."

"What if he's the one who poisoned Acito and murdered Chac, and now he wants to be punished? What if he's trying to tell you how to catch him?"

Bo balanced the phone between her chin and shoulder while putting the finishing touches on a corned beef and swiss cheese sandwich on the kitchen counter. "I don't know," she said. "What if he is?"

"He'd be dangerous. You said he was just a teenager. He could be crazy, Bo. Maybe he was in love with her and killed her rather than lose her. A first love can be awful, and now he has nothing left."

"You've been reading gothics again, and anyway, he's not going to be out in the desert," Bo said with finality. "Talk to you later."

At the door she realized one more call was in order, given the altered nature of her relationship with a Cajun pediatrician.

"This is Bo Bradley," she told Andrew LaMarche's answering service. "Please tell Dr. LaMarche that I will be out today, but will call him tomorrow." She was glad he hadn't been at home. The gesture made her feel caring, even noble. A do-right sort of person.

After loading Mildred, the desert gear, and a cooler of edibles into the Pathfinder, Bo backed the vehicle into the sand-strewn alley behind her apartment building and got a garden hose from the locked laundry room. Fastening the coiled green plastic to a hose bib, she unscrewed the lid of the water jug in its frame attached to the car, and filled it. The jug's lip was bent, making it difficult to resecure the lid.

"Shit!" she exhaled forcibly, jamming the lid crookedly several times before succeeding in getting it straight. There would have to be a new jug, she decided. Next week, no later.

Driving east on I-8 into the mountains surrounding San Diego, Bo thought about Chris Joe Gavin. Raised in Kentucky foster homes since his toddler days, he wouldn't remember the troubled girl who had been his mother. Or would he? Had Chac's resemblance to some barely remembered image brought up powerful and conflicting feelings his adolescent psyche couldn't handle? Chac's devotion to Acito might have triggered a resentment, Bo thought. A resentment intensified by puppy love gone ballistic when he realized the new recording contract would take Chac away from Tijuana, and from him.

Bo sighed. "Freud is dead," she told Mildred, sleeping in the passenger's seat. "And all I really know is that boy was in love with Chac, and she trusted him. I don't know why he was in Tijuana or why she was living with him when she obviously had enough money to rent something a cut above that plywood tent."

Flipping on the radio, Bo watched as boulders replaced hillside houses beside the highway where it climbed out of Alpine toward the last suburban village. In the distance behind her a light sea-haze hung over the city. From a distance, San Diego looked shrunken and cramped inside a cage of white freeways. Ahead lay the Anza-Borrego Desert, silent and frozen in time. Bo sighed, feeling a tightness in her hands relax. A loosening of clamps inside her shoulders and behind her ears. The desert, its stark, swift dangers and dizzying lack of human reference was to her a sanctuary. Probably, she grinned at her reflection in the windshield, because it mirrored the landscape of her neurobiologically peculiar brain.

An hour later she passed the last landmark on a deserted road called S2, before the offroad descent into a canyon so desolate its Spanish name meant simply "without name." The landmark was an informative marker beside the road noting the existence some two million years ago of giant camels, rhinos, and sabertooth cats in the area of the Anza-Borrego desert now called the Carrizo Badlands. Bo dreamed of finding giant camel bones there one day. Maybe doing a Georgia O'Keeffe–style painting of a fossilized camel skull in the sand, red-orange Western sunlight blazing through the eye sockets.

At the gravelly, unmarked turnout, she engaged the four-wheel drive and nosed the Pathfinder over the canyon's rim. Just a jeep track angling straight down through sand and rock. Bo had been to Canyon Sin Nombre once before with a group from the Sierra Club, but never alone. A sense of adventure rushed like a cool breeze along her bare arms. It was hot at the canyon's rim, but below was a splendid jumble of sandstone corridors and exposed fossil-shell reefs, narrow granitic slot-canyons and wind-carved amphitheaters. Less scorching down there in the jagged shadows that, more than anything, cooled Bo's mind.

Andrew wouldn't approve, she knew. Estrella and Henry had long ago accepted her need to seek out lonely places. Places where the racket and incessant interpersonal demands of normal life did not exist. Her friends could not understand the needs of a brain that, even when medicated, was still prey to stimulus in a way normal brains were not. But they could offer their presence at the periphery of her strangeness, and simply agree to call the authorities if she didn't come back. Andrew LaMarche, bound to her by the complex attachments of masculine romantic love, would fight against the distance, the inscrutable difference between them. He would want to protect her. A male, he was programmed by nature to do so. He would not understand that protection from sensory overload, even at the cost of desert dangers, was to her a lifeline.

"I may be in over my head this time," she told Mildred. "I don't want to hurt him, but eventually, just because I'm the way I am, I will."

The dog nodded somberly, sniffing the air from the open window.

On the canyon floor Bo experimented with the four-wheel's capability in sand, then rock. Numerous fresh tire tracks snaked along the jeep trail, indicating the presence of what seemed like hordes of other people somewhere in the craggy silence. Bo crossed a vestige of an old stagecoach track, and tried to remember what the ranger had told the Sierra Club group. Something about a particularly dangerous area at the end of Arroyo Tapiado. An area of twisting caves and blind valleys ending in swallow holes. The caves, the ranger said, were safe in dry weather. But the tortuous, water-cut valleys accessible only through sinkholes in the cave ceilings were an invitation to lonely death. Other sinkholes had formed in the impassable valleys above the caves, covered only with fragile plates of worn sandstone. A fall through one of these would leave the victim trapped in an uncharted cave under a blind desert gorge where no human had been since the 1800s when scouts for the stage line went into the area searching for shortcuts, and never came out.

Shuddering, Bo stayed widely east of the area, and selected a slot canyon off the Arroyo Seco del Diablo creek bed, now dry and glistening in the sun. Parking on firm, rocky ground, she let Mildred run on the clear creek bed for a while, and then lifted the dog into a modified infant carrier strapped to her back. Desert canyons were no place for domestic animals to run free. And the temperature in the parked car would soon surpass tolerable limits for a small, old dog. Over her shoulder Bo gave Mildred some water in a paper cup, drank some herself from a canteen clipped to her belt, and hiked into the canyon.

Its walls, one hundred fifty feet high in places, cast layers of shade on a floor littered with the bulbous, connected concretions that were like strings of stone pearls. Softball-sized and valueless, they formed themselves of minerals around a nucleus in sedimentary rock, and then merely sat there for millennia. Bo thought of them as a discarded first attempt at pearls, formed by nature in its childhood and then forgotten. Like the lumpen clay pot made by small hands that would later shape a Ming vase. The canyon ended a half mile later in a dry fall that captivated Bo's eye with its play of subtle color. Only a deep growl emanating from the backpack alerted her to a coiled form in one of the wind-carved grottoes in the canyon wall twelve feet from her right shoulder. A rattlesnake. Its tail, hanging languorously from the ledge, snapped upward at Mildred's growl, the rattles vibrating with a sound at once unobtrusive and absolutely bone-chilling.

"Oh, shit," Bo whispered. Frost seemed to be crawling up the back of her neck, under her skin. The ancient enmity between snake and woman. "We were just leaving," she said politely, and meant it. The rattler didn't look, but flicked its tongue, tasting their intrusion on the air. In its niche, it might have been some holy sentinel, Bo thought. Placed there as a warning. Its image seemed carved on the backs of her eyes.

Back at the creek bed Bo ate lunch, spritzed a wide arc of straight ammonia on surrounding rocks from a spray bottle, and unfolded a cot in the shade cast by the Pathfinder. She'd read about the ammonia trick somewhere, but doubted its efficacy in defining territory as an animal would do with urine. It might at least momentarily confuse a predatory mammal, she thought. But mostly it allowed her an illusion of shrewd outdoorsiness, like a pioneer woman or somebody in an ad for thermal underwear.

Grabbing the book on Maya hieroglyphics and settling with Mildred on the cot, Bo shifted her attention to the problem at hand. A dead singer and an orphaned baby with too many fathers.

In 1492, the book began, there were eighty million indigenous people in the Americas. A century later only ten million remained, thanks to diseases brought by European invaders. In Guatemala there were less than four million Maya left today, working as near-slaves on plantations or being absorbed into the predominant culture as *ladinos,* acculturated Maya who no longer observed the old ways. Locked between the past and future, *ladinos* were shunned by the traditional Maya as traitors and ignored by the dominant, Spanish-speaking culture. Chac, Bo assumed, would have been one of these. Acito, as an American baby of Maya birth, would have no standing in his mother's homeland at all.

The Maya glyphs, carved over centuries in cities now lost beneath jungle overgrowth, were fascinating. Bo studied the strange faces, bird heads, and dismembered hands. Arcane and puzzling, they told of a world in which time was the reason for being. In which time was measured, honored, and symbolically carried by the ritualized behavior of its people, the Maya. Even contemporary Maya, Bo read, are self-effacing and modest, preferring to allow time itself to order events. The concept was difficult. Bo felt her eyelids drooping as a pleasant breeze swept the image of the snake and its warning from her mind.

"We'll just take a little nap," she told the already-sleeping dog beside her, and sighed into the vast and nurturing desert silence.

Chapter Twenty-three

"Just let it be found . . ."
    —Popol Vuh

On Saturdays the Torrey Pines State Reserve was crowded with joggers, cyclists, hikers, birders, and, it seemed to Andrew LaMarche, everyone else in San Diego who could claim any interest whatever in fresh air. Trails that on fogbound weekday mornings were home only to wood rats and mule deer now resounded with shrieking children and keen-eyed senior citizens yelling, "It's a brown towhee, Marvin! Fourth one today."

He had just wanted to be alone. To revisit the scene of that first lovemaking and search for Bo's earring. After a quarter century of monklike emotional austerity, he thought, it was time to permit himself the luxury of some fanciful behavior. To celebrate the first step in his claiming for his own the most spirited, courageous, warmhearted, and stubborn woman he had ever met. Hard to accomplish amid hordes of weekend nature buffs.

On a sturdy lookout platform below the trail a wedding was in progress, the bride and groom in traditional attire, the clergyman's robe billowing in Pacific sea winds banking off the eroded cliffs. Andrew followed the sandy path to its curve near the grove of pines that had survived drought and bark-beetles, waited to see if the cleric would be borne aloft in his black gown, and smiled. He would marry Bo there, he decided. The unorthodox setting would please her with its wildness. Her hair would catch the wind and glow like copper . . .

"Have you noticed that some of the sea dahlias are still in

bloom?" a brisk voice asked. "And I'm afraid you really can't go off the trail here, tempting as that may be." The speaker was a tiny woman with short gray hair and a tan suggesting much time spent outdoors. Her khaki sunhat was adorned with pins and badges from nature preserves on three continents, and her green polo shirt bore a cloth badge saying, "Torrey Pines Docent Society."

"Ummm," Andrew replied, sharing with the docent a view of his left foot damningly placed beyond the trail edge in a patch of what must be, he feared, sea dahlias. "My, uh, mother lost an earring up here yesterday, in that grove. She was, uh . . ."

"Collecting pine needles?" The woman's sparkling blue eyes left no doubt as to the failure of his schoolboy alibi. "I'm sure she'd be interested in our Native American basketry seminar at the lodge. The Torrey pine needles, as you probably know, are long and attached in bundles of five. The Kumeyaay Indians may have used them for decorative baskets, but we aren't sure. In any event, your mother should not have gone off the trail."

From beyond a sandy mound to his left, Andrew heard something call "Chi-ca-go" in a reedy alto voice. His foot seemed frozen in the dahlias.

"California quail," the docent stated with enthusiasm. "Nests on the ground in grass-lined hollows. You can see what damage tramping around might do."

"Of course," he conceded, pulling the offending foot back onto the trail. "I suppose there's no way of retrieving the earring. I probably couldn't have found it, anyway."

A kind, if knowing smile lit the docent's face. "It's irregular," she nodded, "but if we go in from the northeast loop of the trail near the birdbath, I think it will be all right. But only for a few minutes. How fortunate your 'mother' is to have such a devoted son."

Unaccustomed to blushing, Andrew's first reaction to the tingling rush of blood into his neck and facial capillaries was to suspect the presence of a rare tumor somewhere in his body, suddenly secreting gallons of serotonin. The substance, he remembered aimlessly, not only caused blushing but was believed to figure largely in the mood swings of manic depression. He wondered how often Bo felt as uncomfortable as he did at the moment. "Thank you," he said to the docent. "I appreciate your help."

There was nothing to do but follow the sprightly woman up the trail and into a now sun-dappled grove of Torrey pines. It wasn't difficult to find the sandy hollow he'd shared with Bo in romantic circumstances now blasted by sunlight and the good-natured docent's running narrative on sandstone formations and the medicinal uses of a plant called yerba buena. Its leaves, she remarked as Andrew sifted quartz sand between his fingers, contained acetylsalicylic acid.

"Aspirin?" he asked in a stab of courtesy.

"Yes," the docent answered. "Most people don't know that's what aspirin is."

"I'm a doctor," he mumbled, wishing the earring would turn up and offer an avenue of escape.

"You'd be surprised at the variety of medicinal plants growing in the chaparral. Why there's conchalagua for fever, poppy root for toothache, and of course the poisonous ones." She appeared to be looking for a particular specimen. "Don't see one in here in the grove, but there's plenty of jimsonweed about. Contains datura. Quite deadly. Did you know that during the French Revolution some of the more foresighted among the aristocracy carried an extract made of this plant so they could commit suicide if they were captured?"

LaMarche couldn't remember when he'd heard such grim information presented so lightheartedly. "No," he answered. "I didn't know that. And I'm afraid the earring is a lost cause. Again, thank you so much . . ."

"Here," the docent said, taking a flier from a canvas bag slung over her shoulder as they walked back to the trail, "let me give you one of our brochures on 'Dangerous Plants of the Chaparral.' I think you'll find it quite interesting."

"Thank you. I'm sure I will." He smiled as the woman headed vivaciously toward a group of German college students watching the conclusion of the nuptials over the sea.

"Guten Tag," she called to them as Andrew LaMarche

hurried around a wind-carved sandstone hill and then sprinted past a hundred yards of sagebrush to his waiting car.

At home he tossed the flier on the coffee table and glanced at the empty spot near the hearth where last night Mildred's bed had created a sense of messy hominess. In the shadow of a smooth knot of driftwood he'd placed there because he liked it and didn't know what else to do with it, something gleamed in the bright afternoon sunlight. A gold hoop earring, half buried in the carpet's pile.

"Great," he sighed, shaking his head and wondering how long he should wait before calling Bo.

Chapter Twenty-four
Broken Place

Bo awakened to a comfortable coolness and noticed that shadows cast by the canyon's western rim had stretched nearly across its floor. The sun was no longer visible, although its pulse still lit the sky and dripped washes of white gold, copper, and silver smoke over the tilted rubble and smooth canyon walls to the east. Nothing moved but the light. She stretched on the cot and watched it fade, breathing deeply and stroking the dog at her side. Throughout her body an unaccustomed sense of peace shimmered palpably, as if beneath her skin she were nothing more than a river of quicksilver, smooth and gleaming.

"It doesn't get any better than this," she sighed as Mildred sat up and yawned. The portrait of Chac she would do for Acito seemed to have formed in her mind like a dream. The singer in her *huipil*, striding through a moonlit desert landscape. From a Maya tumpline across the figure's forehead would fall a sling at her back, cradling a turtle whose shell would be a swirl of stars. The picture felt oddly real, as though Bo had actually seen it in her sleep and was remembering rather than imagining it.

Reluctant to leave the silent, darkened desert, Bo gave Mildred more water, drank some herself from the canteen, and found a bag of trail mix in the car. Raisin-peanut with carob chips. An acceptable dinner, she thought, even though the carob chips had melted. Lacking only an appropriate wine.

"Next best thing," she smiled at Mildred, taking a fat pink pill from her pocket and swallowing it with warm water. "Ycchh." The Depakote, lacking not only bouquet but social elegance, would nonetheless contribute to a chemical

143

equilibrium in which Bo could continue to function. But for how long? Eventually, she knew, the mania would come rushing again like debris-laden floodwater in the neural ditches of her brain. Or worse, the depression. Lighting a cigarette, she inhaled deeply and then blew smoke against the night sky. For the moment, it didn't matter.

When this case is over you'll quit smoking, Bradley. You'll take up figure-skating or tai chi as a replacement, and lose ten pounds in a month by living on tofu and exotic grains. Just find Chac's killer, and everything will fall into place.

Watching the smoke dissipate, she noticed another column of smoke rising from the valley floor to the northwest. A campfire, she realized. Just south of West Mesa in one of several rock-strewn amphitheaters formed by a million years of flash floods and earthquakes that were not recorded because there was not yet anyone around to take notice. Curious, Bo loaded the cot and Mildred into her car and drove south along Arroyo Seco del Diablo to its barely discernible intersection with the old overland stage route. She didn't turn her lights on. Why alert the distant camping party to her presence? They might be a bunch of gun-happy drunks. They also might be, she grinned in the dark, Munson Terrell and his macho workshop. Too tempting.

Turning onto the old stagecoach road, she followed it in the dark until cutting off at Arroyo Tapiado and heading northwest again, toward the ancient caves and a flickering fire. A hundred yards from the edge of the amphitheater, from which rhythmic drumbeats could now be heard, she eased the Pathfinder into an eroded cleft. Putting Mildred in her backpack infant carrier, and locking the car out of habit, she snapped the keys to the edge of her jeans pocket and crept closer to the scene unfolding a hundred feet down a sandstone wall.

Bo felt her lips pull toward her ears in a broad grin saved from its destiny as a laugh only by decorum. Indelicate to sneak up on people and then laugh aloud, even if they did look like the casting call for Indians in a grade-school Thanksgiving pageant. Martin St. John actually seemed rather svelte in his leather breechcloth, dancing with the others about the fire. And Munson Terrell, his lock of white hair gleaming in firelight, could have won the competition for a *Playgirl* centerfold. Still, the spectacle of fourteen white men in nothing but breechcloths and ankle bells, chanting and dancing around a fire, gave Bo something that felt like mental hiccups. A need to giggle.

Breathing from the diaphragm, she crawled backward far enough to be unseen, and sat on the ground. There was no point in staying. She couldn't hear anything they might say, and Martin was there to glean any useful information Terrell might drop, anyway. Shaking her head with amusement, Bo had just started back toward the hidden car when she saw it. Something moving beyond a wind-carved window in a mudstone pillar. Something dark, narrow, and perfectly straight. As she watched, the object arced downward from a pivotal point behind the pillar and came to rest gently just above a boulder at the amphitheater's rim. A rifle barrel. Aimed into the group below.

Scuttling back to her vantage point, Bo tried to assess the situation. The men were moving faster now, bobbing and stamping erratically. Only one remained stationary. The drummer. Munson Terrell. If the rifle were equipped with a telescopic sight, any one of them could be picked off easily, but Terrell was a sitting duck. A slight movement of the rifle barrel recalled the message implicit in the snake's tail earlier. "Warning," it said. "Now!" In two seconds, Bo realized, somebody, probably Munson Terrell, would be shot. Would be dead.

Grabbing a chunk of loose sandstone the size of a college dictionary, she tossed it with both hands over the side of the amphitheater wall. It tumbled to a stop fifteen yards down, lodged against an outcropping of metasedimentary schist from the ancient topography below the sandstone. In seconds the scrabbling landslide of smaller rocks in its wake ceased. The dancers had neither seen nor heard it. But someone else had.

Mildred, sensing Bo's fear, began to climb out of her carrier. Bo hooked her left thumb over her shoulder in the dog's collar, and watched as the gun barrel angled silently away from the scene below. It seemed to be following a magnetic tug created by the frenzied drumbeat echoing in Bo's heart. The rifle was now pointing at her!

"Oh, shit," she whispered as the drumming abruptly stopped. In the silence that followed she merely crouched in the ground amid the rubble, and didn't move. The gun barrel swept snakelike back and forth, seeming to smell rather than see her presence. A rifle shot now would alert Terrell's group below, Bo realized. But the drumming might start again at any moment. Better to make a move now than later. But what move?

An open space of about twenty-five feet lay between her and the nearest broken mass of rock in the direction of the car. Even in the dim light of a waning quarter-moon, the flat expanse seemed endless and perfectly deadly. Her blood, she noted without wanting to, would look black, spilled in this eerie light.

The rifle's owner was invisible behind the windowed pillar, and had the additional advantage of being able to stand. Still, there was no indication that Bo was any less invisible among the rocks. Slowly she inched backward from rock-shadow to rock-shadow on her knees and one hand, still holding the trembling dog firmly on her back.

"Don't bark," she hummed through her teeth in a barely audible and patently fake falsetto. The "nice dog" voice. "Don't bark, don't growl, don't whine. Good dog. Good dog, Mildred."

As abruptly as it stopped, the drumming started again. Slower this time, accompanied by a sort of whooping chant in which the men called something that sounded like "kowa key" into the dark, over and over. Their voices seemed dramatically gravelly. It occurred to Bo that she hadn't survived a terrifying brain disorder for forty years only to die to the ludicrous soundtrack of a male-bonding ritual. No, it would be Bach, or nothing.

On her feet now, she dashed for the shadow of a boulder to her right. Footsteps from the area of the pillar made it clear that the rifle's owner was moving in the same direction. An acid taste filled Bo's throat. The only safety lay in getting to the car, and that was impossible. Running, she darted between rocks and broken slabs that had once been canyon walls. Overhead a thin cirrus cloud dimmed the moon's light to a uniform gray that almost obscured the immense hole in the canyon wall before her. One of the caves the ranger had mentioned to the Sierra Club group. Dark and featureless as the world behind a mirror. Bo scrambled through the opening and slid twenty feet down a sloped ledge to land on the dry floor of a subterranean wash that angled narrowly upward. Far ahead she could see a lessening of darkness that would mean a sinkhole in the cave's ceiling, and she crept toward it, following the narrow walls carved by floodwater rushing under collapsed desert sandstone. Looking over her shoulder, she saw the dimly lit cave mouth stabbed by a dark, straight line. The rifle barrel.

Fighting panic, she moved steadily toward the break in the ceiling. A shot in here would be muffled by tons of debris. Terrell's group wouldn't hear it. She and Mildred would die. Their bodies wouldn't be found for years, if ever.

"If we survive this, I'm going to buy a gun," she breathed to the dog panting over her shoulder. "I hate guns and nobody with a history of depressive episodes should have one, but at this rate I won't live long enough to commit suicide."

A lick on the neck was sufficient motivation to climb the wash beneath the sinkhole, and emerge in a landscape Bo hadn't imagined in her worst psychosis. Slender ridgelines intersected each other in a maze of blind canyons leading nowhere. Dry falls plummeted fifty to a hundred feet into sheer-walled holes full of broken rock. At her feet Bo saw cannonball-sized concretions, some worn free and movable. One, about five yards ahead on the ridgeline, seemed to be staring at her in the faint light.

"Oh, not *now*!" Bo said angrily to her own brain, prone to symbolic overinterpretation of everything even under normal circumstances. Whatever those were. The round white rock continued to stare as falling pebbles below indicated the presence of a second climber in the wash leading up through the collapsed sinkhole.

It *was* staring, Bo realized as panic made her head feel as though it were floating. Because it wasn't a rock at all, but a skull.

Moving toward it on feet that felt glassy, she tried to make sense of it. Why would a skull be sitting on a ridgeline in an impassable badland without its skeleton? Beside it on the ground was a single black feather. And halfway down the adjacent valley wall was a scrubby mesquite bush with an abandoned nest in its branches, its roots hanging like pale threads into blackness beneath. Bo ran and fell the fifteen feet to the mesquite, grabbed its trunk with one hand, and slid into the hole beneath it, her knees on the jagged edge of the slumped sandstone slab that had probably collapsed a century after an explorer had first fallen through it. His skull would have been carried to the surface by a coyote or mountain lion exploring the recently accessible tunnel below. Above, someone kicked one of the round, white concretions off the ridgeline. Bo heard it crash over her head and come to rest at the bottom of the blind valley. Then silence.

An eternity of silence in which the pain in her knees became a kaleidoscope of throbbing color, a surgery with no anesthesia. But she couldn't move. Any sound would alert the watcher above, and any movement might dislodge the precarious balance of the slab. The fall below could be five feet and could be two stories. It scarcely mattered.

The footsteps walked to the end of the ridgeline, then back, but no further. Whoever it was knew of the danger in traversing these hidden valleys, Bo thought through the flashes of light her knees were creating behind her tightly clenched eyes. Whoever it was, wasn't stupid. Or patient.

After Bo had counted to sixty twenty times, stroking Mildred's neck with her left hand in time to the count, the footsteps noisily descended the wash into the big cave, and were gone. Bo waited for five more counts of sixty before pulling herself out of the collapsed sinkhole beneath the mesquite, and then lying flat against the valley wall to distribute her weight evenly.

"We're not budging from here until it's light," she whispered to Mildred. "Whoever that is may be sitting down there in that cave, waiting to blow us out of the opening when we go back down."

The dog stirred uncomfortably in the backpack, and then draped herself over Bo's shoulder and went to sleep.

Hours later Bo felt the personality of the sky shift in that way only discernible to those who have been awake all night for reasons not related to work. The ill, the grieving, the manic, and the terrified. A sudden absence of weight, felt in the ears, followed swiftly by murky grayness where before there was only black. Dawn. Often employed as a symbol for the slow crawl of the human race out of an evolutionary darkness in which reason was not an option. Standing again on the ridgeline of a lost desert escarpment, Bo wondered exactly how far that race had come. From the east radials of pale orange light spilled over a tattered horizon and through the eye sockets of a human skull lying on the ground at her feet.

"Thank you," she addressed the empty, protective shell of someone who had died here alone and long ago. "You saved my life." Turning the skull to face a sunrise that seemed symphonic, she adjusted Mildred in the carrier and started toward the open sinkhole. The little dog's eyes were somewhat filmy, Bo noticed, and the skin beneath her fur was slack. Dehydration. To be expected in a frail, old mammal unaccustomed to eight-hour spans in zero-humidity desert warmth.

"Don't worry, we've got five gallons of water strapped to the car," she told the dog. "Hang in."

At the lip of the sinkhole Bo threw down a rock, then waited to hear responsive movement in the cave. There was nothing. No sense of anything alive in the stony silence below. Carefully Bo descended the wash and hurried through the vaulted chamber at whose end a round opening now seemed to pulse with light.

Terrell's group was still asleep, mere rumpled forms in sleeping bags surrounding a dead fire. Bo tried to identify Martin among them, but failed.

In minutes she was at the Pathfinder with its needed water jug. But as she reached to unclip the bungees holding it in its wire frame, she noticed something anomalous. She was sure she'd succeeded in fastening the troublesome cap on the plastic jug correctly. She remembered standing in the alley behind her apartment, struggling with the damn thing after she filled the jug. It had taken several tries to get the cap on straight. But now it was crooked. Someone had opened the water jug, but hadn't removed it, then carelessly replaced the defective cap. The water level was the same as it had been yesterday. Bo remembered a poisoned baby, a shot of tequila laced with almond-scented death. The memory made her back away from the plastic jug as if it were radioactive.

Unlocking the car, she gave Mildred the last two ounces of water left in the canteen, and backed out into Arroyo Tapiado. If she were right, someone had just come close to killing the closest thing to unconditional love Bo had ever known. An animal, but nonetheless there when the symptoms of a brain disorder drove everyone else away. Bo felt threads of ice shoot along a thousand neural pathways and pool in her hands. She could kill, she realized as the veins in her hands stood out, throbbing. She could actually kill anybody who would poison her dog.

Chapter Twenty-five

"The crowded life"

—*Popol Vuh*

Dewayne Singleton sat upright and carefully shook the sand from his shoes again. The shoes were important. He couldn't have left the hospital like he did if he'd still been wearing those thin slippers. But the big man, the nice one who kept getting Tylenol whenever Dewayne complained about the pain in his legs, that one had said shoes might help the pain. He'd gone and got a pair of tennis shoes for Dewayne even though it was time to go to bed. He'd said he wouldn't be there in the morning because his shift would be over at 11:00, and he wanted Dewayne to have the right shoes. They would play volleyball on Saturday morning outside, he told Dewayne. Important to have the right shoes, especially with the Haldol giving him those muscle cramps. Dewayne just nodded and decided not to tell the man he didn't know how to play volleyball.

And then on Saturday morning, when he was outside in the courtyard wearing those shoes with that red plastic visitor's badge still in his pocket, Allah sent a miracle. Or something did. A big group of black people came. They didn't come all at once, but in groups of three or four pretty close together. Dewayne didn't know why they were there, but he knew they didn't know each other. Something about the way their bodies moved around inside the group, leaving spaces that said they were strangers. Something about the way they cut their eyes when they were watching each other do their thing, which was about talking about God.

Without really meaning to do it, Dewayne watched one of

them in a nice shirt and shiny brown shoes go up to a woman and start talking. It was so easy to start letting his body move just like that man talking, sort of pick up on him and his little gestures. Mama always said it was some kind of gift, the way Dewayne could do that.

After a while he rolled down the sleeves of his plaid shirt over the plastic hospital bracelet on his wrist, and went up to a white boy who kept pacing up and down, staring at the ground.

"Do you know about the love of God?" Dewayne said to the boy just like the man in the nice shirt had said it. "Do you know the Bible has answers to all your questions?"

The boy didn't look up and just whispered, "Get fucked, asshole."

But one of the women in the group heard and smiled at Dewayne, her wide, dark face nodding like a mechanical fortune-telling Buddha he saw once at a carnival he and Buster went to in Breaux Bridge. "Praise," she said.

Dewayne smiled at her and nodded just the same and said, "Praise," right back. Then he followed the boy up and down, saying anything he could think of once in a while, but mostly just pretending. Finally the boy stopped and whispered, "Man, you don't leave me alone with this fucking shit, I'm gonna kick your balls off."

"Praise." Dewayne nodded, and drifted toward the woman, whose flowered dress and perfume reminded him of Mama. The staff people, even Mr. Rambo, were playing volleyball with the patients in the center of the courtyard while the rest of the patients and the visitors milled around the edges. On a stone picnic table somebody was setting out lemonade in paper cups, and cookies.

"Wish I could stay for refreshments," the woman said, "but I can't. Got to be going." Dewayne could hear the fear hidden in her voice. She was afraid, wanted to get out.

"I got to be going, too," he answered softly, duplicating her pronunciation. "Praise, got to meet my wife."

"You from the South?" she asked, looking around to see if any of the other visitors were ready to leave yet. The way her eyes just slid over the patients let him know what she was afraid of. Like if she really looked at one, it would do something terrible to her.

"Praise, yes I am," he answered, and then added, "My wife from aroun' here, though."

The woman was making a decision. "Well, you sure do have the Lord's spirit, praise His name. I think I'm ready to go."

Dewayne smiled at her while looking for staff out of the corner of his eye. The only one who really knew him was Mr. Rambo, still playing volleyball, facing away from the door with the guards. "I'll walk with you," he said, pulling the visitor's tag from his pocket and palming it so that the woman could see it, but no one else could.

"You s'posed to have that fasten to your shirt," she told him, getting ruffled as a way of not noticing her own shaking hands and the way she was leaning with her whole body toward that door. As an afterthought she said, "Praise God."

"It kep' fallin' off," Dewayne answered, following her to the door. "His name be blessed." Mama had said that a lot. It seemed to fit in.

The guard opened the door and took their badges. He was listening to the radio and talking to another guard who was counting some kind of papers. The woman in the flowered dress signed her name on the clipboard, and handed the pencil to Dewayne. He signed his name next to one that said, "Daniel Glover," and then realized he should have signed "Daniel Glover" instead of "Dewayne Singleton." But his handwriting was messy, and the guard didn't look. Later they'd see that Dewayne Singleton had signed out, and that was honest. The guard had pushed a buzzer then, and let them out the second door.

Putting his shoes back on, Dewayne sat in the sand and tried to remember what he'd done after that. It was all blurry. He'd run, once he got away from the hospital parking lot. Tore off that plastic bracelet. Run to a big freeway ramp, got a ride in a truck with a fat Mexican man who wanted him to work someplace planting palm trees. When Dewayne said he hated palm trees, the man stopped and put him off next to a park that was on some kind of bay. And some people at a picnic gave him a whole plate of fried chicken and a can of orange pop when he said he couldn't drink the beer because of his religion. That was yesterday, before he spent the night walking in sand. Back and forth. Wondering what to do next.

People seemed pretty nice here in California. Dewayne found himself bowing to the east when the sun came up and asking Allah where all the evil ones were, that the Angel Jabril was going to kill. Then he watched some boys on little sailboats just big enough to stand on, riding the blue water. Even though the muscles in his arms were jumping like snakes in a hot zinc bucket, he didn't think that was because of the infidels. He thought maybe Jabril had already been here, and the evil was gone. He would need to leave, too, he decided, and headed toward the freeway.

Chapter Twenty-six
Spilt Water

After stopping for water at a closed gas station, Bo drove straight home. Only after Mildred was fed and comfortably curled like a white fur donut in her basket beside Bo's bed did Bo go back outside with a pair of tongs and an empty spice bottle. The bottle had, she remembered, contained whole cloves before she'd used them all in an abortive attempt to rescue a mildewed beach towel from its characteristic stench.

After baking for two weeks inside a plastic bag in the sun on her deck, towel and cloves had been tossed in a dumpster, now smelling like mildewed cloves. So much for herbal remedies. Bo wondered why they never worked for her when they seemed to work for everybody else. Especially for somebody poisoning mothers and babies, and getting away with it.

Holding the bottle with the tongs, she dipped water from the jug attached to the Pathfinder's rear door, and then capped the bottle with its plastic stopper. If she were right and the water were poisoned, she realized, the jug should be emptied before somebody got into it. Maybe a child, or one of the beach-area homeless. Bo hauled it out of its cage, carried it to a storm sewer on the street, and dumped its contents. Then she backed the car over it and tossed it in the same dumpster that had received the ruined beach towel a year ago.

Smashed, she figured, nobody scouring the dumpsters for usable trash would be tempted. If she were wrong about what had happened to its lid out in the desert, then she had just completed an elaborate and wholly senseless ritual, which if witnessed, might create suspicion about her sanity. Bo grinned as she climbed the stairs back to her apartment. That suspicion could easily be documented as fact.

Heading for the phone, she realized 7:00 A.M. was really too early to call Dar Reinert at home. She'd wait a while before calling the detective to find out how one arranged forensic tests for poison on a Sunday. The answering machine light was blinking frantically. Six calls from Andrew in escalating degrees of possessive concern about her whereabouts, one from Estrella merely asking Bo to call before noon on Sunday or else she and Henry would phone the sheriff's department as per agreement, and one from Eva Broussard saying a group of expatriate Guatemalan Maya were camping on the property and might be a source of some background information on Chac. Estrella, Eva suggested, should come along since the Indians seemed to know some Spanish, but no English.

Estrella answered on the second ring, relief audible in her voice. "*Madre de dios*," she exclaimed. "Bo, I'm not sure I can cope with your desert camp-outs in my delicate condition, and Henry's even worse. Remember the girl that mummified out there? I kept seeing you turned to leather like an old suitcase, and Henry dropped several references to the habits of vultures. You *said* you weren't going to stay all night . . ."

"I'm sorry, Es," Bo said. "I didn't have any choice. Somebody was trying to kill me."

In the ensuing silence Bo heard her friend marshaling the resources necessary to remain calm while cultural habits learned with her first language clamored for emotive expression. The battle took more than a half a minute. "*What?*" Estrella finally exploded.

"Look, I need for you to go with me up to Eva's to interview some Guatemalans she's snagged crossing her property on their way north from the border. I'll tell you about it on the way, okay?"

"I'll be ready in an hour." Estrella sighed. "Have you called Andy? He's not used to this, you know."

"I'll call him right now." Bo nodded. "And thanks, Es."

Bo found a cup, a museum souvenir from Santa Fe, in the dishwasher. Unclear as to whether she'd run the dishwasher since last week, Bo rinsed the cup and admired its Kachina doll design. Missing as usual from all the popular Kachina souvenirs was the Stone-Eater Kachina, Owanja-Zrozro. The mad one.

The Hopi had recognized and reified the reality of psychiatric disorder in their mythology; but the museum had conveniently left the mad Kachina off their spiffy cup. Bo filled the flawed item with freshly brewed coffee and phoned Andrew LaMarche, whose relief was mixed with predictable anger. Bo decided to spare him the real story in the interest of a more pressing issue.

"This is the reason I avoid serious relationships," she explained, not masking the annoyance she felt. "Of course you were worried, but you *can't* be. Not with me. I'm different, Andy. I care for you, but I can't bond with you at the hip. My life works as long as I have a good shrink, the right meds, and the freedom to take care of myself in ways you're going to find weird. Peace and quiet, being alone, painting—are like oxygen to me and come before everything else. Without them, I fall apart. Normal people in relationships don't like to play second fiddle to anything, especially to something as embarrassing as a psychiatric disorder. But that's the way it is."

Come on, Bradley. Attila the Hun could have handled that with more delicacy. What are you trying to do, drive him into the arms of perky size 6 grant coordinators who will enhance his career while keeping him up nights for reasons more attractive than stark fear?

Maybe she should have been a little pathetic, she thought, played on his sympathy. Except that was dishonest, and he needed to know the truth before things got any more complicated.

"In that case," he pronounced somberly, "I need to rethink a few things."

Bo's heart lurched. She didn't want to be rethought, just accepted. Always the stumbling block.

"Pine-needle basketry is a possibility," he went on, "although I've given some thought to music. Always wanted to build a harpsichord. And then learn to play it, of course."

Bo wasn't sure whether his deadpan delivery reflected a by-now incomprehensible anger or a controlled, if arcane humor. "Harpsichord?" she said, lost.

"Yes. I'm going to need something to do during those long nights when you're prowling snake-infested wastelands in pursuit of peace. When the harpsichord's finished, I may start on a pipe organ. The condo will be too small, of course, but I've been thinking of buying a house . . ."

"Oh, Andy," Bo breathed, relaxing. "I thought . . . well, you know what I thought. Can you really put up with this, with me?"

"Only if I start on the harpsichord right away. Incidentally, aren't we supposed to have dinner with Rombo and Martin tonight? My flight for New Orleans leaves at eight twenty. Dinner will have to be early."

"I'll phone them and move the time up," Bo answered, simultaneously making a judgment call. "And, uh, Andy, two more things. I've changed my mind about going to Louisiana with you. I'd like to go. I need to talk to Dewayne Singleton's family, and they're there. Maybe somebody at the prison where he was, too. So is the invitation still open?"

He was delighted. "I'll arrange for your tickets immediately," he said. "We'll spend the night in the Quarter. Now what was the second thing?"

"The real reason I didn't make it back last night was, well, I was sort of hiding out in a blind canyon from somebody with a rifle who seemed to be, uh, trying to kill me. I'll tell you all about it at Rombo and Martin's, okay?"

"Bo, I'm not a young man," Andrew mentioned raggedly. "I'm not sure my heart can survive too much of this. Are you sure? Who was it?"

"I never saw the face," Bo explained, "just the gun barrel. And I think whoever it was may have put something in the water jug on my car, too. I've got a sample of the water and I'm going to call Dar to find somebody to test it." She felt her voice drop a half octave. "I almost gave some of that water to Mildred, Andy. There are rules about things you simply cannot do in the desert. Poisoning water is probably at the top of the list. I want to kill whoever it was. I really do."

"I'll be at your place at three." He sighed. "Pack the coolest clothes you have. We'll talk about this at Rombo and Martin's, and then I'm getting you out of here before it's too late."

In the shower Bo thought about the boy Chac had lived with before her death. Of everyone involved with the singer, Chris Joe Gavin was the most enigmatic. A runaway teenager with a history that almost always produced troubled, insecure personalities. How many foster homes had the Kentucky social worker said he'd been in? Enough to leave a gaping hole where a sense of security should have grown. A sense of being wanted.

In her work Bo had met scores of adults raised in the foster care revolving door, all of them burdened for life with a need for belonging that would never be met. And Chris Joe was still an adolescent. Volatile. His feelings and perceptions distorted by inexperience and hormonal surges that could at times induce depression, delusions, obsessions, the trappings of madness.

Squishing creme rinse through her hair, Bo enjoyed the pounding of hot water on muscles strained by the night's exertion. Had Chris Joe been the stalker in the desert, she wondered? Had his puppy love for Chac exploded at her death into something vengeful, murderous? The rifle had at first been trained on Munson Terrell. Why would Chris Joe want to kill Chac's manager when Chac was no longer alive? The boy might have known that Terrell was Acito's father, and his longing for Chac had been only too obvious at the time of Bo's visit last week. Did Chris Joe think Munson Terrell had poisoned Acito and then Chac? Maybe Chris Joe *knew* that Terrell was the murderer, and was hell-bent on vengeance.

Remembering her own response to the mere possibility of Mildred's death by foul play, Bo acknowledged the universal human proclivity for revenge. But then why had the boy sent her Chac's bank statements and the strange note saying, "Chac names her murderer in music"?

Stepping out of the shower, Bo wrapped herself in a yellow terry cloth robe and stared into the vanity mirror. Wet, her hair was redwood-colored, laced with silver strands that were rapidly becoming streaks. Time to start dyeing it, or just capitulate to a Mrs. Santa Claus look that would require checkered aprons and tiny, round wire-framed spectacles. Contemplating that option, Bo felt a sudden realization stir to life in her mind. Of course!

"Hair dye!" she yelled at the steamy mirror, bringing an interrogative woof from Mildred in her basket. "Why didn't I see it before?"

Chac hadn't been dying her own hair, Bo now understood clearly. The bottle of aerosol hair color spilling from Chac's backpack shortly after her visit with Chris Joe to Acito in San Ysidro hadn't been for Chac, it had been for Acito! Chac was disguising the baby's telltale white streak, his what-had-Andy-called-it? Piebaldism. She'd been hiding the genetic marker that would document Terrell's paternity of her baby. But hiding it from whom? Chris Joe had been with her, would have seen her dyeing Acito's forelock. Chris Joe obviously knew the truth.

Kee, then. Chac would not want her lover's wife, also his partner in a business that promised to elevate the singer out of prostitution and poverty, to know of his indiscretion. Except Kee had said she'd only heard of the baby. And since she had little contact with Terrell's Mexican musical venture and seldom went to Tijuana for Chac's shows, there was no chance of her seeing Acito, who was kept over the border anyway. So from whom was Chac going to such lengths to hide Acito's paternity?

Her long-lost husband, Dewayne Singleton? Bo wondered how news of his wife might have traveled to the man, fenced behind razor wire in a Louisiana prison. Was there some kind of secret communication service available to the imprisoned? Probably, Bo thought. Even in a prison, information might be purchased. But Dewayne Singleton would not have had the resources necessary to buy, and the manic irrationality of his motivation was inconsistent with that scenario.

Dewayne was no Machiavellian plotter. He was ill and delusional. Unless that was an act. Bo was sure it wasn't, but even if it were, Chac could not have known that Dewayne would turn up. And masking Acito's paternity could do nothing to hide the fact most likely to enrage an absent husband, the simple existence of a baby not his own.

Pulling on clean but rumpled khakis from a stack of clothes under a dusty ironing board, Bo shook her head in confusion. The only one from whom Chac could logically have been hiding Acito's noticeable hunk of hair was Munson Terrell. But why? And who had been lurking in desert shadows to kill him as he drummed for the dancers celebrating manhood? With a gasp of horror Bo remembered a cluster of forms in sleeping bags on the desert floor. One of them Martin, her friend. None had moved in the pale gray light of early dawn. Had the killer gone back while she was hiding, and killed them all?

"Don't overdo it," she warned herself while struggling into a sports bra. "Martin's going to be fine. This will all make sense later. Right now just call Dar and find out if the water was really poisoned, or you just imagined it."

Reinert would pick up the bottle from inside Bo's screen door, he said. But he probably couldn't get it tested until tomorrow. When Bo told him what had transpired in the badlands, he said simply, "It's got to be Gavin. The kid's nuts, Bo. And running on empty since the hooker bought it. I'll put out an APB, see if we can pick him up on suspicion. Weapons or something. But there's not much we can do on a charge of chasing you around in the desert. Not likely we'll find him, anyway. Kid's used to lying low. Makes ya wonder why."

Bo phoned Rombo at home and arranged for an early dinner, then left a message at work for Madge saying she had to fly to the funeral of an aunt in Mississippi. A descendant of William Faulkner, actually. On Bo's mother's side.

Chapter Twenty-seven
The Bundle of Flames

The Maya refugees, a band of six men and two women, were waiting on the tiled veranda of Eva's classic mission-style adobe when Bo and Estrella arrived in the Pathfinder. Eva introduced them in halting Spanish, then sat politely to listen. For a while Estrella conversed with the group in Spanish as Bo searched their wide, oval faces for hallmarks of personality. There was courage in the faces. But then, Bo thought, there would be. These were survivors, the ones who would move on rather than stay and be crushed. The pioneer stock. Some would walk a thousand miles only to die. But others would survive and their children would flourish in new places. Chac had been one of these. A survivor.

As the Spanish conversation continued, Bo turned toward the mountains to the south. Still lost in mist, they seemed to echo with the million footsteps of a soft-spoken army moving northward in tattered clumps. A Third World, it was called, the world beyond U.S. borders, extending through one continent and then the next. A world of people who had been there long before the first European invader. Now quietly invading back.

None of the Maya looked at Bo as Estrella translated what they had told her. Shy, they stared at the ground and waited to learn what this might be about. Dressed in an odd conglomeration of outdated American clothes—polyester bell-bottoms, T-shirts from athletic events five years ago, a maid's uniform from a downtown San Diego hotel long since converted to single-occupancy welfare housing—they seemed unsure of how to position their arms and legs. One of the women wore a shawl woven of brightly colored yarn, its workmanship still lovely under the grime of a long journey. She alone appeared sure of herself as she gazed at the military field boots on her feet.

"They're from a village called San Juan la Laguna," Estrella began, "and among themselves they speak a Maya language called Tzutuhil. They—"

"That's the language Chac said she spoke," Bo interjected. "Remember? She told us at the bar in Tijuana right before she died. Maybe they know who she was. Maybe they know if Acito has relatives who're still there. Chac's real name was María Elena Bolon. Ask them, Es. See if Acito has relatives!"

As Estrella engaged in a conversation that seemed to embarrass the group, Bo indulged in a fantasy. There would be a strong young uncle for Acito, a brother of Chac's. His name would be Jaguar Tooth, or something like that, and his witty, athletic wife, who would remind everyone of Tina Turner, would love Acito. They would welcome their handsome nephew as a son. They would rear him to observe the old ways, to be a splendid Maya Indian.

The look in Estrella's eyes didn't quite match the fantasy.

"They didn't know Chac," she began, "but they've heard her story. Apparently it's reached the status of folklore along the immigrant trail."

"They're proud of her." Bo made up the myth. "She survived countless hardships and became a popular singer, a success. Right?"

Estrella now looked at her feet just like the Maya. "No," she answered softly. "They call her *la puta* in Spanish. It means 'the whore.' I don't quite understand all they're saying, but apparently the Maya lifestyle, what's left of the old one passed down from pre-Conquest times, is quite rigid." Estrella sighed and glanced bitterly into the hills. "Chac is to them an example of disgrace. They don't care that she survived alone, or that she found a way to bring beauty to the world. They say it's good that she's dead because she was worse than a *ladina*—she's a Maya who abandons the old ways. They say time will stop when the last Maya does what Chac did, and becomes . . . the word means something like 'arrogant.' "

"And Chac's family?" Bo asked, disheartened.

"Dead. Her mother was a teacher in their village, something discouraged by the Guatemalan government because literacy diminishes the pool of underpaid labor necessary to keep the plantations raking in bucks. The story is that Chac saw her mother shot by a government soldier when she was just a kid. The father took her to a city called Antigua and left her at a convent school. Then he went back to their village and drank himself to death. The woman in the shawl—her name's Julia Ixtamel—says supposedly the nuns there taught Chac to sing, but she doesn't believe it because Chac's singing was not the singing of a holy person."

"Yes it was!" Bo insisted, jumping to her feet and running to the car. "Just listen to this," she yelled, cramming Chac's tape in the deck and turning the ignition key. As Acito's song drifted on the air, Bo realized she was crying.

"What's the Spanish word for 'holy'?" she asked Estrella.

"*Santo.*"

"This music *es santo!*" she told the Indians, pointing to invisible notes over her head. "That's as *santo* as it gets. Can't you hear it? Why can't you hear it?"

The eight bronze faces stared assiduously at the ground. Bo could feel them turning away, going behind some impenetrable wall that excluded her totally. From the group came the whispered word, "*loca.*"

"Oh boy," Estrella breathed, and wrapped an arm over Bo's shoulders. "This wasn't such a good idea. They never knew Chac, Bo. You have to get to know somebody before you can see that they're not just one thing."

Eva Broussard had hurried to join Bo and Estrella. "Chac is just a myth to these people," she said. "But she's real to you. They can't be changed by the truth of her life. You already have been."

Bo leaned to turn off the tape, and sighed. A dry mountain wind ruffled her hair in the silence. "I wanted," she began, "something to be there in them for Acito. Some kind of heritage. Not this."

"If Chac had wanted their world-view, she would have stayed in Guatemala," Eva stated flatly. "She has left her son something different. Respect that, Bo, and let go of your Hollywood fantasy."

In their brief friendship Eva Broussard had never spoken so directly. Bo considered it a compliment. "Okay," she agreed, feeling silly about her earlier outburst. "But I don't know what to do next."

The Indians had stood and were walking slowly toward a campsite visible in a rocky hollow a half mile behind the house. Some of the members of Eva's group, just arrived from New York, beckoned to the men to help them dig a nearby foundation. Julia Ixtamel lagged at the rear, glancing over her shoulder. In the open sunlight Bo saw that the woman's shawl had ribbons woven among its bright strands of yarn. Black satin ribbons, swallowing the yellow light and setting off the colors like fireworks in contrast. Slowly she turned and walked toward Bo, taking off the shawl and folding it carefully.

"*Para Acito,*" she whispered, pointing to the sky where a lullaby had flown above them. Then she handed the shawl to Bo and left without taking her eyes from the ground.

Chapter Twenty-eight
Snatch Bat

Eva agreed to join the group gathering at Rombo and Martin's that afternoon, along with Estrella and Henry. Bo's hurried call to Rombo confirmed that pizza, while undoubtedly an embarrassment to Martin, would be the only way to feed the crowd assembling to determine the next step in their unorthodox investigation of Chac's death. Near the end of the call, placed from Estrella's kitchen phone, Rombo dropped an informational bomb in Bo's lap.

"I'm afraid Mr. Singleton walked off Saturday morning, yesterday," he told her. "I know you're going to be upset, but imagine how I feel. For the first time in his life he was getting help, might even have stabilized in a few weeks on lithium. Now God knows where he is or what's happening to him."

"He was in a locked unit!" Bo exploded. "How could he walk off?"

"He's smart," Rombo replied. "After he broke out of a Louisiana prison, I doubt that the hospital was much of a challenge. We notified the police and sheriff's departments, but he's probably far away by now. Maybe he went home."

"Nobody wants him at home." Bo sighed, remembering what the sheriff's deputies in Franklin, Louisiana, had said. "But I'm going to be there tomorrow. I'll teach the family what to do, how to get help for him if he shows up."

Bad news. Bo paced the length of the Benedicts' kitchen, drinking water from a Tommee Tippee cup Estrella's sister had brought for someone who was at the moment no larger than a thumbnail and still in possession of his or her embryonic tail.

"Dewayne Singleton eloped from County Psychiatric

yesterday morning," she told Estrella and Henry. "I have a bad feeling about this. Really bad."

"Maybe he was the guy out in the desert last night," Henry suggested.

Bo sat the baby cup on the counter and watched it rock on its rounded base. "Right," she said. "He just manages to slip out of a locked unit in a psychiatric hospital and find his way to a camp-out on a trackless waste seventy-five miles away and unreachable without Bureau of Land Management maps and a four-wheel drive. Your basic, resourceful psycho. Equipped with radar so he can track down his hapless victims anywhere and hack them to shreds with the lightweight, collapsible meat cleaver he carries everywhere. Of *course* that's what happened. Why didn't I think of it?"

"I'm sorry, Bo," Henry said. "I didn't mean . . ."

"I know you didn't. Look . . ." She ran both hands through her hair and shook her head. "If it's okay with you, I'll just leave Mildred here and make a little visit to the Terrells before we all meet back at Rombo and Martin's, and then Andy and I will go straight from there to the airport. It wasn't Dewayne out in the desert, and there are only two people left who might be desperate enough to murder Munson Terrell or somebody watching. I want to see one of them."

"You mean Kee," Estrella stated.

Bo merely nodded as she left.

Kee Terrell was working on the cantilevered deck attached to the side of the house when Bo arrived. Painting something on a tarp-covered table. In the bright morning sun Bo could see intricate designs in magenta, lavender, dark blue, and gold.

"Mundy's not back from the workshop yet," she told Bo at the door. "But I'd love company. Let me show you what I'm doing."

Bo followed the slender woman to the deck, marveling at the casual confidence with which she greeted an unexpected guest. That welcoming insouciance bred of an assumption that she was, in fact, interesting and attractive, even to surprise visitors on Sunday mornings. Bo wondered how that felt.

"At first I combed a bright blue over the magenta," Kee began without preamble, gesturing toward a three-foot square of wood atop the tarp. Short table legs nearby, as yet unpainted, suggested that this was to be a low table, obviously a child's. "But the combed lines interfered with the design, so I started over again and ragged it in a darker shade. That way I can just lay on the designs slapdash, without the background dictating which way. What do you think?"

Her dark eyes were glowing, and Bo noticed a blaze of magenta paint in the expensively cut hair over her right ear. The object on the sawhorse table was delightfully covered in folk figures, mostly animals. A gold and white Mimbres rabbit in the center was surrounded by a blue coyote, several buffalo, a Haida bear totem, a smiling fish, Koko Peli with a golden flute, a Kachina whose name Bo couldn't remember, and a fat magenta lizard with blue polka dots and three toes on each foot.

From long experience Bo drew up a finely honed sensitivity to the reactions of others, and threw out her line. "Are you going to include any Maya figures?" she asked brightly.

Kee Terrell cocked her head abruptly at the question like a large bird. The gesture threw into relief a pale collarbone under skin that appeared to have no heft to it, no muscle. It seemed to Bo that for a moment the woman's eyes reflected a birdlike glassiness that mirrored the angle of her head. A momentary lapse. But with the sudden movement of her skull Kee had effectively obliterated all evidence of response, if in fact any had been present.

"Maya? I hadn't thought of it, but maybe," she answered. "Mundy and I have traveled in the Yucatán—*great* skin-diving off Tulum, by the way—but I don't remember any of the folk imagery."

Was the reference to Yucatán a deliberate avoidance of reference to Guatemala, or was Kee really just recalling a vacation trip? Bo strolled to the edge of the deck and couldn't contain a gasp as she looked over the side. The house was on the rim of a deep canyon. The drop was about five stories, straight down. "Wow," she breathed, wide-eyed. "Killer drop!"

"Yeah," Kee agreed. "It's just too dangerous for a child. The contractors will be here next week to take out the rail and benches. We're having a three-and-a-half-foot solid wall put in, topped with plexiglass. We'll still have the view, but nobody will be able to fall off."

The concern in her eyes, Bo noted, was real. Almost a kind of panic.

"Maybe we should have gone with chain-link fencing," she went on, jamming a paintbrush behind an ear. "You know about child safety issues. Do you think the chain-link would be safer?"

Bo had not thought of her job as involving child safety before, child endangerment being a rather more common topic. "Chain-link's too institutional," she answered, feeling herself being drawn into the conversation as if she and Kee Terrell actually knew each other. As if she weren't really there to assess the woman's potential for murdering her husband. "I think three-and-a-half-foot walls and plexiglass will provide sufficient safety without making your deck look like a tennis court. By the way, when do you expect the child, and how old is he, or she?" Bo was certain that her radiant smile betrayed nothing but the sort of womanly warmth portrayed in TV diaper commercials. Kee's response confirmed it.

"Oh," she began, "there's no telling, but I . . . we . . . well, everything's ready and it's so hard . . . the waiting's just so hard." A quaver in her voice suggested that she was near tears. "Mundy and I have actually talked about just giving up and having our own child. I mean, you know, genetically ours. But we just think that's so *disgusting,* don't you?"

"Um," Bo hedged, caught off-guard, "I've always supported the concept of zero population growth." The response was several degrees upwind of Kee's politically correct position, but it didn't seem to matter.

"Absolutely!" Kee nodded violently. "Why should European imperialism continue to dominate the planet, enslaving indigenous people and destroying centuries-old cultures? We should adopt their ways, not the other way around."

Bo saw no point in mentioning any of the many situations in which trying to go backward in time doesn't work, nor the failure of the woman's remarks to have anything to do with the topic at hand. "The child you're adopting is from an indigenous population, then?" She smiled, recognizing that the term "Indian" would undoubtedly send Kee into orbit. And elicit a lecture on the Spanish Conquest that might go on for hours.

"Oh, yes." Kee beamed. "Let me show you the nursery. And by the way, have you had any success in locating Chac's family? I asked Mundy after you were here before, and he said he didn't think she had any family."

"We're still working on it," Bo said. Kee appeared to be interested in the search, but Bo felt nothing else hidden in the question. The politically zealous young woman either didn't know that her husband fathered Chac's child, or didn't care. It was almost, Bo thought, as if Kee had created a psychic distance between herself and whatever her husband did in Mexico. As if in Kee's mind Chac, the business, the music, Acito, all of it, were not quite real. But why would she have gone to such lengths to dissociate from it, to pretend it wasn't there, if she didn't know the truth about her husband's activities?

Following Kee through the house toward the nursery, Bo read the label stitched to the back of her Levi's. "25 x 30," it announced. The jeans size of a skinny, long-legged boy, not a woman in her thirties. Bo wondered how she did it.

"You're going to love this," Kee said, opening a distressed pine door on which the lock rail and panels were stenciled in an Indian pony design. The room beyond was a decorator's dream. Particularly, Bo thought, a decorator from New Mexico. Even in its mission days California had not had this much atmosphere.

The soft vinyl floor looked like a mat of pebbles, and was covered at one end of the room by a fluffy acrylic "bear" rug complete with a huge teddy bear head. Beside the rug a carousel horse had been refitted with Indian gear and draped with a real Navajo horse blanket. When Kee flipped a wall switch, the horse moved slowly up and down on its pole.

"There are three speeds," she told Bo. "And of course there's music, too."

"Of course," Bo said, eyeing a collection of antique puppets attractively draped over the sides of a fanciful, color-washed wooden armoire with seemingly hundreds of little doors, drawers, trays, and cubbyholes. The sort of furniture a child would love, with plenty of places for secret treasure. The room's indirect lighting highlighted the armoire, the rug, the Indian horse, several framed originals of Western scenes, and a large, hand-carved crib set against a wall in the center of the room. Something about the crib made Bo uneasy.

"We commissioned this," Kee explained, polishing the footboard with the hem of her paint-stained T-shirt. "It's from my hometown. Jenner. It's up north of San Francisco on Highway One. The woodcarver was this marvelous old man who'd lost a leg on a fishing boat when he was a boy. He said he always carves himself another leg in all the pieces he does, but Mundy and I have looked, and we haven't found any leg in this yet."

"Interesting," Bo mumbled. It wasn't the possible presence of a carved leg that made the crib spooky, but something else. Bo stood near a small stone fireplace across from the baby bed, and tried to pinpoint the source of her discomfort. Kee was saying something about having to order a custom-made mattress, as well as sheets, since the crib was so much bigger than the standard size, when the reason for the odd impression dawned on Bo.

On the wall behind the crib was the painted silhouette of a mission, complete with Spanish bell tower. Against the flat blue paint the crib had the atmosphere of a reliquary rather than a simple sleeping nook. Together the crib and the painted shape framing it created a shrine!

"My God," Bo whispered to herself.

"What is it?" Kee asked. "Is there something wrong? Do you think the bigger mattress will cause a problem? God, I worry about crib death all the time, even though they say now it's some kind of allergy. Is there something that should be changed?"

"No, no. I'm just so impressed with the detail in the carving," Bo babbled. "And the planning you've put into this. What a lucky little, uh, boy or girl!" Bo had barely stopped herself from saying "little Indian."

"Yes," Kee replied flatly. "And I'm so tired of waiting." Her eyes seemed to look straight through Bo to a point not easily discernible. "Just so tired."

Retreating from the nursery, Bo tried to remember what she'd planned to accomplish by coming here. Difficult just to say, "Oh, and yes . . . did you happen to be stalking people in the desert with a rifle last night?" She wondered how the cops did it. "Well, I'd hoped to interview Mr. Terrell," she lied. "But I've certainly enjoyed talking with you. And the baby's room is really lovely."

Kee Terrell's eyes betrayed a sense of hurt as Bo eased her way out the door. "I wish you didn't have to go," Kee said, waving now-dried paintbrushes from the deck with a trembling hand. "I'm sure Mundy will be home soon." The last word was pronounced in two syllables, the way a child would say it.

Bo felt as if she'd just been through a house of mirrors in the company of something costumed. That sense of just having missed a sight that's really still there if only you look over your shoulder. Glancing in the rear-view mirror, Bo saw Kee bend to the painted table again. Nothing unusual in the scene. Except for the loneliness of Kee's childlike figure, dwarfed by a cloudless blue sky.

Chapter Twenty-nine
Heron Feather

"Look, I still think it was Terrell," Henry Benedict insisted from behind the slab of pineapple and Canadian bacon pizza he was about to demolish. "Just because somebody was out in the desert training a rifle on him doesn't mean he didn't poison Acito and Chac. The guy could have enemies who have nothing to do with this case. If he's into messing around with the ladies too much, the stalker might have been an irate husband."

"But he's not like that," Martin St. John insisted. "Trust me, I just spent two days running around in a breechcloth with this guy. I know him. He wouldn't kill a baby or a woman, and he wouldn't use poison even if he did. He's into this meaning-of-manhood thing in a big way, and I can tell you the very last thing manhood means is killing your own son. He couldn't do it, even to save his marriage. Believe me."

Bo grabbed another piece of the thin-crust Thai ginger chicken pizza before it was too late, and surveyed the group. Martin had returned from the desert sunburned but untraumatized. In fact he'd enjoyed the group, he said, especially after Terrell explained that throughout time a stable percentage of men had been gay, and that somebody had to remain free of childrearing in order to advance civilizations, especially in the arts. Munson Terrell had made a convert of Martin.

"Just exactly what did you *do* in your breechcloths?" Rombo inquired from the kitchen door. "Or is that one of those 'men's secrets' we don't talk about?"

"They went off alone in the heat to find personal totems, came back, named their totems communally, built a sweat lodge, blessed the sweat lodge, ate, did a sweat lodge ritual, and then danced around in a circle, Rombo," Estrella answered over the top of a beer mug full of sparkling water. "Martin's already described the whole thing. But I don't know why everybody's overlooking Chris Joe Gavin. He's the only one with a motive to do in all three of them—Acito, Chac, and Terrell. Jealousy."

"I'm afraid the boy is the most likely suspect." Andrew sighed. "Bo has checked him out with social services in Kentucky and he's got a troubled history. I wouldn't be surprised if—"

"Wait a minute," Bo said, washing down a bit of spicy chicken with cold beer, "his history seemed pretty impressive to me. Good grades, no problems with the law, people wanting to adopt him. The 'trouble' in his history belongs to a legal system that couldn't get him freed for adoption, and a social services definition of 'foster home' that always means 'not a permanent home.' And why would he have sent me Chac's bank statement and that business about Chac naming her murderer in her music if he'd killed her?"

"Well," Rombo interjected, "why did he run away and hide if he *didn't* kill her?"

Eva Broussard had been admiring the new wall unit in Rombo and Martin's living room. Leaning against it, she crossed moccasined feet before her and stretched. "We're being somewhat less than methodical," she suggested. "Bo, didn't you tell me the name under which Chac kept her bank account was Rother?"

"Yeah," Bo answered, taking a seat on the couch. "Elena Rother. Why?"

"It may be that Chac knew something, feared something, and constructed symbolic messages in odd niches of her life like this one. Messages that may reflect her world-view, or her wishes for her son, or even information about her murderer. Remember that her mind was not that of a contemporary Westerner, but rather that of a Maya."

"I'm afraid I don't see how a name on a bank account can tell us anything," Henry said, expertly tossing a beer to Andrew.

Bo watched as the man in whose arms she would lie tonight popped the beer can's tab and sprayed the length of his pure linen tie with foam. It seemed safe to hypothesize that Andrew LaMarche in a domestic situation would not be prone to nursing beer cans in front of a television. He couldn't even get one open.

So what, Bradley? The fact that he's several evolutionary steps up from Stanley Kowalski doesn't mean you need to start shopping for his'n'her recliners. These thoughts can pave the way to hell. Don't think them.

"Father Rother was a missionary priest," Eva explained, stifling a smile as Martin whisked the sodden tie off to the kitchen for soaking in cold water. "He was murdered by Guatemalan soldiers after a meddlesome visitor from his own home parish in Oklahoma contacted the Guatemalan government. This man told the Guatemalan authorities that Rother was helping the Maya to organize and fight back against the system enslaving them. The government responded to this news by ordering Rother killed. He's a folk hero now among Guatemala's native people. It's said that they buried his heart near Lake Atitlán before sending his body home to the States for burial. I can't help wondering what Chac meant by hiding her money under his name."

"Something about betrayal?" Martin suggested from the kitchen. "Maybe she was betrayed by somebody the way Rother was."

"Or perhaps she just wanted a symbolic connection to a strong, heroic figure," Andrew said.

Bo rolled her eyes. "We're never going to know why she used Rother's name, but we *can* figure out what's in those song lyrics. Es . . . ?"

"The verses are about a white orchid that shelters a turtle with its heart," Estrella explained, sitting on the floor beside Eva and taking a red paper napkin from her purse. "Lots of stuff about forests and a monster called a *duende* that wants to hurt the turtle, but the orchid protects it. A *duende* is an evil spirit, sort of, and there are lots of them. This one has something wrong with its feet. The choruses are just the orchid saying, 'I love you, my little turtle,' over and over. The last verse that Chac sang the night she died is strange, though. Something about how sinful it is for a man to eat in front of a pregnant woman. That part doesn't fit with the earlier story. It doesn't make any sense. And then the words are garbled, something about the orchid dying, the *duende* trampling the orchid. That was right before she . . . she died."

Eva Broussard was nodding slowly, her white hair framing her bronze face like that in a classic Greek portrait. "The *duende* with its feet on backward is the Maya version of the Northwestern Indian Wendigo story," she said. "It's 'the spirit of the wild,' the madness that can overtake and destroy someone lost in a wild place, in nature. Both versions of the tale involve mutilated feet, although nobody knows why. And there is a Maya folk tale about a lazy man who eats in front of a pregnant woman, offering her nothing. Her hunger pangs are so great that she aborts. The man's punishment is that he must take her home, where he already has a wife, impregnate her, feed her for nine months, and return her to her husband pregnant. Among the Maya, no man will eat in the presence of an expectant mother without offering her some of his food."

"Henry, did you hear that?" Estrella grinned from her seat on the floor.

"Chac specifically wanted Bo to hear that song," Andrew said thoughtfully. "Remember? We were about to leave the club, and she called to Bo from the stage."

Eva arched an eyebrow expectantly at Bo.

"The answer is in Chac's song, isn't it?" Bo concluded.

"I think so," Eva said. "Especially if the lyrics she sang that night were altered to create a message. Didn't you say you had a commercial tape that includes Acito's song?"

Bo was out the door in seconds, grabbing Chac's cassette from the tape deck in her car. Back in the house, Martin slid it into their sound system and Chac's voice filled the room. Bo could see the singer again, her sequined *huipil* flashing blue sparks in the smoky bar. As the taped lullaby reached its final verse, every eye in Rombo and Martin's living room was on Estrella, the only one who could understand the words.

Estrella was listening intently. "It's not the same," she whispered over the music. "The business about the *duende* is still there in the beginning, but the last verse is just about the orchid watching the little turtle grow into a *cerro grande,* a great hill, and giving shade to his people. There's nothing about men eating in front of pregnant women or the orchid dying. That's not in the recorded version."

"Wow," Rombo said, puzzled. "So what does it mean?"

Bo watched five people staring blankly at each other. "We don't have a clue," she admitted. "But we will. We'll figure it out."

"We'll do that on our way to New Orleans," Andrew said. "We need to get to the airport, Bo."

On the three-hour flight Bo drifted in and out of sleep as Andrew read a new paperback on the Maya called *The Road from Xibalba,* waking her regularly to share significant pieces of information.

Over Yuma, Arizona, he frowned and read aloud a description of Guatemalan army officers removing Maya babies from the government-run refugee villages. Some of the babies would be "adopted" by army personnel, some would be sold to orphanages that would quickly resell them in the international baby black market, and some would be sold directly to baby brokers. The illiterate parents, often unable to communicate even with other Maya refugees because of differing community languages, had no legal recourse, he told Bo.

"Chac was trying to escape from all that," she mumbled. "Look what she got for her effort."

Somewhere in New Mexico he said, "Ah. In Maya astronomy the constellation we know as Gemini was called Ac. It means 'The Turtle.' "

"Yeah," Bo answered, not really waking up. In the darkened plane cabin she imagined Acito asleep in his crib at the Dooleys', a turtle made of stars shining in the sky outside his window.

By the descent into New Orleans, she'd freshened her

makeup in the plane's lurching cubicle of a restroom, and was ready for a cigarette.

"The *huipil,* the sort of blouse Chac was wearing for her act, is actually a Maya symbol for womanhood itself," Andrew explained as they waited to exit the plane. "The opening for the head is the interface between the worlds of myth and reality, the worlds before and after birth. Many of them are woven in a diamond design that has remained unchanged since the seventh century. A shame to think that the entire Maya culture will be lost now."

Bo gasped as warm, humid air engulfed her in the raised walkway from the plane to the airport terminal. "It's worse than a shame," she replied. "But it's something that can't be stopped. The best we can do is to protect what's left. For us, that's Acito."

A short cab ride later, Bo was seated beneath an enormous potted ficus in a French Quarter bistro called Galatoire's, inhaling the rich scent from a plate of crab- and shrimp-stuffed eggplant.

"The city is fascinating if history interests you," Andrew mentioned over a double order of steamed crawfish. "Perhaps you'd enjoy a brief walking tour of the Quarter tonight, or a moonlit visit to the tomb of Marie Laveau in St. Louis Cemetery. She was reportedly a voodoo queen and many people still believe—"

"Andy," Bo smiled, trailing her fingers down the sides of his face and across his trim mustache, "no graveyards. Let's just let tonight be lovely."

The tiny Rue de Chartres hotel he'd chosen surpassed Bo's fantasy in opulence. Beyond the open balcony of their room a magnolia tree sent washes of fragrance from its white blossoms, while somebody on the street a block away played bluesy notes on a saxophone. Dimming the light of a fringe-shaded lamp beside the Louis Quinze bed, Bo decided a magnolia-colored silk gown would have been superfluous. Totally.

Chapter Thirty
Dark House

It was dark, and Dewayne could feel the damp ocean air chilling his lungs in a sick, clammy way that felt like a fish market smells. Like dead fish on top of crushed ice, their eyes staring at you like they still were afraid of dying. That dim smell of fishiness everywhere, filling his chest with cold.

He was on a beach. Some guy with three kids in his car had picked up Dewayne and dropped him here. The guy had said this was "Oceanside." From what Dewayne could tell, everything around here could be called that. The ocean stretched off into nothing, with just a little white line of bubbles where it stopped at the land. The line of bubbles looked like a string wrinkling on forever.

There were some people on the beach, doing something around a fire. The people kept moving back and forth, and the black stripes following them seemed to dance and stretch across the cold sand toward Dewayne. Even when he moved around to the other side the shadows kept reaching at him. They were devils of some kind. And the Angel Jabril had left California already. Left Dewayne Singleton alone here.

The people were talking about him. He could tell by the way they made patterns like a jumble of dark letters around the orange fire. They thought there was something wrong with him. Maybe they thought he should have stayed in that hospital. Dewayne couldn't put together a reason why they thought that because his mind wouldn't stay still. It was like a picture book when you grab the edge of all the pages and flip them.

There was a blue heron, he thought, standing beside a trash can on the beach. Or was that the heron Buster shot down on the Teche, and Mama cooked because it was a sin to waste food worse than it was a sin to kill a *grosbec*. You could go to prison for killing them. Dewayne had gone to prison even though it was Buster that shot the blue bird. But he couldn't remember which prison was the real one, or the last one, the one he'd run off from.

He did remember getting write-ups for aggravated disobedience a lot of times in one of them. They put him in solitary for ten days at a time, over and over. Sometimes he thought he'd die in solitary, and beat his head against the wall to make the thoughts slow down. And then they took him to another one. Wade, it was called. Dewayne thought Wade was the wrong name for a place where you didn't have wet feet. But he knew what it meant. There was plenty of water here.

He hurried to the ocean to wade, and splashed and jumped in the bubbles, feeling his feet grow sloshy and cold in new, white tennis shoes that seemed to glow in the water. As long as he ran up and down in the waves he was doing right, and Allah would be praised by this and the people at the fire couldn't hurt him.

"Bastard's fucking crazy," he heard one of them say. "Better call the cops before he kills somebody."

That made his heart pull up with fear. One of them was going to kill somebody. One of them was going to kill him!

Dewayne ran faster up and down the beach, kicking up sheets of water that would be like prayers to Allah, the one, the true God. Allah would protect him from the infidels. This running was necessary to stay alive.

The people at the fire were moving faster, picking things up and moving away. A car drove into the parking lot, and one of them yelled something at it. Dewayne's side hurt, and he stopped running and walked to the trash can where the blue heron had been. There were no heron tracks in the sand, just some beer cans and a Big Mac box. He looked in the box to see if the sandwich was still there, but it wasn't. Just two pieces of pickle and a little white plastic knife. He didn't see his right hand curl around the little knife when the two demons came toward him shining bright lights in his eyes.

"What the hell you doing in that trash?" one demon said.

"We got a call, said you were havin' some trouble out here. Better come with us, now. Just do like we say and there won't be any trouble."

"Jabril!" Dewayne screamed as he ran toward the prison, the cement building sitting a block away on the sand. It had a bathroom, he saw. A big bathroom with no roof and sand all over the floor. Behind him he could hear crunching footsteps running so he turned on the water in all three sinks to keep them out, and then he stood on top of one of the toilets with his back against the light blue wall.

There were things written in there, he noticed. One of the things said, "Eat my pussy," and he wondered if you could go to prison for eating cats like you could for eating herons. Except he was already in a prison. And the demons were there, with guns pointed at him.

"Get down," one said in a voice that sounded quavery, like it wasn't a human voice, but a demon voice. Then they started toward him.

"Mama!" he called as he tried to climb over the cement wall, and slipped back down, and turned to try to jump over them from the rim of the toilet. His arms were in the air as he jumped, and he could see the little white plastic knife still in his hand. Except all of a sudden he couldn't hear for the ringing in his ears and the burnt white flashes where he used to see. He was on the floor in something wet, and there was a hole in the front of his plaid shirt. And a hole in his chest underneath.

"Mama," he tried to say, but his mouth wouldn't work. And then a silence came where his thoughts had been, and he was dead.

Chapter Thirty-one
The Blue-Green Bowl

Andrew was up and moving briskly about the room when the Monday morning light was still hazy and peach-colored. Or else Bo's vision, unaccustomed to purposeful movement at this hour, was hazy and peach-colored. She wasn't sure which. The scent of soap wafting after him alerted her to the fact that he'd already showered. From his carry-on he took a starched shirt wrapped in cellophane and folded over a piece of cardboard with "Li's Laundry" printed on it in red. The sound of cellophane being wadded into a ball seemed to go on interminably.

"How can you wear a long-sleeved shirt in this weather?" she groaned, admiring the lean physique more than adequately emphasized by his skimpy underwear. Today's low-cut briefs were of bright red cotton knit with black pinstriping.

"Mmmm," she murmured appreciatively. "Come here."

In seconds the desired effect was in evidence, causing a distortion in certain pinstripes.

"I had thought we'd have breakfast at Brennan's," he said huskily, "then a walk in the Garden District before my conference and your trip to Dewayne's prison."

"We'll skip breakfast," Bo decided, and then watched as a wad of red knit fabric was tossed across the room to land on a rosewood escritoire already littered with magnolia petals blown in from the balcony.

The Garden District, seen an hour later from beneath a flowered umbrella donated by the hotel for the protection of its delicate female guests from a hazy sun, was lovely. Like a collection of leaded glass jewel boxes preserved in steam. Bo admired what seemed like several miles of cast iron fences, gallery balustrades, doorway capitals, and supports before admitting to herself that she was feeling funny.

The incessant buzz of cicadas in the air was disturbing. The heat and humidity sickening. And there was something terrible and sad about the old houses. A brave hopelessness in the face of a future that would not see their kind again. They were like the Maya, Bo thought. Still here, but almost gone.

"At first all the cast iron had to be brought in from New York and Philadelphia," Andrew told her. "But then a foundry was opened in Holly Springs, Mississippi, and . . . Bo, are you all right?"

"I'd like to sit down," she said irritably.

This could happen. Like a drug flashback, some symptoms could break through the fragile normalcy provided by medication. Stress, exhaustion, emotional excess—any of these could stir up a flurry of weird, intense perceptions out of nowhere. It was embarrassing to realize that an unaccustomed erotic activity had probably been the last straw, following on the heels of a terrifying night being stalked through primordial desert wastes. Bo was less surprised than angry at herself for failing to take precautions. Like getting some sleep.

"Here," he said, leading her across the street to what looked like a park full of little houses. "I used to play in here as a boy. We can sit in the shade until you feel better."

Bo restrained an urge to tell him she wouldn't feel better until she was no longer carrying an absurdly coquettish umbrella when there was no rain. Sitting on the ground beneath a large magnolia, she leaned against the whitewashed brick wall enclosing the area. The old bricks were cool and smelled of the moss growing in their mortar.

"The *Ellen Lincoln*, 1895," she said to herself. "The *Hannah E. Schubert*, the *Ethel Maude . . .*"

Atop one of the little houses, Bo noticed, was a draped statue whose head had fallen into the weeds below. Headless, it nevertheless seemed to be staring into the sky where gray clouds were gathering. On the black iron gates guarding the space she noticed iron faces of lions, their mouths open in silent ferocity. From the mouth of one dangled a dead daddy longlegs.

"Andy," she said quietly, "this is a graveyard."

"Lafayette Cemetery Number One," he agreed nervously. "At sea level burials must be above ground because the groundwater would float anything . . . It doesn't matter. Why don't we go back to the hotel, Bo. I'm not doing well at caring for you, am I?"

Smoothing the legs of her navy knit slacks, Bo remembered too late that dark colors absorb heat. Good thing the matching top had been at the cleaner's. Her white cotton shell could no longer be described as "crisp," but at least it wouldn't parboil the flesh beneath it. Near a trash can beside one of the little house-graves a faded yellow ribbon hung limply from a wreath of dead flowers thrown there. Bo thought she could smell the flowers, rotting.

"Yes, the hotel will be fine until my flight to Shreveport for the interview with Dewayne's friend in prison," she answered. "And this is something I hope you'll understand. Sometimes I just feel a little, well, overengaged with things. It crops up when I'm too tired and for a zillion other reasons. When it happens, all I need is to be let alone. This is one of those times. I'll be okay after a while if I just have total peace and quiet, don't have to talk or be polite or even be aware that there's anybody else around. Can you handle that?"

"Yes," he said with reassuring confidence, and helped her to her feet.

Bo was glad he hadn't said, "Oh, you don't have to be polite with me," or "Don't worry, you won't even know I'm there." Just being in the same room with somebody else, even if they were perfectly quiet or even asleep, was at times a sort of low-velocity drain on her psychic resources. Bo wondered if the magnetic field generated by bodies was supposed to drain mental energy from everybody who happened to be around, or just from those already weakened by psychiatric stress.

"Did you say you used to play in here?" Bo asked. "Doesn't seem like a fun place for a kid."

"It was prettier then," he answered. "My family's house is just around that corner."

"Oh, I want to see it, Andy. Another fifty yards in this heat isn't going to make any difference."

Andrew's gray eyes were liquid with concern. "I think we should return to the hotel immediately," he said.

"We will. We'll just walk by your childhood house on the way. I really want to see it."

With the crumbling tombs behind her, Bo felt somewhat better. The air felt cooler, too, or at least darker. Peeking from beneath her umbrella, she noted that the sky was uniformly gray now, and a light breeze rattled the stiff, almost plastic magnolia leaves littering the ground. Impossible not to think the sound was like old bones moving. Brittle bones, fragile and forgotten. Like Chac's would be in the Tijuana graveyard. Like everyone's would be, eventually.

A sign on the cemetery's brick wall announced that the superintendent of cemeteries was someone named Clementine Bean.

"Oh, my darlin'," Bo sang softly, "Oh my darlin' Clementine, you are lost and gone forever . . ."

"Bo?" Andrew's face bore telltale signs of panic.

"Sorry." She smiled, pointing to the sign. "Just one of those inappropriate responses to stimuli we of the straitjacket set are prone to. I'm taking my meds, Andy. Nothing major's going to happen. You can relax. Now which one's your house?"

"There," he said, indicating one of the traditionally galleried facades half hidden by a spreading oak rooted in a small front yard. "Twelve twenty-one. It's been painted, but other than that it's just the same."

Bo didn't miss the note of resigned bitterness in his voice. The boy who played in a graveyard had not been happy in this house. Behind the cast iron railing of its four-pillared lower gallery, Bo saw two long windows, their deep green louvered shutters closed. Had they been closed thirty-five years ago when a social-climbing Cajun couple lived here with their children, Andrew and Elizabeth? He'd told her he joined the Marines and went to Vietnam to get away from them. Beyond the second-story gallery the shutters remained open, and Bo could see rivulets of condensed water running down the interior faces of the tall, old-fashioned windows. An air-conditioner hummed.

"What was the worst thing?" she asked.

"That my sister Elizabeth and I were supposed to be their tickets into a world that didn't even know they existed," he answered quietly. "Just one more piano recital, fencing match, debutante ball, or school award, and they'd be accepted into what they thought was 'society.' Except they never were, and so to them we were failures. *Mon dieu,*" he sighed. "What a waste."

Deciding that a serious rally was in order, Bo took his hand and looked hard into his eyes. "In my terms you're as far as it gets from failure," she told him. "I think you're wonderful."

In his smile as he wrapped his arm around her waist Bo felt something breaking, falling away. Like a film of glass.

"Then I am." He laughed. "And we'd better get to the trolley. Hear that thunder?"

Turning left onto Camp Street, Bo stumbled on the uneven brick sidewalk, set in a herringbone pattern now outlined in moss. In the odd, prerain light everything seemed bathed in grayish gold, like a faded daguerreotype. Set in the rumpled brick design was a gleaming circle the size of a dinner plate, embossed with a moon and nine shooting stars. It seemed incongruous, even magical there beneath a delicately overhanging crape myrtle hedge.

"Andy, look at this," she said.

"I know. When we moved here I was only about five, and I thought they were giant's coins stuck in the sidewalk. It was a real blow when I found out they were only water meter covers."

"They're not; they're giant's coins," Bo insisted. "And we're going to get wet."

A filament of lightning threaded the eastern sky, followed by distant thunder. No birds could be heard, and in the dimming light the pink petals of a huge crape myrtle in the lawn of a tattered Greek Revival mansion appeared magenta, then charcoal gray. Bo allowed the deliciously moody imagery to flood her mind. Why not? Hadn't Dr. Broussard suggested that she should respect her own experience? This experience was suffocatingly hot, lush, and fantastical. Bo memorized the details in case she wanted to paint them someday. But how did you paint air that seemed made of transparent mercury?

The streetcar still named Desire rumbled beneath the dense canopy of oaks shadowing St. Charles Avenue, its headlight feebly yellow in the gloom. As Bo and Andrew climbed aboard, the first dime-sized drops of rain made whispery thuds against the windows.

Chapter Thirty-two
Cornmeal Woman

On the bus ride from the tiny Shreveport airport to Wade Correctional Center in the middle of nowhere, Bo sifted images of New Orleans and wondered why the city was so appealing. It must be an innate artistry, she thought. A blatant celebration of mood, facade, presentation.

In the hotel room after Andrew had left for his conference, she'd listened to cracking thunder and watched the city deluged with rain. An umbrellaed woman in a beautiful long skirt striding the length of a brick wall had been a painting. Everything in New Orleans was a painting, a scene, a play of style and texture. Its doorways, courtyards, balconies—all iron-laced and dripping with rain—suggested secrets, slow corruption, a sad, accepting wisdom. These lay beneath the perennial gaiety, she mused. It was a distinctly European atmosphere, and one that had resonance in her mind. The same could not be said of her feeling for Tijuana, and in that moment she'd understood why.

The world south of the U.S. border, while influenced by its Spanish invaders, had retained a distinctly un-European mythos. Its gated courtyards and baking, lizard-scratched walls hid something quite different from the world-weary sophistication of New Orleans. Something unknown to minds nurtured by Western European ideas, and therefore frightening.

As the bus pulled through two cyclone fences topped and lined with razor wire, Bo wondered how much that disparity would inhibit her ability to understand what had happened to a Maya singer in a Mexican bar. She would have to try harder, she decided. Really breach the barrier between her reality and the one in which Chac and Acito had lived. She would start now.

Climbing down from the bus, she took note of where she was. A prison. Dewayne Singleton had been sent here after bombing out in two others closer to home. His prison master record sheet and conduct report, faxed to San Diego from the Louisiana Department of Public Safety and Corrections in Baton Rouge, had said he was a discipline problem. Not surprising.

What was surprising was that he'd been judged criminal, when the cause of his troubling behavior was an illness. Bo wondered where the defense attorney's head had been during Dewayne's most recent trial. Who wouldn't suspect a psychiatric disorder in somebody who stole insects and then sold them as vitamins? Louisiana, Bo remembered, wasn't exactly on the cutting edge of psychiatric care *or* public defense.

In a cement tower overhead, two guards watched the razor wire. One carried a riot gun, the other an M-14 rifle. On a path between the stacked spirals of shrapnel a row of men in jeans and white T-shirts filed noisily into a side door. Names and numbers were stenciled down the sides of their pants legs and across the backs of their shirts. The bright red stenciling, Bo observed, matched almost exactly the red-orange vincas planted in tidy, geometric arrangements beside the battleship gray cinder block buildings. She wondered if they'd hired a decorator to coordinate the color scheme.

On a southerly breeze Bo sniffed evidence that Wade Correctional Center maintained its own hog lot. She hoped the hogs had a traditional mudwallow, because even in sunlight flies and mosquitoes were omnipresent, droning and whining in the sultry air.

Inside, Bo showed her CPS ID badge to a guard in a blue-black uniform with red stripes down the pants legs. A decorator *must* have planned this refreshing use of red accents, she grinned to herself. Or else they were using discarded costumes from the chorus of *The Student Prince*.

"This way," the guard roared as if she were not the only

person standing in the twenty-foot-square lobby. "The Imam's been brought up. I'll stay in the room if you want."

"No, that's all right," Bo replied. "But what's an Imam?"

"The prisoner you requested an interview with. The Muslim dude."

Bo sat in one of the plastic bucket chairs surrounding a narrow table in the tiny interview room, and waited. Soon a second door opened at the back of the room and a large black man in a white skullcap entered and sat down across from her. Even in prison jeans and T-shirt he exuded a sort of immaculate dignity, tinged with contempt. He looked straight through her and said nothing.

"Hi," Bo said, extending her hand across the table. "My name's Bo Bradley. I'm an investigator from Child Protective Services in San Diego. Dewayne Singleton is connected to a case I'm investigating."

"Yes," the man replied softly, and did not take her offered hand.

Oh, shit, Bradley. Remember the guy's a Muslim. In his view women, especially white women, are on a social par with rabid dogs. You'll be lucky to get two words out of him.

Bo retracted her dangling hand and wondered how to proceed. The Imam merely sat and gazed at a point above and behind her head.

"Look," she began, "I know that you've been brought here against your will to be interviewed by a creature you regard as loathsome. I'm sure it's terrible for you, but this is the way it is. Dewayne Singleton is in California and may or may not have poisoned a child that is legally his, and murdered his wife. For what it's worth, I don't think he did either. The baby, a *male* baby, by the way, has no one in the world now but Dewayne, who has a psychiatric disorder and has eloped from a hospital. I need your help. I need for you to talk to me about Dewayne."

The man appeared to be considering her words, although it was hard to tell since nothing about him moved or changed. He didn't sweat, didn't even seem to be breathing. Finally his eyes focused on hers. The experience was transparently distasteful.

"Mr. Singleton's conversion to Islam was very dramatic," he said in well-modulated English. "I suspected a problem of psychiatric nature, but even that cannot stand between a man and God. Mr. Singleton was devout. There was no conversation between us about a child, although he did say that he had a wife in Mexico. In Islam he came to understand his responsibilities to her. If what you want is my assessment of him, I will say that in my personal opinion he was not capable of the deeds you describe. Will that be all?"

"No, it won't," Bo answered, stifling an urge to reach across the table and pull his white cap over his nose. "I need to know if he said anything about his wife before he escaped from here. I need to know about his family, particularly. You're his spiritual leader and the last person to have any close contact with him. A baby's future is on the line. Can't you just lighten up and talk to me?"

The Imam remained motionless.

"No," he said.

Bo sighed, facing yet another cultural barrier closing her off from an elusive truth.

"What are you in here for?" she asked bluntly, expecting no answer.

"Murder," he replied in the same, soft voice. Nothing in his face betrayed the slightest interest in that, or in anything else Bo might say.

"I appreciate your time," she said, rising and moving toward one door as he moved toward the other.

The encounter had been a perfect void. An absolute absence of connection, providing not one shred of help. An expensive, tedious waste of time. Bo fondled the pack of cigarettes in her purse and thanked an oblivious universe that she hadn't been born in Pakistan.

"Miss Bradley," the Imam said from the other door where a guard stood ready to escort him back to wherever he came from, "in the Qur'an are many repetitions, many ways of saying only one thing—that there is no god but God."

Bo was sure she saw the tiniest twinkle in his eyes before the guard ushered him away, and the door clicked shut.

The Qur'an, she assumed, would be the Koran. And there

were many repetitions in it. So what? There were many
repetitions in the Bible, the Talmud, and the Yellow Pages,
too. Was he trying to tell her something, trying to be helpful?
Or was he just being facetious in his inscrutable Muslim
fashion?

Bo called a cab, which would come from the town of
Minden, thirty miles away, and stood in the hot shade of the
roof overhang, smoking. Were there repetitions in this case, all
pointing to one thing? The only repetition she could see was,
literally, poisonous. A baby and his mother, poisoned.
Different poisons, but obtained from natural sources.

Exhaling, she watched cigarette smoke drift through razor
wire. Smoke could not be cut, and so merely floated through
the murderous metal as if it weren't there. Bo thought the
answer to the puzzle might be found in the same way. If she
could just change her own perspective into something entirely
different. If she could just think like Chac, and understand the
meaning of the Maya folk tale.

Instead, she thought about Dewayne Singleton. His conduct
report said he escaped from a farm crew working outside the
fence cleaning ditchbanks. Had the ditches contained a
poisonous plant that grows wild in streambeds? And why had
he run to California? The heat must be getting to her, Bo
guessed, because the thought of Dewayne brought with it an
empty gray feeling. The feeling she got after tearing the house
apart looking for something only to remember it wasn't there
anymore.

Going back inside the prison's cement-floor lobby, she
breathed the weak air-conditioning and tried to think about
nothing until the cab came.

Three hours later she awakened from fitful napping at
another steamy airport, this one identified by a member of the
cabin crew as Lafayette, Louisiana. The home of Andrew's
sister, she remembered groggily. Part of her elaborate, failing
investigation. Only a few miles from Franklin, where
Dewayne Singleton's family lived without a phone.

Elizabeth was waiting for her, looking a great deal like

Andy would look with an extra fifteen pounds and a sex-change operation. And a measurably different taste in clothes.

"I'm Liz Barrileaux," she told Bo through an unaffected hug, layers of gauzy lavender material draping her well-endowed frame. "I don't know what you've done to my brother, but it's a damned miracle. Welcome to Lafayette."

The woman dressed like a 1960s folk singer, and exuded the unsentimental warmth of somebody who has no illusions and enjoys life anyway. Bo liked her immediately.

"I didn't know your name was Barrileaux," she said. "Andy's only told me you're a psychologist, and that you've got three kids."

"*Two* kids and a clone of Miss Manners," Liz chuckled. "Our oldest, Jeanne-Marie, is her Uncle Andy all over again. Born in the wrong century. We were terrified she was going to be a nun just so she could spend her life observing an elaborate etiquette, but she's finally fallen in love, thank God. Gorgeous boy with the brain of a small reptile. She's only seventeen. The boy won't last, but the inclination will, we hope. Stoney secretly ordered a case of champagne the day she told us she wanted to be called "J" because that's what the boyfriend calls her. Say, am I boring you?"

"No." Bo grinned. "I've just come from a color-coordinated prison with a hog lot. Hearing normal stuff about normal people makes me feel less like dancing naked on the baggage carousel. Who's Stoney?"

"Gaston Barrileaux, father of my children. He would've been the mother, too, if he could've figured out how. We have a nontraditional relationship. I earn money; Stone does everything else. Far from 'normal.' Have you had anything to eat today?"

Following the woman to a battered Volvo station wagon in the airport parking lot, Bo was surprised to remember that she hadn't.

"No," she answered. A gray sky glowered at her personal incompetence. People with psychiatric problems were supposed to take care of themselves. Exercise. Eat right. Be constantly on guard against lapses in routine that could pave fools the way to dusty death, and worse.

"Bummer," Liz Barrileaux intoned while driving at breakneck speed through what seemed to be a nondescript middle-sized town. "I don't suppose I have to tell you that you know better. Fortunately there's some kind of twenty-grain soup in the fridge. Gus—that's our fourteen-year-old—is into being politically correct, only eats things that don't bleed. He made the soup last night out of lawn clippings or something. It'll hold you through a nap until Andy gets in from New Orleans and we can find a restaurant that serves real food."

Andrew's sister, Bo decided, could give Erma Bombeck a run for her money if she ever tired of the psychology business.

"Don't you see clients on Monday afternoon?" she asked Liz.

"Nope. I teach at USL until one thirty Monday/Wednesday/Friday. Only see clients Tuesday/Thursday. Also evenings and weekends. Jeanne-Marie's got a scholarship to Smith, but the other two are going to require money. Stoney's picking up a few bucks, too, doing historic restorations. He practices on our house. Wait'll you see."

Bo relaxed, admiring an enormous oak in the yard of a large red-brick church.

"Biggest damn oak tree in the country," Liz mentioned. "Close to five hundred years old. Has lights on it at night and its own social club called the Live Oak Society. Real snobby. Only oaks over a hundred years old can join. Dues are twenty-five acorns."

"You're not serious." Bo chuckled.

"Yes, I am. You're in the South here, honey. Eccentricity's a way of life."

In a few minutes the car made a swooping turn into a narrow driveway, nearly demolishing a cardboard sign taped to a grape stake pushed in the ground. "Three Twenty Seven Stevenson" it announced in perfect Times Roman letters painted hot pink.

"Angela," Liz sighed. "Our 'surprise baby,' as they say. She's only eight but already planning to join her dad in the architecture business. Right now she's obsessed with typefaces, designs these house number signs all day. Says she has to 'live with' a design for a while before painting it on wood to sell to the neighbors."

Bo grinned. "I think that color could use a bit of forest green outline," she suggested. "Just on the verticals."

"My God, another one." Her hostess groaned. "I'm not letting the kids near you until you've had something to eat and a nap. They'll *adore* you!"

Three hours later Bo awoke on the hide-a-bed in a book-lined den over Liz's office, a converted single-car garage. A spiral staircase snaked around a brass pole, connecting the two rooms. Taped to the pole was a sign saying "Welcome" in dalmatian-spotted Old English lettering. The musical pounding rain above suggested that Gaston Barrileaux had practiced the early-South art of tin roofing on his own house. Bo wished she had a tape recorder so she could hear it again and again. Especially at the office, she grinned, when Madge was talking.

From some distance below drifted numerous voices, including that of Andrew LaMarche, laughing more frequently than was his habit. After popping a Depakote and freshening her makeup in a cypress-paneled bathroom with an Italian tile floor, she went downstairs. The living room, deserted, held more books, two desks, a couch and overstuffed chair. There was no TV.

Tracking the voices, she entered a breezeway off the open front door. Paved in flagstones, it led to a detached family room in which six people sat at a table playing Monopoly. This room also boasted no television, Bo observed with approval. A man who looked like a brown bear appeared to be winning the game, given the piles of miniature money tucked under his side of the board.

"Bo!" Andrew called, delighted, "you're up."

Bo noticed something just under the surface of his bon vivance, hidden behind knitted brows and a shadow deep in his eyes. He knew something she didn't know. And it wasn't good.

The bear stood and wrapped her in arms the size of lawn mower tires.

"I'm Stoney, the brother-in-law," he growled fondly

through a curling black beard topped by a moderate handlebar mustache. "You must be the Irish filly that's hauled Ole Doc here down from his ivory tower. Helluva job."

In a blue-striped dress shirt and jeans held up with red suspenders he reminded Bo of Dickens's Ghost of Christmas Present.

"And these are the kids," Liz interjected, "although you'll have figured that out by now. J, Gus, and Angie."

Shyness, Bo noted, was not a characteristic of the Barrileaux family. The youngsters flocked to her, asking questions about California, movie stars, graphic design, and the ecology movement as Andrew beamed and put away the Monopoly equipment.

After fifteen minutes Stone clapped his hands and said, "Hey, how about some chow?"

"Laissez le bontemps roulez," Angela giggled, and then raced out the door to the car.

"That means 'Let the good times roll,' " Andrew explained as he hurried Bo through a light rain. "It's a Cajun thing."

"I can see that," Bo answered. Then she whispered, "Andy, what's going on? There's something you're not telling me. What's happened?"

"We'll talk later," he said tersely.

At a restaurant called Randol's Bo inhaled a bowl of corn and crab chowder, then couldn't finish her crawfish étouffée. After several rousing two-steps on the restaurant's raised dance floor with Andrew, Stoney, and then Gus, Bo felt her social obligations were adequately met.

"Liz," she whispered as Andrew waltzed with Jeanne-Marie, "I don't want to be rude, but the reason I'm here is that I'm investigating a case. Andy knows something he isn't telling me, no doubt because he thinks it will upset my fragile psyche. I'm afraid I'm running out of patience. I'd like to go home."

"About time," Liz answered, fanning her glowing face with a napkin. "My brother's going to lose you if he keeps pulling this protective crap." The words were tinged with sadness, not anger. "He can be a royal pain in the tail, Bo, but he's a good man. And I probably shouldn't say this, but his level of pompous nonsense invariably goes off the scale after he's been in New Orleans. Did he tell you he always visits his daughter's grave when he's there?"

Bo shook her head. "Sylvie's grave? He didn't mention that."

She remembered the two-year-old who'd died so long ago. A child he'd never seen, whose small ghost had directed the course of his adult life. Medical school, then a specialty in criminal pediatric trauma. Child abuse. He wanted to save the rest of them.

"And here's something a little lighter, in case you need it." Liz grinned conspiratorially. "Our name isn't really LaMarche, it's Lagneaux."

"What?" Bo said. "Why . . . ?"

"Dear old stuffed-shirt parents changed it so they'd seem less Cajun. But deep inside, your Dr. LaMarche out there in the mother-of-pearl cufflinks is a Cajun boy named Jacques Lagneaux who used to sit on top of graveyard mausoleums with a curtain rod, pretending he was back fishing in a bayou." She adjusted a wide bracelet on her wrist and smiled at Stoney and Angela on the dance floor. "A terrible grief can make people forget who they are," she sighed.

"Wow." Bo nodded. She had no idea what she could do with the information.

Later Andrew provided more, germane not to himself but to a poisoned mother and baby.

"I phoned my service this morning from the conference," he began, "and there's a great deal of news. First, Acito's test results are in from the lab. He isn't HIV positive, Bo. We're not out of the woods; it could conceivably turn up later. But the likelihood of that is very small. It looks like he's going to have a life!"

"All right!" Bo grinned, sighing with relief. "But why didn't you tell me that before dinner? We could have celebrated. And what's the rest of the news?"

Andrew clasped his hands between his knees and stared at several shirt cardboards littering the floor, covered with alphabets drawn in Bodoni type. "There was a message asking me to call Detective Reinert."

"Yes," Bo said. "I told him that was the only way to reach me, in case he got the lab report back on the water in my desert jug, or something else broke on the case that I'd need to know about. Which is it?"

"Both." Andrew LaMarche's need to exercise control had never been more in evidence. "I'm afraid the news confirms the identity of the killer, but Bo, there's absolutely nothing we can do about it. There's no way to prove it, no way to prosecute. It's just one of those situations that slips through the cracks. And there's something else . . ."

Bo found sitting in Stone Barrileaux's oversized recliner suddenly unbearable. Struggling out of its oxblood leather depths, she paced up and down before a coffee table made of an old paneled door mounted on two stubs of what had once been an Ionic column.

"Something else! You haven't told me *anything* yet. Do I need to call Reinert myself to find out whatever he told you? Who do you think you are, Andy? And what in hell are you trying to do?"

Andrew stood up from the blue plaid couch where he'd been sitting on the edge, and then sat down again. His face bore signs of misery. Bo was not appalled at the extent to which she didn't care.

"I didn't want you to be upset," he began. "I wanted . . ."

Bo felt her ears moving, flattening against her head as her nostrils flared. "You do not control whether I am upset or not," she pronounced in a deliberately sibilant voice. "Can you understand that? You . . . do . . . not . . . control . . . me. Not in San Diego, not here in your sister's house, not anywhere! Now, are you going to tell me what Reinert told you or not?"

"He said that the water sample you gave him for analysis contained cicutoxin. That's the same hemlock-derivative poison found in Chac's shot glass. But—"

"No buts," Bo interjected. "Just tell me what else Reinert said, and then I'm going to go to bed in your sister's study and think about it. Tomorrow I'll go to Franklin and interview Dewayne Singleton's family. I have a case to work on here, Andy. A baby's whole future depends on how I handle this, and all you care about is playing Victorian patriarch to my

Little Nell. Except I'm not Little Nell. What else did Dar say?"

Andrew LaMarche's eyes had turned a color so flat it couldn't be called color at all.

"Dewayne Singleton attacked two police officers with a knife on the beach at Oceanside," he muttered, tracing the paneling on the coffee table with the side of his thumb. "It happened in a public restroom at the lifeguard station. They shot him, Bo. Dewayne's dead."

"Oh, shit," she whispered, biting her lip. "I'm going to bed, Andy. I've got to think."

On the dimly lit stairway wall she saw her shadow and imagined it crumpled and falling from the impact of a police bullet. It could happen, she knew. It happened all the time when untrained, authoritarian police types encountered people who were psychotic, who wouldn't, couldn't, obey them. Dewayne had been a brother, his picture with the others on her bulletin board at the office. At the moment, nothing else mattered.

As she snapped on a light in Liz's study, Bo realized that she could never forgive Andrew LaMarche for withholding the truth while she danced to a fiddle and accordion. For deliberately controlling her experience of reality, which was not his to control.

Chapter Thirty-three
Cave by the Water

At breakfast Bo was somber.

"What did you mean last night when you said the news about the poison in my water jug confirms the identity of the killer?" she asked Andrew, dressed in polo shirt and jeans to spend the day with his nieces and nephew. "I assume you mean Chris Joe Gavin?"

The kitchen, a long, glass-walled room with a view of bamboo fronted by hollyhocks in the backyard, smelled of coffee, bacon, and the cinnamon vanilla French toast Stoney was frying on an iron grill. Gus and Angie, having already eaten, were hanging around making a production of loading the dishwasher. Bo could hear Jeanne-Marie on the hall phone, saying, "Oh, *gross,* Rosalee. Doesn't your mother know nobody's worn those creepy long gloves since the fifties? Tell her you *can't* go to Julia's stupid tea unless you have the short kind with the pearl button at the wrist. Then you cut out three fingers on each hand, and . . ."

The teenager's need to define herself as an authority. Be seen as knowledgeable, with-it, dependably trendy.

"Out," Liz told the lurking children. "We need to talk about things that don't concern you."

Bo was pleased when Gus and Angie trooped into the yard, accepting that adults own certain privileges not granted to the young.

"Tell me about this case," Liz said over her coffee. "Maybe I can help."

Bo outlined the high points as Andrew filled in details. At the end he said, "You can see that the culprit must be the boy. No one else had the means and motivation to eliminate all three—the baby, the mother, and the father. He couldn't find Bo after he'd tracked her into the blind canyon, and he probably thought she'd seen him. He poisoned the water at her car so she couldn't identify him."

"Chac as the woman he loved and couldn't have," Liz said, frowning. "The family formed by her, Terrell, and Acito as doomed as his own biological family had been. It could happen, I suppose. If he were a ticking bomb, a social isolate wrapped up in his own world. What do you think, Bo?"

Lighting a cigarette, Bo moved to sit near Stoney, who was smoking a pipe. The mingled smoke wafted over their shoulders and out an open screen door into the backyard.

"What matters is what Chac thought," Bo answered. "She's left us clues about her life, about what happened to her and Acito. She trusted Chris Joe, lived with him, put his name on her bank account. He's Jeanne-Marie's age. Just a kid."

Bo exhaled and watched a sparrow pull a worm from beneath the Barrileaux's hollyhocks. Angie was climbing a huge podocarpus tree while Gus did something with a can of 3-in-1 Oil to a ten-speed trail bike.

"And like a kid," she went on, "he sent me Chac's bank statement as proof that somebody treated him as a responsible adult. The phony name Chac used isn't relevant. He sent that so we'd know how grown-up he is. How competent. I just realized that, listening to Jeanne-Marie on the phone. And there's nothing we know about him that suggests he was an isolated character living in his own head. I don't think Chris Joe's our killer. I think it's somebody else."

Andrew poured more coffee for everybody. "Then why did he run, Bo? Why's he hiding and sending arcane messages?"

"He's *seventeen*, Andy. A runaway from a life in foster care. Who knows what he thinks will happen to him if he shows up?"

Bo remembered razor wire and cinder block walls. "To a kid, foster care can seem like a prison," she said. "No control over your life, no sense of belonging to the real world where other kids have parents that don't change every year or two."

"Well, *I* think it was the wife, this Kee," Stoney volunteered, checking his watch. "Philandering husband sires a woods colt on his sexy singer, the little wife goes ballistic. Seems obvious to me. By the way, Bo, we need to get over to Franklin soon if we don't want to steam ourselves on that bayou."

"I'm ready," Bo agreed, tucking one of Gus's T-shirts into the loose waist of a pair of khaki shorts borrowed from Liz. "And I'd suspect Kee, too, except for one thing. She'd never harm a baby, especially an Indian baby. She literally worships a sort of romantic ideal of native cultures, native people. She won't even have her own kid because she wants to devote herself to indigenous children. Kee would no more poison Acito than I'd poison a dog. It's not possible."

"Then who do you think it is?" Liz asked as they prepared to leave.

"It's got to be Munson Terrell," Bo answered. "He's the only one who fits the folk tale Chac sang to me right before she died. I thought it through last night. It has to be Terrell."

"Impossible," Andrew insisted, handing Bo her briefcase. "Somebody was out in that desert training a gun on *him*. And if he'd left the group long enough to poison your water jug, Martin would have noticed. But he said Terrell was with them the entire evening."

Bo stopped at the door on her way to the car with Stoney.

"I was asleep with Mildred on a cot out there most of the afternoon," she admitted. "And Martin said they went off alone on a quest for totems or something in the afternoon. Munson Terrell could have poisoned the water then, while I was asleep."

"Assuming he happens to carry rare natural poisons with him everywhere on the off chance that nosy investigators will be sleeping nearby? That's a bit farfetched, Bo," Andrew said.

"And what about the stalker with the rifle?" Liz asked, puzzled.

Bo felt her interpretation of probable events in Canyon Sin Nombre deserved a careful hearing, even if everybody else did not.

"The wilds around San Diego are full of, well, marginal types, especially on weekends," she explained. "Survivalists, right-wing wackos, gun-freaks who go out there to shoot anything that moves. There's nobody to stop them. The guy stalking me may just have been some half-drunk loner with a cheap rifle playing soldier, pretending he was on a secret mission to wipe out liberals or something. Remember, he didn't fire a shot."

"I want to hear about this folk story Chac sang," Stone said. "But right now we've got to head out."

In less than an hour Stone eased the Volvo into a service station in Franklin, and went inside to arrange for the rental of an aluminum skiff. The boat, he told Bo, was the only way to reach the Singleton residence other than miles of muddy canefield roads on which they'd surely get lost. With the skiff they could float the Bayou Teche straight to the shotgun shack on the edge of a canefield only five miles away, as the crow flies.

Driving to the bayou, Bo noticed a beautifully restored Greek Revival plantation home complete with fluted capital columns and enough Southern atmosphere to cheer the corpse of Robert E. Lee.

"Franklin was full of Northern sympathizers during the war," Stone Barrileaux mentioned with a trace of animosity. "That's why the plantations here weren't burned to the ground."

Bo decided she wouldn't touch that topic with a mine detector. The Civil War, she observed privately, would probably always be a source of bitterness to the inheritors of a lost way of life. But at least Southerners had their landmarks, their Confederate flags and recipes for pecan pie. The banished Maya would have nothing.

"I'm certain Chac meant Munson Terrell when she referred to a man eating in front of a pregnant woman," she told Stone, thinking it through again. "She had been pregnant with his child, yet the distance between them was incredible. The have and the have-not. I think she was saying his wealth and sophistication had no right to tantalize her poverty and desperation. I think she was saying he was selfish and blind."

Stone parked the car in a bare area beside the bayou, paved with broken oyster shells. Bo stepped into the boat and tied her briefcase to an oarlock with a length of wet rope lying on the boat's floor.

"She might have been saying he was a total bastard," the big man noted. "But she didn't say he was going to kill her."

"But that's implied," Bo answered, wondering why she didn't feel more confident of her interpretation. She'd gone over and over it half the night.

The swamp was nothing like what Bo had expected. Instead of green slime and fetid odors there was dark, clear water matted with lavender water hyacinths. The boat moved through them with a slooshing sound. Cypress trees and their above-water roots called "knees" rose smoothly toward the sky. Among them Bo felt like a visitor at a convention of sorcerers. From the watery field of flowers she saw a blue heron rise and fly to a distant cypress. A snapping turtle slid off a log as the boat passed.

"This is lovely." She smiled. "I had no idea. And what are those black swimming birds? They look like chickens."

"They are chickens," he nodded. *"Poule d'eau,* they're called. Water chickens. Make a great gumbo."

"Pool-doo?" Bo repeated.

"Oui." The Cajun smiled. "I can feed my family from these swamps if I need to. At least until the runoff from the canefields kills everything."

"Runoff?" Bo splashed her face with the cool water and waited for an explanation. Two swimming chickens further betrayed her assumptions about chickens in general by taking wing and flying away. The swamp might have been a storyboard for the Disney version of the Uncle Remus Tales.

"Insecticides," Stone muttered. "The sugar-growers spray the fields *and* the sharecropping families who live along them, like these people you're going to see. It all percolates down, runs off in the bayous."

As he slowed the boat in its approach to a rickety dock, Bo wondered if insecticide poisoning had contributed to Dewayne Singleton's ruined life. When he had a life.

"I'll wait in the boat," Stone said as he tied it to the dock and helped Bo climb out. "These folks aren't used to company, and they've just lost a son. It'd be rude for me to go in there."

Bo couldn't recall ever feeling quite as ungainly as she did standing on the Singletons' wobbling dock in tennis shoes and borrowed shorts, holding a briefcase with a wet rope hanging from its handle. The word "unprofessional" came to mind but was quickly dispelled by the fact that there was nothing professional about what she was doing, anyway. Madge Aldenhoven would be the first to point that out.

"Mr. Singleton, I apologize for intruding on you in this way," she said to a wiry black man in corduroy pants and a tan work shirt who looked like Dewayne would have looked if he'd lived to be sixty, sitting in a webbed lawn chair on the dock. "I've come all the way from California to see you because your son's wife had a baby, and there are some questions . . ."

The whites of the man's eyes were actually a creamy yellow, and bloodshot. A lifetime of anger looked out from them. For a split second Bo thought he was going to hit her.

"Don't know nuthin' about that," he said, glaring at Stone sitting in the skiff. "The sheriff's man already come to tell us Dewayne be dead. My wife, she talk to you if she want." He gestured toward a ramp leading into the house, which was on stilts.

Bo couldn't help thinking of the Russian folk-witch, Baba Yaga, and her house on fowls' legs. And then the Irish story of Maurya Ni Keerwaun, the dying witch in her hut like this beside a lake, who made Paudyeen O'Kelly a rich man because he bought Masses to save her soul. Witches always lived in houses like this. The cypress trees, dripping with Spanish moss, cast unnerving shadows in the bright sunlight. The night world hidden inside the day.

Shape up, Bradley. Stoney's right there in the boat, and your name isn't Gretel. Do what you have to do, onerous as it is.

"Thank you." She nodded, and climbed the ramp into the house on stilts. In the hazy interior light a woman in a faded red sweatshirt and flowered cotton skirt sat reading a Bible, her thin fingers following the words as if smoothing them on the page. She could have been any age between fifty and seventy, and behind drugstore reading glasses her eyes, too, were bloodshot. She was not a witch, but a woman still in shock from the news of her son's murder by police in a state two thousand miles away. Bo cursed herself for not bringing flowers, a sympathy card, something, to Dewayne's mourning parents.

"I'm so sorry," she began, and felt tears spilling on her face. Whether they were for Dewayne or for herself and every other "mental patient" the world wouldn't miss, she didn't know. "I met Dewayne briefly while he was in the hospital. He seemed like a gentle man. My name is Bo Bradley, by the way. I work for Child Protective Services in San Diego."

"And my name is Sarah Mae Singleton," the woman said, looking up from her Bible slowly. "I just had me the two boys, you know, Dewayne and Buster. Now they both gone."

Bo walked across the bare board floor and took Sarah Mae Singleton's hand. It was all sinew, and trembled slightly in Bo's. After a while the woman said as if closing a prayer, "His name be praised. Miz Bo Bradley, what you want with me?" In the grieving face Bo saw an enviable willingness to face just about anything.

"It's about a little Indian baby," she began, and settled on a wooden stool to tell Sarah Mae Singleton the whole story.

Forty-five minutes later Stoney and the husband, William, were invited in for sweet chicory coffee so strong Bo was surprised it didn't dissolve the spoon. When Stone admired a collection of bamboo fishing poles leaning in a corner, William Singleton insisted on giving him one.

"You done brought good news to this house," he said, staring at his steel-toed work boots. "I always thought Dewayne had the devil in him. But I was wrong. Sarah Mae know now at least one of her boys weren't bad, jus' sick in the head. That be a comfort to her."

Bo couldn't imagine what comfort until William Singleton described events leading to Dewayne's brother, Buster's, life sentence at Louisiana's maximum-security prison at Angola for the murder of a convenience store clerk in Breaux Bridge.

"I wish we could take in that little baby, even though

Dewayne weren't the real daddy," Sarah Mae Singleton said as Bo and Stoney were leaving. "But we jus' too old. Buster lef' five children we tryin' to help as it is. You let me know what happens to that little Indian now, won't you?" she asked Bo.

"I will," Bo promised.

On the way back she and Stone Barrileaux admired the swamp in silence, lost in their own thoughts.

Later she and Andrew did much the same thing on flights to New Orleans from Lafayette, and then to San Diego. At the airport she hugged him briefly in the cool evening air, and then took a cab alone to her Ocean Beach apartment. The solitude was worth every penny of the twenty dollar cab fare. And she needed it to plan her next move, which involved a visit to the well-appointed Rancho Santa Fe home of a cold-blooded murderer.

Chapter Thirty-four

"But their faces did not die."

—*Popol Vuh*

Bo phoned Estrella from the chipped phone on her kitchen counter as soon as she got home. Mildred, Es reported, was doing fine. Madge Aldenhoven wasn't. Nick Paratore, the other investigator in Madge's unit, had tangled with an octopus while skin-diving Sunday afternoon, and wouldn't be out of the hospital until Thursday. Cases up for investigation were being shuffled all over the system. Madge's case census was down by two thirds with Nick and Bo out, threatening her weekly lead in the number-of-cases-petitioned race.

"You'd better show up early tomorrow," Estrella warned, "because she'll expect you to file two more cases this week and that means one Wednesday and one Friday. You're going to have to haul ass, as they say."

Bo had long ignored Madge's insistence that every case under investigation required intervention by the court and the removal of children from their homes.

"You know I don't file petitions for court custody unless I really think it's necessary." She sighed. "That isn't going to change just because Nick Paratore never got over his first reading of *20,000 Leagues Under the Sea.*"

"There's more bad news," Estrella went on. "When Madge heard that Dewayne Singleton was . . . had passed away, she personally gave foster care the go-ahead to move Acito to a pre-adopt. They picked out a couple, and the authorization from the court came through yesterday afternoon. I told foster care I had to interview the new parents in order to close the investigations file on Acito, and they bought it. I got the address and made a visit."

"And . . . ?" Bo lit a cigarette and exhaled angrily at her refrigerator.

"And Acito's going to a pre-adopt foster home where he will eventually be adopted by the only Latin people I have ever met who hate music. Their name's Estan. And get this— they both work for the county. He's in revenue recovery and she's a guard at the county jail. His boss is the brother-in-law of one of the supervisors over in adoptions, who just happens to have been the one who kept the new foster care worker from getting fired when somebody noticed she'd lied about her education on her initial application. Turns out the foster care worker is living with the adoptions supervisor's husband's son from a previous marriage. Are you tracking this?"

"I'm tracking it," Bo answered through clenched teeth. "The bureaucracy's finest hour. They can't get away with this, Es. We can't let them."

"The Estans already have two kids of their own, two girls." Es sighed. "The missus told me they want to adopt so they'll be sure to get a boy. They plan to send him to military school."

"Oh, shit. When do the Dooleys have to relinquish Acito?"

"Tomorrow afternoon."

Bo glanced at her kitchen wall clock, a yard-sale find shaped like a coiled plaster snake. She'd repainted it in a beige and cream diamond design and glued tiny sunglasses to the snake's head. With the two-hour difference between New Orleans and San Diego, the time was still only six o'clock.

"I need to see the Dooleys," she told Estrella. "And somebody else. Could you keep Mildred until tomorrow morning? I'm going to pay a visit to Munson Terrell. It looks like he poisoned Acito and Chac, Es. I'm going to confront him. If he's guilty, I'll know it."

"It's not Terrell, it's Chris Joe Gavin. You're just going to make a fool of yourself. Stay home, Bo. I'll bring Mildred with me to the office tomorrow, and you can take her home on your lunch hour. Promise me you won't do anything rash, that you'll just stay home."

Bo had stretched the phone cord around the end of the counter so she could reach the refrigerator. Inside, what had once been a slab of pizza was now a landscape of greenish gray mold, but the skim milk was still okay. In a cabinet she found enough Golden Grahams to fill one of the new stoneware cereal bowls she'd found on sale at a china outlet only last month. Dinner.

"Can't promise," she told Estrella. "I don't lie to friends. But there's something I need for you to do. Would you mind calling every guitar store in South Bay and central San Diego? I've got the phone book right here. There aren't that many."

Estrella's tone could only be described as resigned. "Why?" she asked.

"It's a long shot," Bo answered through stale cereal, "but Chris Joe lives for music, and he uses silk-wrapped guitar strings. I noticed that the day I went down to Tijuana alone. Those strings are only available at special stores that cater to musicians. I know because my mother used to take me with her to get violin strings. He'll be in and out of one of those stores if he's still in San Diego, probably in the evening when the manager's not there. That's when the young guys hang out, talking about music until they go off to do gigs in the clubs starting at nine or so. Somebody may know him, know who he is. I want to get a message to him."

"What message?" Estrella asked in a singsong voice meant to reveal her dim view of the task.

"Just say Bo Bradley has a gig for the Ghost Pony, backing an Australian heavy metaler, and he should call right away."

"Heavy metaler?"

Estrella was beginning to sound deeply edgy.

"Yeah." Bo laughed. "I thought that was a nice touch. Terrell wears a silver bracelet inlaid with polished stones. Heavy metal. Get it?"

"Bo?"

"Yeah?"

"You've been taking your medications, right?"

"Religiously," Bo answered. "Don't worry, Es. I'm not losing it. And I'll call you when I get home."

"Roger," Estrella sighed, and hung up.

After a quick shower and a change into sweater, jeans, and tennis shoes, Bo drove the beach route from her apartment to La Jolla. In the long park fronting Mission Bay people clustered around barbecue grills, backlit by fading yellow light. The water seemed black and fathomless, its smooth surface ruffled only sporadically by a weak breeze. A smell of charcoal starter hung in the air.

Bo watched the picnickers, the teenagers on Rollerblades, the elderly couples walking fat little dogs, and wondered what these people would do if there were no such thing as a government agency called Child Protective Services. Would they rescue children from cruelty, or would they look the other way?

"My job shouldn't exist!" she yelled from her car window. "And what does it say about *you* that it does?"

No one heard across five lanes of traffic. And no one could have answered, anyway. In Africa they said it took a whole village to raise a child. But American cities weren't villages, Bo thought, so it took a whole bureaucracy just to keep children alive. Raising them, the decades-long process of socialization, had been forgotten.

But not for Acito. An unlikely sprout from a dying culture, this Maya baby was going to get a fair start in life if Bo had to break the law to ensure that. But how? Once set in motion, the CPS bureaucracy would be supported by the courts. It could not be stopped or altered.

Adoptions had certified the Estan home as suitable for a child. Foster care had changed Acito's status from long-term unadoptable to pre-adopt because the Court Unit, in the person of Madge Aldenhoven, had notified them that both the mother and the legal father were dead and there were no relatives. The actual adoption would take months to finalize, but in the meantime Acito would be moved to the adoptive home as a foster child for the sake of continuity. The plan was, on paper, in the best interests of the child.

Legally, the facts that one parent hadn't been a biological

parent at all, and that one biological parent had apparently attempted to murder the child, were irrelevant. The system, like an enormous, blind hamster in its exercise wheel, simply ran. Bo pounded her fist on the steering wheel as Mission Boulevard became La Jolla Boulevard. The monster was running over Acito.

The Dooleys were home when Bo arrived unannounced. She'd half expected them to have left, taken Acito and run to Mexico where the idea of "kidnapping" an orphaned child from the jurisdiction of a court would still be met with disdain. The Latino culture would have sheltered Davy and Connie Dooley, but they hadn't grabbed that desperate option.

Connie was giving Acito a bottle as Davy limped to the door and invited Bo to enter. The softly lit room pulsed with sadness held in check, a sense of inevitability. The Dooleys barely looked at Bo.

"Have you come to take him now?" Davy asked. "They said—"

"No!" Bo blurted in the quiet room, startling the baby in Connie's arms. "I just found out what's happened. It's not right. Estrella, my officemate, checked out the adoptive parents. We don't think . . . she doesn't think . . . oh, hell, this whole thing sucks."

"We knew what the rules were when we signed on as short-term foster parents," Connie pronounced as if she'd said this several thousand times already. "And it's ridiculous that we think of Acito as ours. We've only had him for four days."

Her voice cracked as Acito reached over his bottle and patted her face. Crying, she stood and handed him to Bo.

"I love this baby," she said through tears. "I don't care what your damned agency thinks. We would have made good parents for him, but we couldn't even be considered. We're not good enough."

Turning her back on Bo, she left the room.

"I'm sorry," Davy Dooley said as Bo sat in the rocker and regarded the baby in her lap. The patch of white hair that would have earned the tiny boy adulation among the ancient Maya was more pronounced now. A deformity indicating the blessing of the gods. Bo wondered when Munson Terrell had figured out this was his son, since Chac had hidden the evidence with hair dye. Acito was watching the door through which Connie had vanished, his rosy brown right hand waving.

"Connie's right." Bo nodded. "But I don't know what to do about it."

"There isn't anything you can do, is there?" Davy said, his shoulders bent under a red T-shirt featuring the black profile of a timber wolf under the words "Save the Wolves." "We won't be accepting any more foster children, though. What's happened to us here . . . it's what they told us not to do. They told us never to think we might really be parents, just to give a little love and be ready to let go. We couldn't do that. We failed."

Bo rubbed her cheek across Acito's soft hair, and thought of Chac. If the mother could have chosen, would she have picked these people to love and raise her son? Bo saw nothing but darkness in the conjecture. No way to know what Chac would have chosen. And Chac was dead. The person who would have to choose was sitting right here.

"I don't think loving, giving the best of yourself, can ever be equated with failing," she said slowly. "It's risky, and pain is always part of it, but it's not failure. I'd like for you and Connie to forget about what they told you in foster care training, and see what a wonderful gift you've been to Acito and Acito to you. You've changed each other's lives. Not everybody can have that experience."

Bo had no idea where her words had come from. Emotional crises usually sent her running for the nearest exit.

"Right," Davy Dooley replied dismally.

"Daaa-daaa," Acito crooned in Bo's arms, pronouncing the syllables that all babies, regardless of the language they would ultimately speak, produced first. Dada. In English, a diminutive for father. Bo let Acito stand in her lap, holding his brown hands and admiring the strong little legs beneath white terry cloth sweat pants. The matching shirt had an appliqué of "The Little Engine That Could" on the chest.

"I think I can, I think I can," Bo quoted from the children's classic.

"Daa-daa," Acito replied, making walking movements on Bo's stomach. "Daaa!"

He seemed to be trying to make a point.

"You've got two dads," she whispered to his drooly smile. "Only I'm afraid one's a killer, and the other one's dead. Legally the dead one was your father, although . . ."

Legally! Bradley, stop emoting and start thinking. That's it. There is a way!

Bo stood Acito on the floor and walked him in sliding swoops toward Davy. The terra-cotta toes still curled inward at every step, she noticed, but that wouldn't last much longer. In another month he'd be walking. Just as soon as the first round of teething subsided.

"I think I can do something here," she told the ex-stuntman. "I shouldn't. The rules absolutely prohibit my interference in foster care and adoptions decisions. If my boss should hear that I did *anything* connected to the placement of a child, I'd be blacklisted in every CPS agency in the country, *capice?*"

Davy Dooley's black eyes sparkled like crystal in lamplight.

"Do anything you can," he said, his voice cracking. "Even if we don't have Acito, he should go to people who're right for him. We'll do whatever you say. We only want him to have the best."

"May I use your phone?" Bo grinned.

"Sure. It's in the kitchen."

In moments Bo had reached a big-hearted Cajun named Gaston Barrileaux in Lafayette, Louisiana. He listened, he agreed, he would do as Bo asked.

"Wanted to do some fishing, anyway," he laughed. "And nothing warms my heart more than beating a bureaucracy at its own game. Liz is right here; she agrees. I'll call you tomorrow, let you know if it worked."

"Thanks, Stoney," Bo said. "I knew I could count on you."

Alone in the Dooleys' kitchen, Bo realized that her attachment to Liz and Stoney Barrileaux felt familial. Comfortable and solid. They didn't question her decision, just agreed to help. Friends. If only Andrew LaMarche, she thought, were more like his own family. But now wasn't the time to worry about that.

Connie Dooley had rejoined her husband in the living room, her composure regained.

"I apologize," she began. "It's just that—"

"Look," Bo explained, "I've just pulled the last available string that may keep Acito with you. That's what I think is best for him, and so that's what I've done. It may work and it may not. The system may never approve your home for a regular adoption, but there's a way to prevent what's been set up for tomorrow. After that, it's one day at a time. Can you handle it?"

Connie Dooley's smile could have sold surfboards to nomadic tribes in the Sahara.

"Did you mean that? That you think we're the best home for him, even though we're not young and Dave's got a bum leg, and we don't work regular jobs, and we don't belong to a church, and . . ."

"I think you're just fine," Bo answered, marveling at the weight given her opinion just because she worked for an agency that distributed a prized commodity—children. "So enjoy your evening with Acito, and let's see what happens tomorrow."

"Thanks," they both said as Bo headed for her car and an unscheduled visit with an Australian entrepreneur. "Whatever happens, thanks."

In her car Bo put Chac's tape in the deck and said, "I hope you'd approve, Chac. It's the best I can do with what I've got."

Chapter Thirty-five
Blood Woman

In dusky twilight the Terrells' house was even more attractive than it had been in sunlight. Like some tasteful high-desert resort patronized by aging movie stars who would lie on the deck in silk dressing gowns, reading scripts. Invisible ground lights illuminated the house, its plantings, and a mailbox Bo had missed on earlier visits. A Frank Lloyd Wright–style mailbox, hewn of local granite with narrow little windows and a hinged door painted flat black. The name "Terrell" and the house number were painted in reflective Garamond type across the bottom of the door. Bo was sure Angela Barrileaux would approve.

A cream-colored Mercedes convertible with the top up sat in the driveway, and there were lights on throughout the sprawling house. Bo parked the Pathfinder and padded stealthily to the door in her tennis shoes, wondering why she felt as if she were breaking and entering. She wasn't. There were plenty of lights; she was going to knock quite properly on the door; she was going to tell Munson Terrell that he might have gotten away with murder, but not entirely. She was going to tell him that she knew what he had done, knew what he was. A pampered, egotistical yuppie who thought easy charm, good looks, and intelligence gave him the right to create and then destroy whatever he chose, including life itself. Bo was going to tell him he was a man who would eat in front of a pregnant woman.

That was what Chac meant, she reassured herself as she rang the doorbell. That had to be what Chac meant. Bo was sure Terrell would merely laugh, and then politely usher this crazy government hireling out his hand-carved front door. But there would be that momentary flash of angry vulnerability when he saw that his victim had sent a message blowing his cover. In the car Bo had practiced the arrogant, superior smirk she would lavish on Munson Terrell in that instant.

"The Indian outsmarted you," she would sneer. "A druggy prostitute who wouldn't know a classic Navajo rug from a polyester doormat beat you at your own game and took her stolen culture back from you. She won, Terrell. She died, but she made a fool of you first."

Bo liked the speech. Delivering it would be her gift to Chac. A message from the grave, sort of. Except nobody was answering the door.

Bo rang the bell again, listening for its chime inside the house. There was nothing. Pushing the bell repeatedly, she pressed her ear to the door. Still nothing. Incongruously in the perfect house, perfectly maintained, the doorbell was broken. And there wasn't a knocker. Ineffectively she pounded her knuckles against the solid oak door. She could barely hear the sound herself. If Munson or Kee were anywhere but standing around in the entry hall, they'd never hear her. Surprisingly, the brushed brass doorknob turned when she tried it. The house wasn't locked.

"It's Bo Bradley," she yelled into the tiled foyer. "Hello?"

A breeze from the open deck doors off the living room ruffled her hair. They might be admiring the view from the back of the deck, Bo thought. With all the lights on and the door unlocked, somebody had to be home. On the glass-topped coffee table with its collection of fetish animals inside, a white rectangle of paper fluttered. Closing the door, Bo padded soundlessly across the carpet and looked at the paper. It was a note from Kee, casually handwritten on ordinary typing foolscap.

"Darling," it said. "I'm helping Dr. Stoa with the orientation group. He says I'm his best advertisement. Back around 9:30. Your Kee."

The handwriting was round and juvenile. A circular smiley face had been drawn after the word "advertisement." Bo looked at her watch: 8:00. Plenty of time to confront Terrell before Kee got home. If she could find him in the cavernous house.

"Terrell?" she bellowed down the hall where the nursery door was now closed. "It's Bo Bradley. I want to talk to you!"

A silence echoed back, making her ears ring. In shadows near the glass wall overlooking the canyon, the lifesize bronze statue of the old Indian woman seemed to be staring at her. Its gaze was not friendly.

Get out of here, Bradley. You're alone in an isolated house with a man you believe capable of murdering his own baby. He knows you're here. He's waiting for you. Go!

Bo looked at her tennis shoe on the carpet, turned toward the door. The foot inside was straining against the leather toeguard, but the shoe seemed rooted to the floor. An image of ambivalence. Bo thought she might do a small pen-and-ink sketch of it if she lived long enough. From a partially open doorway across from the nursery, yellow light spilled in a fan shape across the hall. Terrell might be in there, she thought. Maybe he was listening to music on a headset. Maybe that's why he hadn't heard her shouts.

Ignoring the fact that there was no earthly reason to use a headset in an isolated, empty house, Bo climbed the three tiled steps from the living room to the wide hall.

"Terrell?" she called again.

The silence now seemed to rush in waves from the backlit doorway. It made a thumping sound in Bo's ears, rushing past her. Her knock on the half-open door was so loud it made her jump. Then more silence. Pushing the door aside, she stood facing an attractive office decorated in Southwest style, and the back of a ponytailed head visible in the colored light of a computer monitor. The room smelled like the marzipan candy her grandmother used to send from Ireland every Christmas. Almonds. That dusky-sweet, unmistakable odor of almonds.

Her shadow, cast by a stoneware floor lamp beside the door, snaked across the motionless body of Munson Terrell as Bo moved on numb legs to look at his face. The foam at his lips had dried to a thin, white line, but its odor was still powerful. An empty cup painted in Kachina figures sat on a coaster beside the computer. The coaster was a tiny Navajo rug, Bo mentally recorded without knowing why, complete with fringe. Munson Terrell's blue eyes were open, but covered with a drying film. In the wrist beneath a silver bracelet inlaid with polished stones, there was no pulse.

Bo felt dizzy, then forced herself to resume breathing. On the monitor screen, a paragraph of words shone yellow against a bright blue background. Reading it, Bo thought Munson Terrell must have dreamed of being a poet.

"I'm sorry, my darling," it said, "but the colored skies of our love have grown dark at my betrayal. The woman, Chac, was nothing. Just a cheap joke told by cheap tequila. I tried to kill the bastard baby she called Acito, too, to save that sky for us. But it's too late. Our sky is closed. Never forget that I loved only you. Mundy."

Bo scanned the desk top for paper. There was none. But in a small, pit-fired pot were several black ballpoint pens embossed in gold with the words "Outback Odyssey." Bo grabbed one and copied the text of Terrell's note onto her left forearm. Then she ran.

Down the hall, past the glaring statue, outside. The car started immediately and drove itself away from Munson Terrell's dead body. Several blocks away Bo saw a brightly lit convenience store, and seized control of the vehicle.

"I have to call the police," she told it. "That's what one does in these circumstances."

The hand that dialed 911 from a pay phone next to an ice machine was shaking, but Bo managed to convey the gist of the situation to an operator trained to remain calm. A dead man. The address. Bo's name. Her address. Her phone number.

"You may phone me at my work number tomorrow," she agreed politely in a voice that sounded like Julia Child's. "No, I will not wait at the address of the deceased for the arrival of the paramedics. Yes, I'm sure Mr. Terrell is dead."

One more call, this time to Eva Broussard, gave Bo sufficient stability to get home.

"I will meet you at your apartment in an hour," the unruffled voice told Bo as if they were talking about dinner before the symphony. "I will give you a mild sedative, phone Estrella and Andrew, and spend the night. We will not discuss this until tomorrow, if then. Agreed?"

"Agreed," Bo replied gratefully.

She hoped the paramedics got there before Kee Terrell got home at 9:30. She hoped Kee wouldn't have to smell the almonds.

Chapter Thirty-six
Laughing Falcon

Bo awoke at an uncharacteristically early hour and found Eva Broussard already drinking coffee on the deck. The marine layer, still dense, sent dimensionless fog-shapes from the sea. Bo watched something that looked like a thin frying pan float diagonally through Eva before dissipating near the deck doors.

"Chickens can swim in Louisiana," she told her psychiatrist, whose bare, tanned feet were propped on the deck rail. "Fly, too. So I guess an Australian murderer might take himself out, leaving what must be the worst suicide note ever written."

She held her left forearm across Eva's field of vision.

"Did you read this? It's awful. Not what you'd expect from a sophisticated international type."

Eva stood and stretched, the sleeves of her oversize black sweater sliding down to reveal muscular arms adorned with narrow woven leather bracelets. With a bronze finger she drew an Iroquois mask in the film of dew on the deck rail. The elongated face lacked a mouth. Eva's black eyes beneath cropped silver hair regarded Bo fondly.

"This is the mask of confusion," she said. "It also teaches the way to defeat confusion. Would you like some coffee?"

Bo smiled at the drawing.

"You mean I should stop talking, achieve inner tranquility, that sort of thing? Sounds like fun. But I'm afraid the best I can do is find tranquil surroundings, Eva. My mind *never* shuts up. And right now it's going over and over what I saw last night. I should probably have closed his eyes, but they were . . . they were dry . . ."

Eva sighed and wrapped an arm over Bo's shoulders, steering her inside.

"Coins," Bo went on as Eva poured coffee. "My grandmother always talked about putting coins on the eyes of the dead, although my whole family's dead and I didn't see coins on any of their eyes—"

"Yes," Eva interrupted. "Your parents and sister are dead and you've stumbled on to the dead body of a man you suspect was responsible for another grisly death you witnessed less than a week ago as well as the attempted murder of a baby, followed by the slaughter by police of a man who suffered the same disorder with which you must live. One might safely say that for a mind prone to emotional and symbolic excess, your situation is less than optimal. How are you going to deal with it?"

Bo eyed the empty Golden Grahams box on her kitchen counter narrowly.

"Go out to breakfast?" she suggested.

"Excellent," her psychiatrist agreed. "And Bo? Wear a long-sleeved blouse. I don't want to read suicide notes over my omelette."

Bo couldn't remember having eaten breakfast at six o'clock in the morning, ever. But the little Mexican restaurant on Newport Avenue in Ocean Beach was already populated with early risers when she and Eva jogged in, ruddy from the three-block sprint through patchy fog. Bo ordered *huevos revueltos* and grimaced at a fading wall mural from which a toreador glared proudly at a gaunt spider plant in an orange macramé sling. The restaurant smelled of cooking grease and old wood.

" '*Huevos revueltos*' looks like it should translate as 'revolting eggs,' " Bo said, scowling at the toreador. "You know, Eva, Terrell's suicide pretty much closes this case. Ties it up in a clean little package. Yuppie idealist dies of self-loathing. Except I don't buy it. That suicide note's just *too* smarmy, and—"

" '*Revueltos*' means 'scrambled,' and suicide notes aren't usually drafted for publication. What are you saying, Bo? That you don't think Terrell's death was a suicide?"

Bo inhaled steam from her coffee cup. "I don't know him," she admitted. "But the picture Martin painted of Terrell during their workshop in the desert was scarcely that of a depressed man contemplating suicide. And I have trouble connecting this . . ." She tapped her left arm under the sleeve of her navy sweatshirt. ". . . to a border-hopping Australian entrepreneur with a museum-quality home, a svelte, adoring wife, and an adoptive child on the way. It's possible that Terrell took himself out, Eva, but I find it hard to believe he wrote what I saw on the computer screen."

"Let me see your arm again," Eva sighed as Bo obligingly pushed up her sleeve.

"I agree that the choice of words is juvenile and affect-laden," she nodded after pondering Bo's outstretched arm. "But I never met the man and my sensitivity to English nuance is permanently compromised by the fact that I've spoken Canadian French since I was five years old. That's fifty-five years. Who do you think wrote the note?"

"I don't know. Kee might have. She has an odd, childlike quality. Except that would implicate her in her husband's death, and Chac's, and the attempt on Acito. And that's the hitch. Kee would not have harmed a baby, especially an Indian baby. It's not possible. That rules her out, even if her apparent devotion to Terrell doesn't."

"And . . . ?"

"And so that leaves Chris Joe Gavin."

Bo spooned a prodigious mound of fresh salsa atop the scrambled eggs placed before her by a waitress in gleaming orthodontic braces and a parochial school uniform.

"Do you think the boy is responsible for Terrell's death, and the others?" Eva asked, attacking her *chorizo* sausage omelette.

"I don't know what I think," Bo sighed. "And there's no way to prove anything. Chris Joe looks like the obvious culprit. An out-of-control adolescent male, jealous, resentful, bitter. But Chac's song, the folk tale in the last verse . . . it seems to point to Terrell, so he probably did commit suicide. Bottom line, we're probably never going to know what really happened."

"Can you live with that?" Eva asked.

Bo grinned at a sprig of parsley adorning the refried beans on her plate. "I doubt it," she answered.

Two hours later she arrived at work on time, wearing a pale yellow cotton-blend shirtwaist bought three years ago for the interview that landed her this job. The social worker costume. Wash-and-wear niceness. The dress seemed to buffer Madge Aldenhoven's voice, now shrill with bureaucratic outrage.

"The *one* case I could have transferred out today has just blown up!" she informed Bo, pacing in the tiny office as Estrella pretended to read a three-page, single-spaced directive from County Administration regarding reimbursement vouchers for repairs on county-owned office equipment. A copy of the directive had been in the mailbox of every county employee that morning. A small forest, Bo thought, had gone into yet another ton of paper that nobody would read. Madge seemed ready to perform acts of violence, a fact that only reinforced Bo's satisfaction in her choice of the idiot dress. No one would assault a kindly social worker in a buttercup yellow shirtwaist.

"We should have sent this damned Indian baby over to Indian Child Welfare in the beginning," Madge went on. "Now we're going to be stuck with this case for months."

More like years, Bo thought to herself, but merely said, "I thought you'd set Acito up for a pre-adopt foster home. What happened?" In the foggy morning sunlight pouring weakly through their office window Madge looked like a puppet being walked up and down on invisible strings. The shadow twitching behind her seemed gnomelike and out-of-sorts.

"The parents of that dead lunatic who was legally the baby's father phoned the hotline this morning from someplace in Louisiana. They left a message saying they can't take the baby right now, but they will under no circumstances release him for adoption. We're stuck."

Bo wished the faces on her bulletin board, every one of them undoubtedly labeled "lunatic" by earlier versions of Madge Aldenhoven, could come to life if only for a moment. She particularly wished Walt Whitman would step down onto her desk and bellow the endless entirety of *Song of Myself* at Madge until she either got the message or locked herself permanently in her office.

"And whoever walks a furlong without sympathy walks to

her own funeral . . ." Bo recited, examining her nails and altering the gender of the possessive pronoun to fit the situation, ". . . drest in her shroud." The shroud part was particularly apt, she thought. Madge was wearing a blousy, belted shift of tan kettlecloth. Easily mistaken for a shroud in the wrong light.

"I'm not in the mood for whatever it is that you're doing, Bo," the supervisor snapped. "And what happened to your arm?"

At Eva's suggestion Bo had stuck a large butterfly Band-Aid over Munson Terrell's suicide note, which had proven resistant to removal. Outback Odyssey's promotional pens had apparently been filled with indelible ink.

"Blood work," Bo sighed dramatically. "Isn't it amazing what modern medicine . . ."

"They don't draw blood from the front of your arm." Madge frowned.

"Psychiatric blood tests are different," Bo lied, smiling at Charlie Parker and his saxophone above her desk. "You know, *lunatic* blood?"

Estrella appeared to choke on a sip of coffee.

Madge stopped pacing. "I'm sick of your nonsense, Bo. You'll get a new case within the hour, and I expect you to complete the investigation today. In the meantime I want a case plan for the Indian baby. Foster care says there aren't any long-term homes available right now. They're going to do a recruitment program sometime this year, but right now there's nothing. Try Indian Child Welfare. It may not be too late to let them take him."

Bo spun her desk chair so the full impact of her social worker costume would not be lost on Madge. "What a mess," she said sympathetically as Estrella bit a half-moon out of her Styrofoam coffee cup. "Those grandparents sure botched things up. Too bad the placement he's in now is only certified for short-term. They seem to enjoy fostering, and might agree to keep him . . ."

"I'll have foster care reclassify them as long-term," Madge said. "What was their name?"

"Uh, it begins with a D," Bo answered, pulling Acito's case

file from the collection on her desk and feigning no memory of the distraught Dooleys. "Here it is—Dooley. David and Constanzia Dooley."

Madge was at the door. "Can you convince them to keep the child until this legal difficulty with the grandparents is straightened out?"

"I'll give it a try," Bo said brightly. "We need to get this case out of the way."

When Madge had closed the door behind her Bo and Estrella mimed high-fives across the space where their supervisor had paced. The legal problem with the grandparents, with knowledgeable handling, could drag on for years. The State of Louisiana would accept jurisdiction over Acito, based on the Singletons' residence there. Then it would grant the State of California, County of San Diego, "courtesy supervision" of its ward, there being no money to transport him to Louisiana and no desire on the part of that state to assume the financial burden of his care. After a few years the courts would insist that permanent arrangements be made for the child, at which time the Dooleys' case for adoption would be insurmountable, particularly if the grandparents made it known that they wished the child to remain with the Dooleys.

An archaic law designed to prevent "bastardy" had given Acito an appropriate home. A woman's legal husband, the law insisted, was legally the father of her children even if that were a physical impossibility. The law said that Dewayne Singleton, imprisoned in Louisiana, had nonetheless managed to father a child in Mexico. When the mother, and then Dewayne, died, Dewayne's parents became Acito's next-of-kin. They could, as had Chris Joe Gavin's mother, prevent Acito from being placed by San Diego County's Child Protective Services under the direction of San Diego County's Juvenile Court, for adoption.

Bo sighed, and then phoned the Dooleys.

"It isn't foolproof," she warned. "But it's the best I can do. Good luck."

The Dooley's understood, they said, and then whooped with joy.

Chapter Thirty-seven
Ancient Word

The new case Madge brought in fifteen minutes later was merely the last entry in a case file already thicker than the San Diego phone book. "Opiela," it said simply on the orange band where the names of children were usually written. The single word was enough.

"Oh, no!" Bo winced. "Not again!"

"Afraid so," Madge nodded, eyeing the case file with a disdain equal to Bo's. "This time a neighbor found one of them, the ten-year-old girl, sleeping in a ramada in his orange grove. The neighbor phoned police when the girl refused to go home, claiming her mother's boyfriend hangs around the house all day in his underwear, drunk."

"Is she afraid he'll hurt her?"

"No." Madge shook her head. "The girl says she's afraid *she'll* hurt *him*. Says it's all she can do to keep from pouring hot coffee into his shorts. Hearing this, the police, of course, took her into custody. I'm afraid the protective issue this time may center on the boyfriend, not the child."

"I'll go talk to Marjorie," Bo told her supervisor. "Get her to throw the drunk out. It doesn't sound petitionable."

Marjorie Opiela and her eight children had been on the receiving end of Child Protective Services for a decade, to no avail. Robustly unconcerned with twentieth-century standards for diet, cleanliness, and school attendance, the Opielas continued to thrive a hair's-breadth short of the cloudy line beyond which the term "child abuse" might legally be employed.

One or another of the children was referred to CPS with astonishing regularity by doctors, teachers, truant officers, neighbors, and police for problems ranging from head lice to petty theft. Nearly every worker in the system had at some point tried to convince Marjorie Opiela to clean her crumbling barn of a house occasionally, and to force her children to wear shoes. The worker who'd decorously left a packet of birth control information on Marjorie's kitchen table had been run off with a broken canoe paddle. Bo regarded the case as an opportunity to ponder Munson Terrell's death, since there was documentably no point in devoting thought to the colorful, recalcitrant Opielas.

"Interview the girl at the receiving home and then go on up to Leucadia and talk to the mother," Madge said. "If there's no grounds for a petition, we'll close it and you'll have another one this afternoon."

"Great," Bo replied without enthusiasm. At least the trip to the northern coastal community of Leucadia would be pleasant. It would take her along the beaches, past Torrey Pines State Reserve, near Andrew's condo. She wondered what she was going to do about Andrew, and decided to table the conflict until later. The decision was rendered moot when the phone's muted bell thumped seconds later.

"Bo," the familiar voice began carefully, "I was pleased when Eva called last night to tell me what had happened. I mean I was pleased that she was with you. It must have been upsetting, finding Terrell's body. But I'm sure you're relieved that the mystery is resolved. I thought you might like to meet me for lunch to celebrate. I mean to celebrate the resolution of the case, not Terrell's death. Ah, *mon dieu*. I'm not doing well, am I?"

Bo smiled and drew a series of collar pins on the margin of her desk calendar. "We do need to talk, Andy, but I've got to run up to Leucadia on a new case. I can't meet you for lunch. How about dinner? You know, I'm not really convinced about Terrell's death. I want you to take a look at the suicide note. I've got it on my arm—"

"You've got it on your arm?" Andrew LaMarche's voice attempted to suggest that suicide-note-laden arms were only marginally out of the ordinary.

"I copied the note on my arm; there wasn't any paper. But I

don't think Terrell wrote it. Why don't you meet me for dinner at—"

"I've got a better idea. I made some peanut soup last night, and an oyster rarebit, as well as a pan of coffee fudge. The soup and rarebit are in the freezer, but you could stop by on your way back from Leucadia and . . ."

Bo recognized the throbbing of her Achilles' heel, and gave in to it with abandon. "Coffee fudge! I'll be there. But you must have been up half the night cooking. How come?"

"I was, um, concerned that you, ah, well, I was worried about you, Bo."

"We'll need a salad," Bo replied. "And a long talk about how I hate it when people worry about me. Nothing, however, could keep me from trying coffee fudge."

"There's a spare key inside the doormat. Just pull up the C in 'WELCOME.' It's fastened with Velcro. The key's right there, and you can leave the soup and rarebit on the counter to thaw."

"Okay, but wouldn't it be quicker just to microwave it?"

"A microwave thaw overcooks everything except the center." A hint of self-congratulation surfaced in his voice. "I rather hoped you'd see the effort I expended in sublimating my need to race to your side and hover last night. Cooking, I think, will do nicely until the harpsichord kit arrives. I do love you, Bo."

"Cooking is brilliant," she agreed. "And tonight we'll talk about the lengths to which I'll go in a lifelong struggle for autonomy. In the meantime Estrella's going to be in the office all day in case Chris Joe Gavin calls."

"What?"

"Tell you about it later. Gotta run."

As Bo placed the receiver in its cradle the Alfred Stieglitz photo of Georgia O'Keeffe pinned to her bulletin board seemed to smile knowingly. Enduring relationships with men tended to be an uphill climb for independent women, the smile suggested, especially independent women riding mood swings that demanded frequent solitude. But it was always fun to try.

Kara Opiela, cooling her heels at San Diego's Hillcrest Receiving Home, couldn't understand what the big deal was.

All she'd said was that she'd *like* to pour hot coffee on Cole Durocher's weenie, not that she was *going* to. Besides, he was always too drunk to feel it, anyway. She would specifically like to get home before Friday, when her oral report on the life cycle of the tapeworm was due at the university-sponsored science camp she was attending. Bo regarded the request as reasonable.

Later in Leucadia Marjorie Opiela joined Bo in a cigarette, and proudly displayed the hand-drawn chart featuring tapeworms made of real tape that Kara had prepared for her presentation. The boyfriend, Cole, had been dispatched early that morning. He wouldn't be back, Marjorie assured Bo through a blue haze of smoke. And keeping Kara away from her science camp was plain stupid. Surely Child Protective Services could see that. Bo could.

"I'll close the case and arrange for somebody to bring her home this afternoon," Bo said. "And Marjorie, tell Kara not to make graphic references to hot coffee and male anatomy in the presence of police again, okay? They freak."

"I'll try," Marjorie said thoughtfully. "Probably won't do any good, though."

Driving back down the coast, Bo stopped at Torrey Pines Beach and practiced skipping flat stones in the splash. The beach and sandstone cliffs were, as usual, evocative. Bo thought of St. Bridget's Well near the sea in the west of Ireland, and the little fish in the well that appeared only every seventh year and that few, her grandmother said, could see. But anyone seeing the fish would be cured of all illness, so people came to peer into the ancient well, and hope.

The story was nice, Bo thought. It would be nice to see a fish in a holy well and be free of the illness that would force her to depend on Depakote, or lithium, or Tegretol, or something, for the rest of her life. Nice even to believe such a well and such a fish were possible, even if she never saw them. All her grandmother's stories were like that. They all felt comfortable, while Chac's story did not. They made what Bo liked to call "deep sense," a vibrato of whole-body understanding that did not require intellectual analysis. Chac's stories of *duendes* and men eating in front of pregnant women were different, not European, impossible for Bo to decipher beyond intellectual guesswork.

Why had Chac written a lullaby for her baby with references to an evil spirit Eva said represented something driven mad by nature? Bo thought about her own brain, programmed by an unusual DNA coding to experience excesses of feeling and intense symbolic interpretations of everything it perceived. Feelings and symbolic interpretations that other people, "normal" people, didn't have and couldn't understand. Madness. But was that nature? Was that what Chac meant by the *duende* in her song? Bo didn't think so. The Little Turtle's lullaby wasn't about psychiatric disorders, but something else. Some evil that Chac had believed threatening to her baby. Was Munson Terrell the *duende*?

Bo sliced a flattened oval of black granite into the receding surf and watched it skip sluggishly three times before sinking. The outgoing wave rattled a thousand smooth stones where the beach sloped down to vanish in sparkling saltwater. The sound, repeating with every wave, was like the breathing of something huge. Bo let the chorus of stones hypnotize her, and merely stood staring south along the coastline.

In the distance beyond the continental hump that was La Jolla, the U.S. coast became the Mexican coast of the Baja Peninsula, ending at Cabo San Lucas. And across the Gulf of California from Cabo, the mainland coast of Mexico stretched south to its terminus in the state of Chiapas. Beyond Chiapas lay Guatemala, where at least a million people might readily understand what a Maya singer's lyrics meant. That she couldn't see that far, Bo thought, was appropriate. She couldn't think that far either.

Walking back to the car she remembered New Orleans, the accessibility of its gated courtyards to her imagination. That bone-deep understanding of cultural imagery because it was European, because it was familiar. An understanding that became useless twenty miles south of this beach where the gated courtyards were dusty adobe, and the mythological bedrock of reality just different enough to be indecipherable.

"Damn!" Bo whispered to the Pathfinder's steering wheel as she drove out of the beach parking lot and uphill toward

Andrew's condo. Somebody had poisoned a baby and murdered that baby's mother in a club full of people, and nobody was ever going to know, for sure, who that somebody was. And either the same person or somebody else had stalked the desert darkness with a rifle and poisoned a water jug. Had it not been for the jug's defective lid, a devoted old fox terrier would certainly have died as well. Bo didn't find it strange that the thought of Mildred's death enraged her more than the thought of her own. Now Munson Terrell was dead, seemingly poisoned by his own hand, leaving a document admitting his guilt. It was too tidy, Bo thought. But it was finished.

There would be a cursory internal affairs investigation of Dewayne Singleton's murder by the Oceanside police, but nothing would come of it. After all, he was crazy. Acito would thrive in the Dooleys' love and probably be adopted by them eventually. Tying up the paperwork to ensure that likelihood would present no problem. The system Bo worked for excelled at bureaucratic delay. Other cases would arrive for investigation. Life would go on.

"I hate it when I feel like this," Bo muttered as she parked near Andrew's front door. "I hate it when I know somebody's getting away with murder!"

The key was neatly tucked under the welcome mat's C, just as Andrew had described. Bo let herself in and quickly removed the only two items in the freezer, placing them on a towel on the counter. In this uninhabited silence Andrew LaMarche's condo reflected his life. Tidy, tasteful, and lonely. Picking at an edge of the flesh-colored Band-Aid on her arm, Bo wondered again what to do about the domineering pediatrician.

People didn't change. He'd always think he had a right, even an obligation to shape her experience as he saw fit. Men always did, which was why it was always best to avoid extended contact with any particular one of them. On the other hand, he did seem to be trying. An intelligent, disciplined man. Maybe he actually could learn to relinquish his need for control. Maybe . . .

And maybe the Wee Folk will dance in your hair, Bradley.

Bridget Mairead O'Reilly had employed the phrase to

suggest irrational thinking. Bo thought her grandmother would in all likelihood have used it now.

The butterfly Band-Aid was nearly off. Bo glanced at the words on her forearm.

"I'm sorry, my darling, but the colored skies of our love have grown dark at my betrayal . . ."

There was still something not quite right about the words. Something *wrong*. Bo found herself staring at two words— "colored skies." What was it about "colored skies" that seemed to be screaming in the quiet order of Andrew's kitchen?

"Colored . . ." Bo pronounced experimentally. "Skies . . ."

The words seemed to jiggle as she concentrated. But they were just words. Spelled correctly. In traditional sequence.

Spelled correctly. *Bradley, you brainless slug, that's it! Terrell didn't write that note, an American did!*

Bo ripped the Band-Aid from her arm and ran to the phone in Andrew's living room. An Australian, Munson Terrell would have written "coloured." Hadn't Kee said he deliberately used British spellings in the promotional materials for Outback Odyssey's workshops? And in the stressful moments immediately prior to killing himself, wouldn't he have automatically written in the form most familiar to him? Bo dialed Estrella's office number jubilantly.

"Es," she yelled when her friend answered, "Terrell really didn't write that suicide note, because 'colored' isn't spelled 'coloured'!"

After listening to Bo's explanation, Estrella agreed. "Then it must be Chris Joe," she concluded, "and you'd better call the police right now."

"I'll do it when I get back. There's no rush."

Estrella was adamant. "I think there is," she insisted. "Because he called you only five minutes ago. I told him you'd be back after lunch. He wouldn't leave a number, but he said he'd call this afternoon. If you contact the police now they'll have time to set up a trace. I told you it was Chris Joe all along, Bo, and now we know it. He's dangerous. You'd better notify the police."

"Umm," Bo answered noncommittally, noticing her own

gold earring, lost at Torrey Pines, lying atop some sort of flier on Andrew's tiled coffee table. "I'll be back in half an hour."

Things were starting to fall into place. Bo made an instinctive judgment merely to watch, and wait for a pattern to emerge. Not to think, merely observe. It wasn't easy, she admitted. Without the Depakote it would be impossible.

Wandering to the coffee table, she picked up the earring and flipped through the flier beneath it. Something from the Torrey Pines Docent Society, entitled "Dangerous Plants of the Chaparral." On the back page was a warning that environmentally unsound interlopers were prone to planting marijuana and other nonindigenous plants in some of the less accessible areas of the preserve.

Only a month ago, the flier said, park rangers had been shocked to find a stand of the tropical *Abrus precatorius* in a sheltered south-facing ditch in Fern Canyon. Bits of sterling silver and a small crucifix found webbed in the plants' roots suggested they had grown from the beads of a rosary probably lost there by one of the undocumented Mexican laborers who hid in the canyons on their way north. The attractive, deadly red and black seeds, called "rosary peas," had once enjoyed popular use in the manufacture of rosaries, especially among Latino populations in Florida where the plant was common. A single seed, the flier warned, was sufficient to kill an adult once its colorful outer shell was broken. Visitors were urged to carry nothing but water while hiking in the preserve, and to avoid consuming *any* of its plants.

Bo felt a gentle snap in her mind as a strenuously maintained adherence to consensual reality was allowed to fall away, like the tarp covering a sculpture at its unveiling. No one would understand how this had happened. No one would see how obvious in this innocuous, badly printed flier, was the design of a universe in which evil might be thwarted if only people would look at what was right in front of them.

In her ears and beneath her right foot the memory of a crunch re-created itself. The crunch of a rosary hidden among blankets in a cement-block pen where a teething baby had been given the paraphernalia of Roman Catholicism to play with. A rosary that had years ago been a deathbed gift to a woman, now a grandmother, who in her anger at Bo's clumsiness screamed what sounded like "Tampa," over and over. Tampa was in Florida. Where rosary peas grew wild.

In Andrew's guest bath Bo bared her teeth at the mirror. Adult teeth, opaque and worn. Not like Acito's two translucent lower incisors and one upper incisor, freshly erupted from a rosy gum. Only two opposing, sharp little teeth, but enough to crack the red and black shell of a pretty, toxic seed.

"Nobody poisoned Acito!" Bo yelled in the empty condominium. "It was an accident!"

The green eyes staring back from the mirror were, she admitted, a bit wild. Just the barest gleam of irrationality there, but what the hell? She was right. A momentary breakthrough of manicky sainthood couldn't hurt anything, as long as she enjoyed it in solitude. Closing her eyes, she let her head fall backward and felt the warp-speed pulsing of a million universal intentions on a grid with more dimensions than the three she could understand. Whatever, she was a part of it. One of the pulses. She'd seen what was there to see, and knew what was there to be known. She was alive!

The manic experience, she reminded herself a few minutes later, was crazy. Time to rein it in, contain the awareness before it got in the way of what had to be done next, which would require icelike rationality. Splashing her face with cold water, she breathed deeply and felt a brief surge of sympathy for people who never had manic breakthroughs. The price was high, but occasionally worth it. Well, very occasionally. Like maybe once.

Back in Andrew's living room she searched for phone books and finally found them in a hinged bench beneath the front windows. Under "Physicians" in the Yellow Pages she found what she was looking for—a sole doctor whose name matched the one Kee Terrell had mentioned in a note left for her husband last night. Dr. Neil Stoa, the Yellow Pages informed her, specialized in eating disorders.

"Dr. Stoa's office," the nurse answered. "How may I help you?"

Bo tried to make her smoker's voice sound twenty years younger than it was. "I, uh, think I need some help," she began. "I've been dieting and working out for a while, and, uh, my period sort of stopped. Is that normal?"

"Are you an athlete, a runner?" the nurse asked.

"No. I just really watch my weight."

"This can happen when a woman's body has an insufficient percentage of fat," the nurse went on cheerfully. "Why don't I make an appointment for you to come in and talk it over with Dr. Stoa?"

"No. Thank you," Bo concluded, and hung up.

She'd just wanted to verify it. That women who starved themselves might sacrifice the ability to bear children. It was all falling into place.

Chapter Thirty-eight

"There will be no high days and no bright praise."

—*Popol Vuh*

The Terrell home had turned mauve in the late afternoon sun as Bo knocked loudly on the door. Kee was there, she knew. The cream-colored Mercedes had cruised past Bo's concealed car only fifteen minutes earlier. And Kee was alone. Bo tried not to remember a poisoned water jug in the desert, and what that death would have been like for a small, old dog. Mentally folding the thought into a tiny packet, she pushed it down again behind her eyes. But she could feel it there, throbbing.

"I'm on the deck," Kee Terrell's high voice called over the front railing. "The door's open. Come on up."

Bo watched her own sandaled feet cross the Berber carpet and pass the mission doors leading to the deck from the left of the fireplace. Kee, barefoot in a loose black jumper, was huddled against what remained of the rear deck rail.

"The contractors came ahead of schedule," she whispered, nodding at a gaping hole where the benches and railing had been removed. "They didn't know about Mundy, of course, and I wasn't here when they came. I was, you know, at the funeral home. It's tomorrow, the funeral. Are you going to come?"

Bo blinked slowly at the question and tried to make sense of Kee's childlike request. It was sincere. Kee Terrell, as usual, was treating Bo Bradley like a friend.

"I'm afraid not," Bo pronounced in a practiced monotone. "I couldn't stand to be in an enclosed space with you."

Kee's dark eyes filled with tears. "It wasn't *my* fault Mundy killed himself," she wailed shrilly. "*I* did everything right. It's not my fault he got that woman pregnant and then tried to kill the baby so I wouldn't know when I saw its hair. The baby has Mundy's hair, you know. That white streak. Mundy told me she tried to hide it with hair dye so he wouldn't know the baby was his. Can you believe somebody doing that?"

Bo felt as though she were gossiping with a thirteen-year-old about the behavior of some heartthrob movie star. That sense of overemotional fantasy. Kee shook her head dramatically.

"What I can't believe is that Chac managed to fight her way out of Guatemala," Bo began softly, "survive prostitution and heroin addiction, make a career for herself singing, and give birth to a lovely, healthy baby, only to be murdered by a selfish brat who thinks she can buy anything, including children to match her artwork."

"I don't know what you're talking about," Kee muttered, but Bo didn't miss the change in her eyes. The self-righteous cruelty there.

"What was your favorite fairy tale, Kee? Snow White? You know, I could have put it together days ago and maybe saved your husband's life if I'd thought about Snow White instead of pretending to understand a Maya story that wasn't mine. But that's what happens when you try to live in someone else's world, isn't it? You screw up, don't you?"

Bo had been moving closer to Kee as she spoke, pacing her steps to her words.

"I didn't screw up," the younger woman answered, casting a sidelong look at Bo and rising abruptly. "She did. She was a liar and a thief. I hate her!"

Bo was again struck by Kee's juvenile peevishness. It was unnerving, attacking what seemed to be a child. Bo had a sense of loose conceptual footing, as if she were roller-skating in grease.

"What did she steal, Kee? Her own son? How could Chac steal her own son from you?"

Kee Terrell turned to face Bo, another change creasing her narrow face with a sneer. She seemed to be taking Bo's measure. And she was taking her time. Finally she spoke, this time in the chilling voice of an angry adult.

"Kylie isn't her son, he's mine. That was the agreement. Mundy arranged it."

"Kylie?" Bo blurted, laughing deliberately. "Kee and Kylie? Sounds like a twin water-skiing act. You've got to be kidding."

An already-present darkness hardened in Kee's eyes.

"Mundy agreed to promote her career, make her a star. All she had to do was let him get her pregnant with my . . . with our baby. But when Kylie was born, she lied. She told Mundy she'd been screwing around with other men, and the baby was one of theirs. She dyed Kylie's hair so Mundy wouldn't know, but I didn't care. That baby was mine whether Mundy was the father or not!

"One night I went down to that filthy bar and told the bartender, Jorge, that I knew she was lying, that the baby was mine. I told him she'd better turn Kylie over to me or I'd make Mundy drop her, pull the money out. That's when she hid Kylie away from me and said he'd been adopted by a family from Mexico City. Then Mundy tried to poison Kylie . . ."

Bo narrowed her eyes. "You're getting your stories mixed up, Kee. Not that it matters. Your husband didn't poison Acito, and neither did anyone else. He was poisoned by a bead in a rosary he was teething on. It was a freak accident, but Chac's death wasn't, and Munson Terrell's death was no suicide. You murdered them both, Kee. Why?"

Strangely, Kee was moving in an arc to Bo's left, gradually getting behind her. "You're crazy," she sneered.

"Sometimes, but that doesn't answer my question. Did you think Chac's death would get you the baby?"

"Mundy's baby," Kee insisted. "I hired a private detective to follow Chac and that stupid boy she moved in with. He followed them to that place in San Ysidro and took pictures of Kylie for me when those awful people brought him outside. Sometimes you could see the white hair in the pictures, when the dye wore off. But Mundy wouldn't do anything to make her give Kylie to me. He said it was all a big mistake and we should just forget about it. He said Kylie should stay with that woman. Can you believe that? Forget about my own baby! You can see that Chac had to die in order for Mundy to bring the baby home to me. He was the father, you see. I'm the mother."

In Kee's face Bo saw the *duende* Chac had described in her song for Acito. Something evil, crazed by nature. Maddened. And dangerous. Bo turned again to face the woman now standing behind her.

"The politically correct poisons were a nice touch," she said. "I especially like the apple-seed cyanide. Poisoned apples are such a staple in our folklore, and it was clever of you to juxtapose the symbol of fertile womanhood, the ripe apple, with the symbol for your self-imposed barrenness, the poisoned core. So poetic, just like that doggerel note you left on the computer monitor. But where on earth did you find the second poison, the one called cicutoxin? The herb it comes from doesn't grow naturally around here."

Kee pointed into the canyon beyond the edge of the deck. "It grows here, if it's planted and cultivated," she snarled, "by the stream down there. But you don't have to take my word for it, you're going to get to see it!"

In that instant Bo understood with disconcerting clarity Kee Terrell's intent in moving between her and the mission doors leading back into the house.

"A terrible accident," Kee whined sweetly. "I may even sue the contractor for the mental anguish I endured because of your death due to their negligence. But not until my attorneys get Kylie out of that foster home and safely in his beautiful bed right here with his mother." Her eyes glinted like coal in a poorly lit cellar. "They tell me my chances for a legal adoption are excellent, since Kylie is all I have left of my beloved husband."

"Over my dead body," Bo said with feeling.

"Yes," Kee replied, and lunged, burying her right shoulder in Bo's upper abdomen and toppling them both to the deck's floor before leaning back to slam her fist into Bo's face. Bo felt blood spurt from her nose and dizzying pain. Kee was holding Bo's ears and pounding her head against the deck floor. Bo pulled her knees close to her chest and then kicked the other woman away. A dull cracking sound created some hope that Kee Terrell now had a broken rib. If so, Bo noted with despair as Kee stood up quickly, it wasn't slowing her down.

Bo struggled to her feet as well, pulling up the hem of her now-bloody sweater to reveal a miniature tape recorder secured to her flesh with adhesive tape.

"You're busted," she burbled through the blood in her mouth. "Everything you said is right here. You're finished, Kee."

But Kee wasn't finished. The wild, adrenaline-pumped glaze in her eyes was sufficient evidence. It occurred to Bo that Kee Terrell was actually going to kill her. In the seconds it took the thin, muscular woman to lunge again, Bo opened the tight little package of rage stored behind her eyes and let its power flood her body. It was that or die.

"Do you know," she yelled suddenly, grabbing the other woman by the arms and throwing her against the remaining bench, "that you almost killed my *dog* out there in the desert?" The words, maniacal and fierce, reinforced a strength Bo had known was there but never touched. A burning anger that pulled her lips back from her teeth and coiled in her hands. An ugly, terrifying feeling. She wanted to kill Kee Terrell, not because Kee had murdered two innocent people, but because Kee had almost destroyed the life closest to her own. The sensation was mindless, and oddly existential.

When Kee rose and came at her again Bo simply shoved her away. The movement was effortless, almost dancelike in its simplicity. But Kee flew backward as if hit by a wrecking ball. Backward toward the unprotected edge of the deck and its five-story drop to certain death.

Oh no, Bradley. She's going over the edge and you're going to prison and you'll never see Mildred again anyway. Stop her!

In agonizing slow motion Bo flung herself facedown and grabbed a thin arm as the rest of Kee Terrell slid off the deck into late afternoon sunlight. A muffled pop followed by screams indicated that Kee's shoulder had dislocated, the arm pulled from its socket by the dangling weight of her body.

"Let go of me!" Kee screamed, invisible under the lip of the deck. "Let me die!" Even in extremis, Bo noted, Kee Terrell somehow managed to whine.

"Not a chance," Bo gasped, wrapping a leg around a deck rail to avoid being pulled over. "I've got a dog to walk, my best friend's going to have a baby, and there's a man in my life who makes coffee fudge. I'm not killing anybody!"

In seconds pounding footsteps crossed the deck behind Bo, and a pair of long-fingered hands grabbed Kee Terrell's pale arm. They were followed immediately by another pair, wide and stubby.

"Let go, Bradley, we've got her," Detective Dar Reinert roared into the lean shoulders of Chris Joe Gavin. "Get out of the way."

"I can't," Bo told him, giggling in a manner she privately thought sounded insane. "I can't let go of her. My fingers won't move."

"Well then, roll out of the way. We're pulling her up."

"Where are the police when you need them?" Bo asked shortly after that when her locked hands had been eased from Kee Terrell's right arm by the practiced skill of Andrew Jacques LaMarche, M.D.

"*Madre de dios,*" Estrella Benedict whispered with genuine spiritual verve. "I never should have let you take this case. I knew it from the beginning. That woman's crazy, Bo. She almost killed you."

Bo sighed through the cold compress Andrew was holding against her nose. "I've got to have a cigarette," she decided. "And she's not crazy, Es. People like Kee give us crazy people a bad name. She's just a rotten, spoiled, egotistical crybaby determined to have whatever she wants at whatever cost."

Chris Joe Gavin was watching Dar Reinert escort Kee, moaning, through her own mission doors to a phone where he would call for an ambulance. "I wish Chac could see this," he said sadly.

"Maybe she can," Estrella replied.

Chapter Thirty-nine
The Keeper of the Mat

Andrew had ordered an immense antipasto salad and tub of sausage-stuffed manicotti in garlic-Parmesan sauce delivered to his condo, the oyster rarebit having barely sufficed as an appetizer. Chris Joe Gavin was helping himself to a third plateful as Estrella leaned back in her chair, beaming.

"I can't believe we actually pulled it off, Bo," she sighed with satisfaction. "If you hadn't talked Reinert into wiring you with that recorder and then waiting—"

"That was the hardest part," Chris Joe interjected, raking the sides of his long blond hair with Lincolnesque fingers. "I thought she was gonna do you, Miss Bradley. Man, I couldn't get there fast enough!"

"Fast?" Bo queried with false sweetness from the kitchen. "You call that fast? You were just outside in Dar's car. How could it take you five minutes to run fifteen yards? I saw my life flash before my eyes."

"It was less than a minute, Bo," Andrew noted, wadding his napkin into a tight sphere. "Although a lot can happen in a minute."

Bo readjusted the icepack on her swollen face as she brought another bottle of wine to the table. It would be best, she thought, never to mention everything that had happened in that minute. From her spot by the fireplace, Mildred glanced expectantly into Andrew's dining area. The possibility of table scraps had created a canine smile on her furry face.

"If you hadn't called us," Estrella told Chris Joe for the fifth time, "she would have gotten away with it. And she would have gotten Acito."

The young guitarist pushed his chair from the table and

strode to the window, his long thumbs hooked in the belt loops of his Levi's. "That couldn't happen," he said angrily. "I would have stayed around. I wouldn't have let that happen. I couldn't prove she killed Chac, but I knew enough to stop her from getting the baby." He turned to gaze levelly at Bo, Andrew, and Estrella. "That is, if anybody would have believed me."

"You're right," Bo agreed. "That's why you ran, isn't it? After Chac . . . after that night at the club."

The shadow of pain crossing his eyes was difficult to watch.

"I just wanted to help her, take care of her," he went on, ducking his head to curtain his face with hair. "She was, you know, like a hooker before Terrell set her up singing. She said she married Singleton because they were both lost souls, but then he went back to Louisiana and was supposed to send for her, but he never did. When Terrell asked her to have his baby I guess she couldn't really say no, could she? I know what it's like when you're just so tired of moving around and not really belonging anyplace or to anybody. She meant to give them the baby like they agreed, but then she just couldn't. I loved her."

His voice dropped to a ragged baritone. "When I knew she was dead that didn't stop, but I didn't know what to do so I ran. Later I thought if I showed you how she'd saved money for the baby, and showed you how she tried to tell you who was after her, you'd, you know, do something."

"That was a smart move," Bo complimented him. "But the best thing you did was returning Estrella's call this morning. Without you we couldn't do anything but guess. You had the critical information. You knew about the deal Kee and Munson Terrell had made to exchange career promotion for Kee's idea of the perfect baby. And you knew Chac was reneging on the deal."

"She loved Acito," Chris Joe said proudly. "She'd never give him up. She was going to keep him right with her, just as soon as she could get away from Kee."

In his voice Bo heard a lifetime of longing for somebody who had done just the opposite. His own mother, who would neither love him nor permit anyone else that role. A sorrow too late now to remedy, for which he found expression in music. The gangly, sullen teenager was, Bo thought, going to make a fine man.

"So what will you do now?" Andrew asked. "We'd be happy to help you settle here, get into school, the military, whatever you'd like."

"Thank you," Chris Joe answered, stuffing his hands into his pockets, "but I'll be eighteen in August. This family I was with, the Springers, they want me to come and live with them in Ohio, go to night school, and finish my senior year. They've been sending me money. I can live with them as soon as I'm eighteen and out of the system. That's why I went to Mexico, so the system couldn't get me and put me in another foster home. I'll be heading for Ohio in a few days." He shook his head. "You know, it's funny, Mundy Terrell wanted to help me, too. He wasn't a bad guy. He just loved the wrong woman."

"Why did she kill him?" Estrella asked, rising and searching for car keys in her voluminous purse.

"When Reinert called while you and Bo had gone to pick up Mildred," Andrew answered, "he said Kee told the police her husband was going to leave her, and she'd never get the baby." He grinned tentatively at Bo. "He also said her hotshot lawyer is already talking about an insanity defense if she's formally charged with Terrell's murder."

"Insanity?" Bo yelped. "What kind of insanity? Ripping off Indians? Since when is personal imperialism—"

Estrella grinned. "I'll give you a ride to your motel," she told Chris Joe. "Time to get out of here before the fireworks."

As they left, Bo watched Estrella's car lights slice the darkness in narrow cones, and then tilted her head to look at the night sky stretching over the Pacific Ocean. The Milky Way seemed to be a hazy road, leading to the past and future at once.

"Andy?" she asked. "Would you mind driving me by the Dooleys' for a few minutes? There's something in my car that belongs to Acito."

"A drive would be nice," he agreed, asking no questions.

A half hour later Bo stood in a nursery lit only by a night-light made of a seashell. In her hands was a fraying shawl woven from colored yarn and black satin ribbons. From it an odor of dust drifted, warm and historical.

"I'm going to paint a portrait of Chac for him," she told Davey and Connie Dooley as the four of them gazed at a sleeping baby with rosy brown skin, a tuft of white hair, and a classic Maya nose. "But right now I want him to have this. It's a gift from the Maya."

As she tucked the shawl over him Bo saw one small hand clutch its fabric and tug it toward his heart.